I0712799

THE YOWANI CHOCTAW SAGA

INTERNATIONAL EDITION

THIS BOOK INCLUDES THE FULL SERIES:

THE YOWANI CHOCTAW EXODUS
WILLIAM CLYDE THOMPSON
AND
HANK THE SYCAMORE INDIAN

LEAFORD LEVEN BLEVINS, JR.

The Yowani Choctaw Saga

by Leaford Leven Blevins Jr.

This book is a work of historical interpretation and narrative reconstruction based on available records and sources. While every effort has been made to ensure accuracy, certain events and dialogues have been interpreted to convey continuity and clarity of the historical experience.

Editions and Translations

This work is also published in international editions, including:
- English (original edition)
- Spanish edition
- French edition
- Portuguese edition
Each edition is published under its own ISBN and may vary in format and presentation.

Publishing Information

Published by Ishkatini Studios

Castle Hills, Texas

ISBN: 9798218861490

Distribution

This title is available through major online retailers, libraries, and global distribution networks, including IngramSpark.

Author

Leaford Leven Blevins Jr. is an architect and author whose work explores the intersection of land, history, and cultural memory through both narrative and design.

This book is dedicated to my Mother, Geneva Darken Blevins, to whom I owe my existence, and from whom I was gifted this heritage, and to my daughters, Haven and Adrienne, and to my grandsons, Locke and Tesla to whom it is entrusted.

"In the heart of every story lies the spirit of a people; may their journey inspire all who read."

SAGA Table of contents

Hank

This book began as a search into the life of my sixth great-grandmother, Margaret McCoy. What started as genealogical research slowly became something more: the uncovering of a story that had been pushed to the margins of history. Along the way, I discovered the struggles of my first cousin, William Clyde Thompson, whose efforts to establish his Choctaw and Chickasaw identity carried him all the way to the Supreme Court of the United States. Tracing his lineage brought me back to Margaret, and to the difficult role she played in guiding a band of Yowani Choctaw from their Mississippi homeland during the years of Indian removal.

As I explored Margaret's story, I became more deeply drawn into the wider history of removal. The federal government's determination to clear Native people from the lands east of the Mississippi, to make way for others, was an injustice of lasting consequence. For the Yowani, as for many, it meant both displacement and the daunting challenge of rebuilding their lives in unfamiliar country.

My mother knew very little of this ancestry, having lost her own father when she was very young. Much of what connects me to Margaret and William Clyde has been reconstructed from records and stories that survived in fragments. Through this book, I have tried to give voice to those fragments, and to imagine the lives behind them.While much of this book is built on documented history, it is also shaped by imagination. The records of Margaret McCoy and her companions leave gaps that no archive can ever fill. Where the trail of fact grew faint, I have drawn upon reason, context, and the lived realities of others who made similar journeys. In doing so, I have tried to create not a literal history, but a truthful picture of what life would have been like for a band of farmers and families forced to leave their Mississippi homelands and carve a new path westward.

It is my hope that this story honors both the resilience of my ancestors and the many others who endured removal. Though we may never know their every word or step, we can glimpse the strength it took to walk that road — and recognize that very few of those who sent them would have survived it themselves.

THE FIRES OF DECISION

The Indian Removal Act was a federal law signed by President Andrew Jackson on May 28, 1830. It authorized the president to negotiate with Native American tribes in the southern United States for their removal to federal territory west of the Mississippi River in exchange for their ancestral homelands.

Key Provisions

Authorization for Negotiation: The act did not order the forced removal of tribes. Instead, it gave the president the power to negotiate removal treaties with tribes living east of the Mississippi River.

Land Exchange: It proposed that tribes would exchange their current land for new, unsettled land in what was called "Indian Territory" (present-day Oklahoma).

Financial Incentives: The act promised financial compensation for the cost of relocation, assistance with the move itself, and protection for the tribes on their new land "as long as they may occupy it."

Historical Context and Motivations

Manifest Destiny: The policy was driven by the desire of white settlers for the fertile farmland occupied by the Five Civilized Tribes (Cherokee, Chickasaw, Choctaw, Creek, and Seminole) in the South, particularly for cotton cultivation.

· State's Rights vs. Tribal Sovereignty: Southern states, especially Georgia, were eager to assert their jurisdiction over tribal lands within their borders and ignored previous federal treaties guaranteeing tribal sovereignty.

· President Jackson's Stance: Andrew Jackson was a fervent supporter of removal, framing it as a way to protect Native Americans from conflict with white settlers and to allow them to govern themselves in the West without interference.

In summary, the Indian Removal Act of 1830 was a piece of legislation that legalized the forced displacement of Native American tribes from the southeastern

United States, leading to immense suffering, death, and the loss of ancestral home-lands. It is widely regarded as a tragic and unethical chapter in American history.

***

The late summer heat lay heavy over the pine ridges and river bottoms of southern Mississippi, the air thick withthe smell of drying cane and the faint sweetness of muscadines ripening on the vine. Families gathered in clearings and along the shaded bends of creeks, the women laying out baskets of dried corn and roasted squash, the men leaning on their rifles or seated cross-legged near the fire. A Removal Act had been passed in the late Spring of 1830.

The Yowani Choctaw had been meeting like this for weeks, all Summer, their councils stretching deep into the night, words circling like smoke, heavy with fear and resolve. Margaret stood slightly apart, her face lit by the fire's edge, her eyes shifting from one speaker to the next. She had been born into the Wind Clan, descended from the ancient line of matriarchs, and though her brother James often spoke in her stead, everyone knew the authority of the family lay with her.

At thirty-five, she carried herself with the quiet certainty of one who had endured much, her voice measured, but her presence commanding.

The council fire snapped as an elder, storyteller, and conscience of the people leaned forward. His hair was silver now, his voice roughened with age, but when he spoke the circle fell silent. It is not only the land that is being taken from us, his eyes glowing in the firelight. It is the bones of our ancestors, the clay from which we shape our pots, the reeds from which we weave our baskets, the canebrakes where our flutes sing to the young women in courtship. All these things our very breath are bound to this place. To leave is to risk losing more than soil; it is to risk losing ourselves.

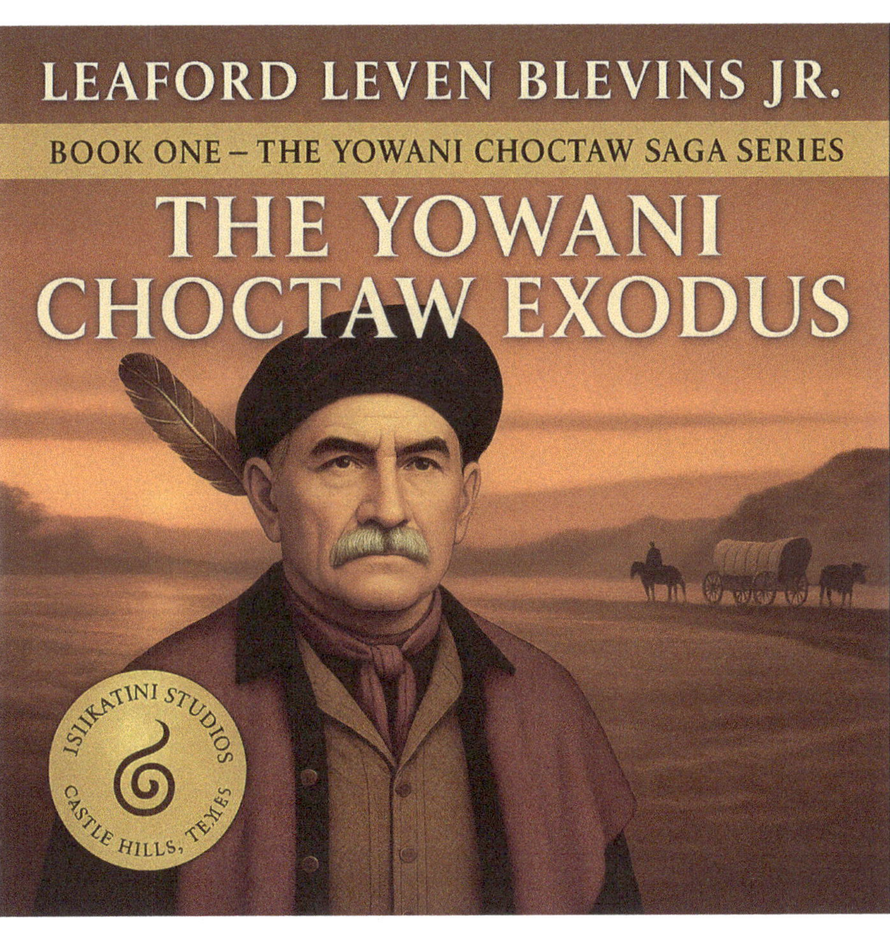

LEAFORD LEVEN BLEVINS JR.
BOOK ONE – THE YOWANI CHOCTAW SAGA SERIES
THE YOWANI CHOCTAW EXODUS
ISIIKATINI STUDIOS
CASTLE HILLS, TEMES

CHAPTER I

WHAT WE CARRY AND WHAT WE LEAVE BEHIND

In the days after the council fire, the Yowani homesteads buzzed with activity. Wagons creaked as they were pulled from sheds and patched, harnesses mended barrels scrubbed clean. Every family faced the same impossible questions: What can we carry? What must be left to the woods and the memories?

Margaret walked among her people, her own wagon already half-loaded. She watched as women packed baskets of dried beans and parched corn, the foods that would keep longest. Deer hides were folded tight, pots carefully wrapped in cloth to keep them from shattering on the rough roads. Tools axes, hoes, knives, flints were tucked into corners where they would not rattle loose.

But the decisions that cut deepest were not about food or tools. They were about the sacred. At one home, an old woman knelt before bundles of bones wrapped in deer hide. They were her ancestors, once set high on a scaffold, later gathered by bone-pickers and preserved beneath the family lodge. The woman's hands trembled as she stroked the bundle. Would they fit in the wagon? Could she leave them behind? To abandon the bones felt like abandoning herself.

Nearby, children scattered seeds into pouches corn, beans, squash, sunflowers. Margaret remembered Ishkatini's words: The seeds must go first. Some seeds would grow in the new land. Others would not. No one could know which. Still, they carried them, because to abandon the seeds was to abandon hope. James argued for rifles and powder above all else. Food we can find. Water we can draw. But without rifles, we are prey. His voice was sharp, but his meaning was plain:

there would be men waiting in the woods, eager to steal from a wagon train heavy with provisions.

There were disputes, but never arguments. Families made their own choices, each bound by its own obligations. Some carried baskets of river cane for weaving, though Margaret knew the canebrakes of Oklahoma would never match the lush stands of Mississippi. Others loaded clay pots, their surfaces incised with ancient designs. Potters worried aloud that the new soil would never yield the right clay, that their art would wither in foreign ground. One evening, Margaret found Ishkatini seated alone, weaving a bundle of river cane into a simple mat. His hands, though old, moved with ease. She sat beside him. You will carry that? she asked.

He nodded. Even if it cannot be remade, it must be remembered. He paused, then added, The cane is more than a plant. It is the sound of our flutes, the basket that holds our food, the shaft of the arrow. Without it, we forget who we are.

Margaret placed her hand on his. We will not forget. Even if the land changes, even if the clay and the cane are gone, the memory lives in us. We will teach our children. Ishkatini gave a thin smile. Then the spirits will travel with us. As the sun sank low and the cicadas began their evening chorus, Margaret returned to her wagon. She looked at the bundles inside: food, tools, her children's blankets, the sacred bones wrapped carefully at the bottom. She knew there was not enough space for everything that mattered. There never could be.

But there was room for what mattered most: the living her children, her brother, her people. And so the packing continued, day after day, each family balancing survival against memory, the future against the past.

CHAPTER 2

THE ROAD TO DANCING RABBIT CREEK

The morning they set out, the air was heavy with late-summer heat. Mist clung to the bottoms, curling off the creeks like smoke from an unseen fire. Margaret stood with her children at the edge of the homestead, staring at the line of wagons creaking onto the trail. Their oxen leaned into the harness, hooves sinking deep in the rutted clay.

Everywhere there was motion: women calling to children, men lifting barrels into place, dogs darting underfoot. The sound of wood and iron groaning mixed with the low murmur of voices.

They moved at a steady pace not fast, but unbroken. James rode on horseback alongside the wagons, scanning the woods. His rifle rested across his lap. Behind him, younger warriors walked, bows strung, muskets slung over shoulders. They knew too well that eyes watched them from the trees.

By midday, the air was thick with sweat and dust. The trail wound through pine barrens and creek bottoms, sometimes narrowing so much that wagons passed single file. Margaret saw children stumble, their bare feet scratched by brambles. Once, near a dark slough, a child strayed too close to the water's edge. In an instant the surface rippled Š the flash of an alligator's jaws. A shout rang out, and the child was snatched back just in time. The screams and sobbing that followed reminded them all how swiftly death could strike.

That night, they made camp near a shallow creek. The wagons were drawn into a crescent with the water at their backs, fires kindled low inside the ring.

Warriors took turns in the trees, sharp eyes watching the shadows. The biskinik the red-headed woodpecker tapped in the distance, a warning in the silence of the forest.

Margaret sat near the fire, her children pressed close. She listened to the low voices around her. Elders murmured prayers, asking the spirits for protection. Younger men whispered of the dangers yet ahead settlers who might lurk in the woods, desperate men who would not hesitate to kill for food or powder.

The next day, they pressed harder. James urged the wagons forward with little rest. The longer we linger, the greater the danger, he said. His words carried weight. The people drove their oxen until foam flecked the animals' mouths, then pressed them on again. On the third day, they came across signs of others. A patch of trampled ground. Broken branches. And then, worse: a body strung from a tree, its hands bound, its face unrecognizable. Bandits who had followed too closely had met the warriors™ justice. The sight chilled Margaret's children, who clung to her skirts and would not let go.

By the fourth day, the people were worn but resolute The land began to slope gently toward the Tombigbee River valley. The forest thinned, and rumors spread through the wagons: Dancing Rabbit Creek is near. That evening, as the sun slid low and lit the pines in fire, Margaret saw smoke rising far ahead not a small fire, but many. She smelled woodsmoke and meat roasting, and, faintly, the sharp, bitter scent of whiskey. James reined his horse beside her wagon. The treaty grounds, he said, voice tight. We are here.

The people fell into silence, each wagon creaking forward into the glow of thousands of campfires, into the gathering place where their nation's fate would be sealed.

CHAPTER 3

THE TREATY GROUNDS

By the time they reached Dancing Rabbit Creek, the air itself seemed thick with tension. The forest gave way to a broad clearing, trampled flat by thousands of feet, hooves, and wagon wheels. Smoke rose from a hundred fires, twisting into the September sky.

Margaret smelled it before she saw it: whiskey, sharp and acrid, mingling with sassafras tea, roasted meat, and the musk of livestock penned nearby. The stench of sweat and damp canvas hung heavy. For miles, wagons and tents sprawled across the fields.

There were Choctaw everywhere five, maybe six thousand, gathered from every corner of the nation. Women carried water and tended children. Warriors sharpened blades or stood watchful at the edges. Elders sat in small circles, speaking in hushed tones. Over it all, the laughter and shouting of men already drunk carried like a warning.

Soldiers moved through the camp in ordered lines, their tents set apart, neat as white teeth. Beyond them, the commissioners' pavilion loomed a gaudy canvas marquee striped in red and blue, guarded by federal troops. This was the place where Greenwood LeFlore and the other chiefs would be called to speak, and where pens and parchment waited to strip a people from their land.

Margaret drew her children close as they passed through the crowd. She had seen gatherings before, feasts and dances that brought joy. But this was different. This was a festival arranged by their enemies, designed to soften resolve. Barrels of whiskey had been rolled out like gifts. The young men who drank too deeply shouted foolish boasts, stumbling at the edges of the firelight.

Near one fire, a group of white traders jeered as an enslaved girl was paraded before them. Margaret turned her eyes away quickly, her face burning with shame and anger. She could not let her children see. James muttered low, This is what they call civilization.

The Choctaw chiefs sat apart, sober, grim-faced. Greenwood LeFlore, tall and stern, moved among them with the air of a man carrying unbearable weight. Nitakechi of Okla Hannali sat wrapped in silence, his eyes on the fire. Mushulatubbe of Okla Falaya scowled openly, as if daring anyone to meet his gaze.

Into this gathering the Yowani wagons rolled, weary and road-worn, but upright and intact. Their warriors flanked them, grim and disciplined, not stumbling drunk. To the others, their arrival seemed to carry a whisper: not all have lost themselves. That night, as fires burned low, Ishkatini stirred within Margaret's thoughts. His voice came like the wind, soft and insistent:

Daughter, do you see? The white man has made a stage for humiliation. They pour whiskey as though it were water, thinking it will drown your spirit. But your people are not so easily drowned. Remember Nanih Waiya, remember the stories of the mound your roots are deeper than this soil, your spirit stronger than their chains. Do not bow your head here. What is signed in daylight will bind their hands as well as yours. But what is remembered in your blood Š that is beyond their reach.

Margaret closed her eyes, tears wetting her cheeks. For a moment she felt the weight of her ancestors pressing steady against her shoulders, holding her upright. By morning, the drums began to sound Š slow, solemn, carrying across the clearing. The people gathered, tensely silent. The commissioners stepped forward, their uniforms bright against the dust. Greenwood LeFlore raised his hand.

CHAPTER 4

THE SIGNING

The morning sun slanted low across the clearing, catching on the dew still clinging to grass and canvas. Drums had ceased. A silence hung over the thousands gathered at Dancing Rabbit Creek, broken only by the restless shifting of livestock and the cough of soldiers in their ordered ranks.

Margaret stood with James and the children on the edge of the crowd. The Yowani wagons rested behind them, wheels still caked in mud from the road. Warriors lingered in a protective arc, watchful, their eyes sweeping the tree line. They were strangers here Š kin, yet apart and all knew it.

At the center, a table had been set beneath the commissioners' striped marquee. Sheets of parchment lay heavy with ink, their edges held down by polished brass weights. Quills waited in an open case. Behind the table, federal commissioners sat in stiff-backed chairs, faces unreadable.

The Choctaw chiefs came forward. Greenwood LeFlore in his tailored coat, his eyes hooded and cold. Nitakechi, older, shoulders sloped as though already bearing the burden of what was to come. Mushulatubbe, his jaw set, anger smoldering just beneath his skin.

The commissioners began to read the treaty aloud. Their words were dry, legalistic land boundaries, obligations, compensations. But to the Choctaw gathered, every clause struck like a drumbeat: cede– remove– relinquish.

Margaret's stomach knotted. She thought of the clay banks of Shubuta, the cane brakes where her mother taught her to weave, the graves of kin resting beneath cedar and oak. With each sentence, those things were stripped away, transformed into mere lines of ink on paper. When the reading ended, silence pressed heavy on the clearing. Then Greenwood LeFlore stepped forward. He took up the quill. For a moment, the world seemed to hold its breath. His hand trembled only slightly as he pressed the pen to parchment and signed his name. Gasps rippled through the crowd. Some wept openly. Others cursed under their breath. Nitakechi signed next, his face a mask. Mushulatubbe lingered longest, but at last, with a snarl, he too scrawled his name.

When it was done, the commissioners smiled thinly, as though concluding a successful transaction of cattle or land. Soldiers shifted their stance, muskets gleaming in the sun

Around the edges of the crowd, barrels of whiskey were rolled forward again. Already some young men reached for cups, desperate to drown the moment in drink. Laughter rose hollow, bitter Š mingling with the cries of those who still clutched the earth beneath them as though by sheer force they might hold it.

Margaret turned away, her throat tight. James stood beside her, his jaw clenched, his hand resting protectively on the hilt of his knife. It is done, he said quietly. The land is gone.

No, Margaret whispered, her voice fierce though her cheeks were wet. The land still remembers us. They can take the paper, they can take the fields, but they cannot take what lives in us. We carry the land with us in our hands, in our songs, in our children.

Ishkatini's voice stirred once more, low and steady, like a current beneath the noise: You see now, daughter. The white man's ink can bind the land on their maps, but it cannot bind the spirit of a people. That spirit walks in you. The choice is no longer whether to stay or go that choice has been forced. Now the question is only how to walk forward, and whether you walk with your head bowed or lifted to the sky.

Margaret lifted her chin. Around her, the Yowani warriors began to form up again, gathering the wagons, steadying oxen and horses. Already whispers of departure passed among them.

The treaty had been signed. The nation's fate had been sealed. And for the Yowani, the road west or south, or wherever survival might yet lie had begun.

CHAPTER 5

DEPARTURE

They broke camp before the sun touched the tops of the pines. Smoke hung low over the treaty ground, a sour mix of last night's fires and spilled whiskey. The commissioners' marquee still loomed like a bleached sail in the gray light, but the drums were silent now. Men slept where they fell. Crows worked the edges of the clearing.

James moved through the Yowani wagons, tapping wheel rims with the butt of his knife, testing spokes, checking lashings. No bundles dragging, he said, voice low. Nothing loose to rattle. Children inside for the first mile. He didn't raise his tone; he didn't have to. The warriors heard him and repeated the words without turning their heads.

Margaret cinched the strap on a deerskin parcel and laid it flat beneath a folded quilt. Bones, wrapped years ago by careful hands, made no sound when she settled them into place. Her daughter pressed close to her skirts. Are we leaving before the others, the girl asked.

We leave when the wind is still, Margaret said, smoothing the child's hair. Quiet ground keeps us safe. On the edge of the encampment, two Chickasaw riders waited by their horses, faces unreadable under sweat-dark hats. They had walked in with the Yowani when the road grew mean old friends of James from hunts that ended with shared fires and bad jokes. Now they held their reins like men deciding where to place a final word.

You ride with us to the river crossing? James asked. The older of the two shook his head. We turn back here. Our own houses are only as safe as we are near them. He leaned forward in the saddle so the others wouldn't hear. This ground is more dangerous than the woods. Too many hands, no one steering. His eyes flicked toward the sleeping soldiers and the scattered barrels. Keep to the low trails. And if a man steps out of the trees alone, assume he is not.

James nodded once. There was no grasping of forearms, no speech. They had said everything that mattered on other nights, with other fires. The Chickasaw put their heels to their horses and were gone, swallowed by the pines as if they'd never stood there at all.

Ishkatini watched them go. He had not slept. The old man's face was creased like bark, and in his lap lay a narrow mat of river cane, half woven, the ends still rough. Margaret crouched beside him.

Come up into the wagon, she said. We're moving. He turned the mat, testing the weave with his thumb. The cane from home bends in your hands, he murmured. The cane out there will fight you. Remember that, and your baskets won't split. He lifted his gaze to hers. You know why I stay.

She did. His legs would not carry him far, and his heart would not forgive him if he left the graves he'd tended. He had said it last night without complaint and without asking her to argue it.

Will you walk back to your people? Margaret asked. I will sit where those who come looking will see me before the sun is high. He smiled and it deepened the creases, made him look like a young man laughing inside a paper mask. Do not look behind you. I am already there.

She took his hand and felt the bones inside it light, dry sticks tied with sinew. She pressed her forehead to his knuckles, just once, then rose. You taught us to weave, she said. We will keep the pattern.

The biskinik tapped in a nearby pine. Sharp. Then again. A third time, spaced like knocks at a door. James raised two fingers and every moving hand went still. The warriors stepped into their places.

The order was simple but never said. Two scouts ahead on the trail one to read the ground, one to read the air. Three at the rear, men who did not hurry even when the rest did, because nothing behind them was allowed to be faster than their eyes. A pair on each flank, walking with the canvas, lifting the wagon skirts with two fingers when they needed a view. Those with best aim rotated through the wagons themselves, rifles braced on folded blankets, canvas slit in neat little smiles that could be held shut with a thumb.

Go, James said.

The first ox team leaned into the yoke. Wood groaned. Rope sighed. The wagon moved, then the next, then the next, a long-boned animal finding its stride. Children peered over the railings with grave faces. A woman crossed herself with one hand and touched a shell necklace with the other, covering both gods in one breath, just in case

They skirted the edge of the clearing rather than cut its heart. Better the ragged ground by the trees than the tidy lanes between soldiers' tents. A drunken shout chased them and then died. They passed a circle where young men had gambled away knives and dignity until dawn; Margaret kept her eyes on the ruts ahead and the way the oxen's hooves set down and lifted.

At the tree line, a shape moved.

The lead scout lifted his palm without looking back. The line slowed, breath drawn in one long body. A man stepped out of the brush, hat low, hands empty and too wide to be empty.

Morning, he called, cheerful as a peddler. You folks got a far piece to go. Be a shame if you took the wrong turn.

James didn't answer. He looked past the man to the darker shadow to his left the second one who thought he could be a tree if he believed it hard enough. Trail's clear, Margaret said, though she was speaking to her daughter, not the stranger.

The man shifted his weight and the woods shifted with him. Then there were three of them. Four. One smiled too much. One did not blink. The third made a show of keeping his hands away from his belt, which meant he wanted them to notice he owned one.

You leave in a hurry, the smiling one said. Hurry makes mistakes. Mistakes break wheels. Broken wheels need help. James lifted his chin and spoke as if to nobody at all. Rear guard, hold your line. Canvas rustled. The man who didn't blink saw it and his smile finally found a job to do: it vanished.

You don't want trouble, the stranger said, and for a moment it sounded almost kind. Lot of it out there. You got children. Let us walk you a stretch. No, Margaret said, and now she was speaking to him. You are trouble. We have enough. It was not loud. It landed like a stone in a pond no splash, just a sure widening.

The unblinking one's hand sank toward his belt. He found his knife but not his nerve. The scout's rifle had not moved but the barrel was already a conversation he didn't want to have. Somewhere behind, a child coughed and the sound made the air more dangerous. The smiling man tried once more. A woman shouldn't talk for fighters, he said, which was the wrong sentence in the wrong world.

Then talk to me, James said. Say the short version. The man weighed that and found nothing in it for him. He stepped back, palms up. Road's yours, he said. For now.

They melted into the trees. Leaves settled. The biskinik tapped twice, quick and light, as if approving a small repair. The wagons moved again.

By the time the sun found the tops of the pines, the treaty ground was a smear of smoke behind them. The trail narrowed into a sandy cut with broom sedge on the shoulders and blackberry canes reaching like little hands. A doe burst from the brush and bounded away, white tail flagging; the children watched it go with the same attention they'd given the soldiers' tents, as if both were creatures that could trample them without meaning to. They made for a creek they had scouted the night before a bend with a gravel bar where wheels would grip and oxen could drink. The wagons drew into a crescent with the water at their backs, just as they had taught themselves to do on the road in. Fires were kept no higher than a man's knee. Meat sizzled in a pan. A woman hummed under her breath, breaking a song into pieces so it couldn't be stolen whole.

James walked the line once more, counting quietly. He didn't count people. He counted rifles, ax heads, whetstones, spare linchpins. He stopped beside Margaret's wagon and rested his hand on the rail. Word's already out, he said. Some of those who stayed are being visited by men without names. The sooner we clear the country, the better for everyone. Margaret didn't ask who told him; news had a way of running ahead of feet. She looked down at her children, at their hands, at the grime in the crescents of their nails. She took the canteen and tipped a palmful of water into each mouth, measuring it so the youngest got the sweetest, because that was how the world kept faith with itself when paper didn't.

Ishkatini was not there. Every now and then, as the wind set the cane mat rustling in the corner of the wagon, she felt his absence the way a tooth feels a missing neighbor tongue pressing into emptiness, finding it still there.

Do we stop long? her daughter asked. Long enough to breathe, Margaret said. Not long enough to grow roots.

They did not speak of destinations aloud. Some said the Red River under their breath. Some said the Nation. A few said both, as if the one could lead them to the other if they kept walking a little farther than tired men would. James had folded a map that did not know their names and pinned it under the seat anyway. It made a good wedge to keep the rifle from rattling.

The sun climbed. The creek threw a little light. A hawk wrote its name over the clearing and then went looking for something that could not read.

Up, James said, and it was as if he'd said it inside each body. Fires were killed with dirt, not water. Ash was scattered. The oxen leaned without being told. The last wagon rolled and the rear guard stepped off the gravel bar, one after the other, so their prints would be the creek's business and not the trail's.

They moved in a long breath. The pines opened their columns to them and the light shifted from pewter to brass. Behind, the treaty ground faded to a story that others would tell. Ahead, the track bent out of sight. The biskinik tapped once, then was quie

No one said go. They already were.

CHAPTER 6

FIRST MILES

The pines accepted them without a word. Wheels found the old cart ruts and settled into them; hemp creaked; oxen breathed like bellows. The morning light fell in tall bars, and in those bars the dust turned to gold. Margaret walked a few paces beside the lead team, one hand on the wagon rail, the other resting against her daughter's shoulder. The child's steps matched the oxen's plant, lift, plant steady as a prayer.

No one spoke of destinations. The trail itself was talk enough. It ran straight until a stand of sweetgum insisted on a bend, then straight again, a muscle under bark. The scouts were shadows at its point, their shirts gone gray with sweat. Twice they lifted a hand to slow the line: once for a wild grapevine fallen low, once for a root that rose like a knuckle and could snap a spoke if given the chance. Each time the wagons drifted, obedient, not a word wasted.

James kept to the outside edge where the light was thinnest, reading the understory the way men read river water eddies, bulges, places where something larger than leaves might be turning in its sleep. Watch that hollow, he said, and two men watched it until it stopped being a question.

A whippoorwill called at the wrong hour and the rear guard turned to see who else had heard it. Nobody laughed. The bird corrected itself and went quiet. They moved like that for a long while one animal with many legs. When the sun leaned higher, the air warmed enough that resin bled from a pine and sweetened the path. A boy in the third wagon rubbed his fingers against the sap and then pressed them to his nose, eyes surprised at the gift of the tree. Margaret saw him and almost smiled.

Ahead, a woodpecker worked a snag tap–tap-tap quick, confident. Biskinik is doing his job, she thought, and let her hand fall from the wagon rail.

The first obstruction was not much to look at, which is what made it dangerous: a long needle-choked slope where the trail narrowed to the width of a wagon and, across it, a pine laid down as neat as a gate. Fresh chips showed pale where the saw had bitten. The scouts had seen it minutes before; now they stood loose-kneed beside the trunk, palms open at their thighs, not moving fast because moving fast is how you let somebody else choose when things happen.

James came up, eyes sliding over bark, over the hollies below the cut, over a low swell above that could hide a man with a rifle and a little patience. He did not look back when he spoke.

Flanks hold. Rear holds. First wagon kneel. Oxen were backed a half-length so a shoulder wouldn't take a stray ball. Two men ghosted into the brush on the high side. One disappeared entirely; the other left a hat on a stump where a hatless man might make a better target. A minute stretched until it lost its name. Margaret could hear the woodpecker again, softer now, like someone drumming fingers against a tabletop to keep from speaking.

James touched the trunk with the toe of his boot. Fresh, he said. They meant us to stop.

We did, Margaret said. Her voice was level. But not the way they wanted.

A leaf turned in the shade. That was all. It was enough. The man behind the leaf had a plan he loved too dearly: wait until the big bodies came close, then step up like a savior and sell the fix. Men who love their plans don't watch the ground as well as men who don't.

Two on the lower side, James said. Three breaths. The three breaths came and went, counted in the passage of a cloud over the sun. Then a twig snapped down-slope, a deer's mistake made by a human foot, and the low brush erupted two men rising at once, palms out, mouths wide and friendly as summer.

Trouble, friends? That's a big tree.

Road's bad this year.

They stopped, not because anyone shouted, but because the rifles that had been sleeping in the canvas were awake now, and there are sentences you cannot finish into that kind of silence. One of them saw the hat on the stump and understood what it meant about the other two. He changed his mind about a lot of things in a very short time.

James did not raise his voice. Stand where you are. They did, not from obedience but because the ground under their feet had suddenly become specific and disappointing.

Who else? James asked.

The men glanced upslope without moving their eyes, which is another way of pointing. Someone above the cut shifted just enough and the scout who had gone high tapped his rifle against bark to let the world know he could see all the way to the man's idea of safety. We can help you move it, said the friendlier of the two, dragging his smile back over his teeth.

We have our own backs, Margaret said. She did not look at him when she said it. Her attention was on the stump where the saw had bit clean. She could read the speed of the cut in the smoothness, the lift of the blade in the way the fibers tore at the end. Whoever had laid the tree had not been in a hurry. That meant they expected time here. That meant they did not know the Yowani. James flicked two fingers and men with axes came forward, not close enough to be easy targets, close enough to do what needed doing. The strangers stepped aside without being told.

Leave your knives, James said.

That got a look. The man upslope made a little sound with his mouth, something between a laugh and a cough, and then let the bone-handled piece he loved fall into the needles.

Belts too, Margaret added.

They stripped them the quick hand finding every small blade a man forgets to count when he promises he is empty. A satchel came off a shoulder and hit the ground with the soft clink of someone else's property. Margaret did not look inside. She would not catalog what had been stolen from the people who would not see it again. She lifted the satchel and set it in the wagon bed. The child with the resin-sweet hands touched the strap and then tucked his fingers out of sight.

Axes made their bright, hollow sound. Chips flew. The trunk was levered just enough that a chain could be run under, then backed by oxen inch by inch until the road was a road again. It took less time than the men who had cut it had counted on. Plans die of that.

When the way was clear, James turned to the strangers. You can go back to your friends and say you tried, he said. Or you can follow us and we can be done with it in a different way.

The friendlier one worked his jaw and found that his words had gone somewhere without him. He nodded, once, twice, as if agreeing with a proposal he wished someone else had made. We'll go, he said, and this time it was true.

Leave a sign, Margaret told the rear guard.

They knew what she meant. No body on a rope flies do that work too eagerly, and she would not give them a feast. Instead, a message carved swift and deep in the trunk they'd dragged Choctaw letters cut clean with a trade knife, the new writing the missionaries had taught pressed into old wood:

NOT PREY.

Under it, a small thing, but sharp: a cane-splint braid, three strands twined and knotted, left hanging where anyone who touched it would feel how unbreakable something thin can be if you teach it to cross itself the right way.

They moved again, and this time the road pulled them faster, as if it, too, were done looking at men who wanted to be trees.

By midday the heat laid its hand on the back of the neck and did not lift it. They came to a seep where water bled out of clay and gathered in a pool no bigger than a pallet. Margaret sent the children up-line to wait with their mouths shut and their hands behind their backs. A dipper went around in the elder's order, not the thirsty one's. No one took more than two swallows. James wetted a scrap of cloth and pressed it to the places where a yoke rubs hardest; the ox flicked an ear as if in thanks.

Near the edge of the pool, someone had left a bit of cane, cut clean at both ends, not much good for anything. Margaret picked it up and turned it in her fingers. It was just big enough to remember itself. She lifted it to her mouth and blew a test note across it, and a thin sound came unsteady, but the right shape. Her daughter's eyes grew. Margaret passed it to her. Not now, she said. But later, when the trees can keep a secret.

They ate standing up corn cakes cold from last night's fire, a strip of smoked meat, a handful of dried berries that survived as if their bushes had been walking beside them all morning. The scouts ate last. Then James looked at the sky and nodded, and the whole animal that was their caravan put its weight forward again.

The afternoon made a long wick of the road. Once, a doe and her fawn stepped into the light and stepped back out of it, and the only sound was a child's breath catch it just before a mother's hand found the back of his neck. Twice, the woodpecker rattled somewhere ahead, not alarm, just work. A hawk drew a dark needle across the bright cloth of the sky and stitched nothing to nothing.

When the day began to lean toward evening, they swung off into a stand of sweetgum and sycamore where a creek braided itself around a tongue of gravel. They shaped the wagons into a crescent with the water biting at its inside edge. Fires were kindled low and mean. Axes bit just enough wood to keep a pan hot. Men with good eyes drifted up into the trees and made themselves part of the bark. The children were counted and counted again.

James walked the line, then walked it backward, because you see different things facing the other way. At the last wagon he stopped. The satchel they had taken from the men at the cut was there where Margaret had set it. He opened it and looked long enough to understand the weight inside. He closed it and tied it twice.

Someone will come for that, he said.

They will not like what we ask in trade, Margaret answered.

What do we ask?

That they leave our people alone.

He considered and found he did not need to. A high price, he said. Cheap, at that.

They ate with the quiet of people whose mouths are not the only place work happens. When the children were drowsy and the oxen had stopped chewing loud, someone asked Ishkatini's name without meaning to, and the silence that followed said all the answers there were. Margaret sat with her back against the wagon wheel. The cane-splint braid the men had tied to the trunk was still in her mind, light and strong. She took three long grasses and began to twist them together the way he had taught, her fingers remembering even where memory hurt. The little flute lay under the folded quilt. Her daughter's breathing settled toward sleep. The road hummed in the bones of the wheel.

From up in the dark, a low whistle came two notes, then a third, shaped like a question. It was not a signal they used. It was not a bird either. James raised his hand and every head tipped to listen. The whistle came again, nearer, then stopped. Leaves lifted where someone passed without asking the leaves' permission. Stand easy, James said, which is not the same as relax. He stepped out from the shadow of the wheel.

A figure appeared at the edge of the crescent small, slight, a girl in a dress that had been white once and was now the color of road. She held her hands out away from her body, empty, careful I kept walking, she said. Her voice was a whisper the creek nearly kept. No one followed me. Her eyes were older than her face. Can I sit in your circle awhile? No one moved to her, and no one sent her away.

Margaret put down the braided grasses and rose. Yes, she said, the word as soft as the place where the creek made itself smaller to go around a stone. If you can be quiet and still.

The girl nodded. She did not cry. She did not look behind her. She crossed into the thin light and sat where Margaret pointed, near enough to the water that its talking might cover breath.

James did not ask questions. There would be time or there would not be. He walked the line one more time, and in the dark between two trees he paused and looked up until the sky became eyes looking back.

The fires guttered to coals. Somewhere, far off, a drunk laughed himself into a cough and then coughed himself into silence. The biskinik tapped once, like a nail being set, and then nothing but creek and insects and the lowpatience of trees.

They were only miles from the treaty ground. It felt like a country.

No one said sleep. They already were, the part of sleep that keeps watch while the rest of the body goes where it can bear to be. The wagons breathed. The road waited outside the crescent like a dog that knows the morning by heart.

When the wind shifted, it brought no smell of whiskey. Only water on stone, and a hint of crushed mint where some wheel had found a tuft and taught it the weight of leaving.

CHAPTER 7
THE LONG ROAD TO THE SABINE

The treaty ground lay behind them, but its shadow stretched long. Ahead was the rst leg of the journey: the road southwest to Natchez, nearly two hundred miles by the old trace. At twelve miles a day, the march might take sixteen days if the weather held, twenty if it did not. For the Yowani, this was no wandering. It was a deliberate passage, the first trial of many, and every detail mattered.

On the last evening before departure, James McCoy called the people together. The relight flickered against weary faces men, women, and children who carried the weight of both loss and determination. His voice was firm. We walk as one. Scouts ahead, guards behind.

Wagons tight but not pressed. Boys at the wheels, men on the flanks. At midday we halt, at night we circle.

Water first for the animals, then for the people. At dawn, we rise and move again. No fire on the open trace. Watch is kept in pairs until morning. This is the way we will live until we reach Natchez. Margaret spoke when the talk turned to food. We carry what we can, but we must make it last. A strip of meat, a corner of bread, enough to keep walking. The land will give the rest: nuts, persimmons, grapes, venison if the hunters are steady. If fever comes, we do not leave the sick by the road. If a wagon breaks, we mend it. We do not scatter. We began together, and we will end together. Her words settled heavy on the circle, but not all were satisfied. William McCoy, James's twin brother, shifted forward in the firelight. His face was weathered like James's, but where James carried calm, William carried grievance.

Twelve miles in a day? William said sharply. Not with children and worn beasts. Better to stop short than drive them to death. And a mouthful of corn won't keep a man on his feet. We'll be starved before Louisiana. James met his brother's eyes without heat. We will not walk to death. We walk to water. Ten miles, twelve, whatever the day allows. As long as we find water and sound ground, we will endure. And gaunt but living is better than full but finished. Margaret added softly,

The hand that carries will be joined by the hand that gathers. Both together will keep us alive. A younger hunter broke the tension with a laugh. William will curse today, but bless us tomorrow, once he's got squirrel bones in his teeth. A ripple of chuckles passed through the circle, though William shook his head and muttered into the fire. They all knew the truth: complaint was another load to carry, but so was hope. Each family dreamed of reaching Natchez whole, with no graves dug along the trace. It was not a guarantee, but it was a reasonable hope the kind that kept people moving. The fire cracked, sending sparks into the dark. Children drowsed against their mothers, dogs curled near the wagons, and the men on first watch adjusted their rifles. The rules had been set, the food counted, the doubts voiced, the hope spoken. Tomorrow, the road itself would test them.

CHAPTER 8

FIRST MARCH

At the break of dawn, they rose. No fire, no lingering. The wagons stood ready, beasts yoked in the dim light, breath steaming against the pale horizon. Men tightened traces, boys steadied the wheels, women tucked children under canvas.

The command was not spoken but understood: move. The wagons creaked forward, one by one, falling into their order on the narrow trace. Guards took the flanks, scouts slipped ahead with rifles on their shoulders. Dogs trotted, tongues lolling, eyes bright. The road itself, pressed into the earth by hundred years of travel, was no more than a worn path, two ruts cut into soil and pine needles, lined by woods that seemed to press close.

Dust lifted with each turn of the wheels, but the cool morning held it low. Margaret walked beside the second wagon, her skirts brushing dew-wet grass. She called encouragement to the children inside, who peered out from canvas, eyes wide, already weary with the day. James rode up and down the line, his voice steady, his presence a constant.

William kept his silence, rifle slung across his back, mounted on the wheel horse. His limp made walking pain, but astride he looked almost whole. The sun climbed, burning off the last of the mist. Birds scattered as the train advanced. They halted only long enough to water the beasts at a muddy creek, filling barrels with slow care.

Margaret reminded them: not long, not here. Danger lived in stillness. When the beasts™ sides heaved less and the last bucket was hauled, they moved again. By midday, they found a patch of higher ground. The wagons circled, not for rest but for order. Men inspected harness and wheel, women passed strips of dried venison and parched corn to hands that reached from beneath canvas.

Children chewed in silence. The halt lasted less than an hour. Then, with the sun still high, they moved again. The road did not end, only stretched before them, mile upon mile. By dusk, the Yowani had walked a third of a mile of wagons into the wilderness. They camped in silence, fires lit low, watchmen set in pairs. And in the quiet that followed, William still said nothing. Stoic, tight-mouthed, bearing the pain in his back as though it were another pack to shoulder. Not supportive, not cheerful but present, enduring, and proud enough to keep the silence.

CHAPTER 9

RAIN ON THE TRACE

The third day dawned gray, the air heavy with promise. Clouds thickened as the wagons rolled, and before the sun was high, drizzle slicked the canvas and speckled the dust. What might have been misery brought relief. The air cooled, the dust settled, and the beasts pulled steady, their hides darkened but their breath easier. Rain was a gift, even in its inconvenience. The trace softened underfoot, slowing the wagons.

Wheels sank deep, oxen strained, men leaned into the push. But there was no complaint. Better the mud than the choking dust of yesterday. Margaret walked close, skirts soaked, her hair plastered against her face. She urged the children to stay beneath the canvas. Out in the open, a misstep could mean more than a bruise a snake shaken from a tree, or worse, a wagon sliding off the path.

At midday they halted by a low creek swollen by the rain. The animals drank greedily, heads thrust into the current. The people, too, lifted handfuls of water to their mouths, cold and sweet. Barrels were filled, skins topped. Margaret pressed the women to use the rain as well, spreading blankets across wagon boards to catch the fall, collecting what the land gave for nothing. Food was passed without fire.

No one wanted smoke rising from the wet wood to betray their camp. They ate from sacks: parched corn hickoha carried dry and chewed soft; strips of venison toughened with age but enough to sustain; hicanina, a sweet from ground nuts mixed with honey, passed from hand to hand. The children devoured it, sticky smiles breaking the gray of the day. Rifles were wrapped in hides, powder horns capped against the damp.

Every man knew a soaked charge could mean death. They checked their weapons again and again, even as rain seeped into seams and shoes. Mothers kept knives close, their blades wiped dry beneath shawls, for a knife would cut true no matter the weather. By dusk the drizzle settled into a steady fall, drumming on canvas, masking every other sound.

The camp was set tight, wagons drawn close, guards wrapped in cloaks. In the dark, William sat astride his wheel horse, silent, rain running off his hat brim, his back stiff but unyielding. He did not speak. He endured. Like the rest of them, he pressed forward, step by sodden step, bound to the road that would not release them until

Natchez lay behind.

CHAPTER 10
BANDITS ON THE ROAD

The fourth morning broke clear, the trace drying under a hard sun. The wagons rolled steady, beasts pulling without falter. It seemed, for a time, that the day might pass without trial. But trouble found them before midday. From the trees ahead, shadows moved where no deer ran. The scouts lifted their hands Š halt. Rifles came forward.

Then the bandits burst from cover, muskets raised, faces streaked with paint meant to mimic Chickasaw war colors. But the gait, the gear, the voices shouting curses were no Choctaw tongue.

These were whites in disguise, preying where law held no sway. The ferrymen guards answered first, firing from theflanks. Smoke drifted, shots cracked, and men fell. William, astride his wheel horse, swung down hard. He would not risk firing from the saddle Š not with a beast bred for pulling, not war.

Using the horse for cover, he leveled his rifle and shot true. One raider dropped, clutching his chest. He reloaded, calm in motion, and fired again. Another fell into the dust. The wagons closed, men shouting, women pulling children down beneath canvas. Dogs snarled, straining at tethers. The bandits, meant to surprise and scatter, found themselves pinned against the road.

A younger guard's ball The struck a man in the throat. The rest broke, fleeing into thebrush as suddenly as they had come. Silence fell but for the moans of the dying. William straightened, sweat on his brow, his back stiff from the crouch but his rifle still firm. The people looked at him differently now not as the brother who complained, but as a veteran whose fire could hold the line. The dead lay in the road. James gave the order without pause.

Throw them in the river. Nograves, no markers, no ceremony. The current would take them. Men dragged the bodies by their boots, heaving them into the water. The river swallowed them, ripples closing without trace. Margaret walked among the children, steadying them with soft words, turning their eyes away from blood on the boards.

Ishkatini's whisper stirred within her: not every enemy wore his true face. She shivered, though the sun still burned. When the wagons rolled again, they rolled tighter, guards watchful, rifles at the ready. The road was no longer just a path Š it was a gauntlet, and they all knew it.

CHAPTER II
TOWARD THE FRENCH CAMP

The wagons creaked into French Camp by late afternoon, a small scatter of cabins standing where the trace widened. Smoke rose from a smithy, iron ringing against iron. Children's voices carried on the air, reciting letters at the mission school.

The place was half stand, half settlement Choctaw still, yet edged with the mark of white traders and missionaries. The Yowani slowed but did not scatter. James gave the order: quick work, no lingering. Wagons drew up near the blacksmith's shed. A wheel was pulled from its axle, a split mended with iron bands.

Horses were checked, hooves scraped clean. The smith worked fast, his hammer echoing across the yard. Margaret moved among the women, trading nuts and venison for salt and thread. She watched the schoolhouse, where Choctaw children bent over slates, their voices rising in unison. English words, Choctaw mouths. William kept his eyes on the road, rifle across his lap. His back ached, but he held himself straight. He felt the eyes of the settlers Š measuring, weighing. Not all gazes were friendly. Margaret sensed it too. This was Choctaw country still, yet already slipping.

They stayed no longer than they had to. When the wheel was set and the beasts watered, James called them back. The wagons closed ranks, the guards mounted. French Camp fell behind them as quickly as it had appeared, the echo of the hammer fading into the trees. Margaret looked backonce.

She saw children's faces pressed to the glass of the mission window, watching as the wagons rolled away. She wondered if those children envied the travelers or pitied them. Then she faced forward, where the road unrolled, and French Camp became just another mile left behind.

CHAPTER 12
THE WHEEL HORSE

Thunder rolled far off the next morning, low and unsettled. The air felt close, heavy, as if the sky itself pressed down on them. The wagons creaked forward, the beasts uneasy. By midmorning, a wheel horse balked Š stamping, snorting, tugging against the traces. The boy guiding it tugged hard, but the beast only tossed its head, eyes white. The wagon lurched sideways.

Shouts rang out. Men ran to steady the load before it tipped. The boy fought the reins, but his arms shook, his voice broke in panic. The horse was stronger, wilder than he could master.

William swung down from his mount. Here, he called, his voice sharp. Let me. He stepped to the wheel horse, his limp barely visible in the mud. Rifle slung across his back, bandoliers heavy on his chest, he reached for the reins with a sure grip. His hand stroked the horse's neck, firm and steady. The beast's eyes rolled, but William's tone was calm, commanding. Easy now. Easy.

The wagon steadied. The boy stepped back, relief plain on his face. William swung himself into the saddle, settling atop the restless beast as though he had always belonged there. He leaned forward, guiding with a light hand, his back stiff but his seat sure. The horsesnorted, then obeyed. From that moment, William rode the wheel horse not as passenger, but as guard. His rifle, his eyes, his skill were now at the head of the wagon.

The people watched, respect plain in their faces. He was no longer just James's twin, no longer the man who carried complaint. He was their shield, their veteran, their proof that endurance could wear the shape of pride. Margaret, watching from her place beside the second wagon, felt something in her chest ease. William had found his role.

Not behind, not apart but at the front, where his strength, scarred as it was, could lead.

CHAPTER 13

STORMS AND STILLNESS

By dawn, the storm broke full. Rain came in sheets, hammering the canvas, drumming against wood until the wagons groaned beneath the weight. The trace turned to mire. Wheels sank deep, oxen strained, men leaned shoulder to wheel. Progress slowed to a crawl, but no one faltered.

The rain was both curse and blessing misery for the flesh, mercy for the beasts. Margaret walked with her skirts clutched high, her feet sodden in the muck. She moved from wagon to wagon, checking children tucked beneath hides.

Their small eyes stared out wide, their bellies grumbling, but they were safe under cover. Mothers handed strips of jerky and cakes of parched corn to quiet them. No one spoke of fire. Wet wood would smoke and betray them, and the storm gave no shelter for flame. Rifles were swaddled in oiled skins, powder horns capped tight. Men checked their weapons again and again, knowing a single soaked charge could mean death. Women kept knives close, their blades wiped dry beneath shawls.

A knife would cut true no matter the weather. Margaret caught sight of one mother, her hand wrapped around the hilt with the same ease she might grip a cooking spoon. Lethal skill lived in such hands, quiet and unspoken. At midday, the rain eased to a steady fall. Blankets were spread across wagon boards to catch the water, funneling it into waiting barrels. Margaret pressed the women to save every drop. Clear water was treasure, rarer than coin.

Children laughed as they held out their tongues, catching the sky's gift in open mouths. Even in the storm, joy flickered. By dusk the downpour lessened, leaving mist that curled through the trees. The camp was drawn close, wagons tight, guards cloaked and hunched at their posts. The fire was banked low, smoke lost in the fog. In the shadows,

William sat his wheel horse, rain dripping from his hat brim. His back burned with pain, but he held his post without complaint. Silent, steady, enduring. Like the rest of them, he pressed on, bound to the road that offered no mercy and no pause.

CHAPTER 14

OLD HICKORY'S MEN

The rain broke at last, leaving the world washed and bright. The wagons rolled on under a sky scraped clean, the sun sharp against wet leaves. The trace widened as they neared the great river towns, and traffic thickened. Drovers drove cattle south. Traders marched with mules laden in packs. Some passed with greetings, others with suspicion.

The Yowani pressed forward, their wagons tight and their guards sharp-eyed. By midday they overtook a party of Choctaw men, older, their hair bound with red cloth. Veterans men who had fought at New Orleans under Pushmataha's command. Their muskets bore scars of that war, their eyes the weight of memory.

One saw William astride the wheel horse and called his name. They had served together, two decades past, when Jackson had led them against the British. The reunion was brief, but heavy. Laughter rang at first, the joy of old comrades meeting again, but it quickly faded to silence. The men spoke of betrayal, their voices hard. They had bled for Jackson, stood with him when the British fell back at Chalmette. Now, the same Jackson signed the papers that drove them from their homes. Pride had curdled to bitterness.

We fought for their freedom, one said, and now we march to our chains. Margaret listened, her heart tight. Ishkatini stirred within her, the whisper of her ancestors: loyalty given, loyalty broken. She thought of Pushmataha, whose death still carried whispers of poison. She thought of Red Shoes, betrayed in his sleep by one who had shared his fire. Bloodlines carried glory and treachery alike. That night, camped by the roadside, Margaret walked apart, her skirts brushin wet grass. She felt the presence of her ancestors like a weight.

Voices pressed at the edge of hearing Red Shoes, Chata, Chiksa, the mothers and fathers of her line. Ishkatini whisper was clear: Betrayal was no stranger. It was the oldest companion of her people. She drew her cloak tight and returned to the circle, where William's laughter echoed low with his comrades, evenas his eyes carried the same fire of hurt.

CHAPTER 15

THE CROWDED PORT

Natchez rose from the bluffs above the river, its white houses gleaming against the sky, its streets buzzing with commerce. But it was the docks below that struck Margaret hardest.

The riverfront was a tangle of ships flatboats, keelboats, steamboats belching smoke all pressed against the landing. Men shouted, barrels rolled, mules strained under loads. And everywhere, the trade of flesh. Slaves crowded the decks of vessels, chains at their ankles, their faces turned blank toward the water. Traders barked prices, inspecting teeth, prodding limbs, shouting claims of strength and fertility.

Families were split before Margaret's eyes a child pulled from a mother's arms, a man shoved into a line of strangers. She turned her face, bile rising in her throat. It was not only Africans. Among the enslaved she saw Choctaw faces Š children with straight black hair, eyes and noses that mirrored the men who stood over them. Margaret knew at once whatshe was seeing.

These were offspring, bred from women held as stock and sold as proof of profit. The fathers stood in the market as sellers, their features stamped on the children at their feet. Her chest tightened, her hands trembling as she pulled her shawl close. William's jaw set hard, his eyes dark with rage. James said nothing, his silence a wall.

The Yowani pressed their wagons close, unwilling to linger. Yet Margaret could not look away. The sound of the chains, the smell of sweat and fear, the laughter of the traders cut deeper than any knife. Ishkatini's whisper rose in her ear. Do not take on the world's burden. Your task is your people. Carry them forward. Margaret closed her eyes, the weight of the whisper heavy.

She knew the truth of it, but the truth offered no comfort. To turn from the suffering before her was its own kind of wound. Still, she did as the ancestors commanded. She drew her cloak tight and followed the wagons through the press of Natchez, away from the cries of the enslaved and the reach of the traders' hands.

CHAPTER 16

SLAVERS

The market beyond the docks was worse than the road into Natchez. Here the slave pens stood in rows, rough timber walls and iron locks. The air was heavy with sweat, tobacco, and despair.

Traders moved like merchants at any fair, their voices sharp, their laughter cruel. But what set Margaret's heart hammering was not only the sight of the captives it was the faces of the men who sold them. Choctaw men stood among the whites, their features unmistakable.

They haggled over prices, boasted of the strength of their stock. At their feet, children waited children who bore their noses, their eyes, their very likeness. Margaret's breath caught. These men were selling their own blood. Some of the children clung to one another, their skin shades apart but their features the same.

They were proof of what had been done: slave women bred like cattle, their children sold as profit. One girl carried a swollen belly proof of her value, the trader crowed. Margaret turned her face, shamed for him. William muttered a curse, his hand tight on his rifle strap. His back burned with pain, rage held him straighter than pride ever could. James set his jaw, his silence dangerous.

The Yowani kept their circle tight, unwilling to let the sight scatter them. The children in their wagons stared with wide eyes, hushed by mothers who had no words. Margaret's heart thundered. She longed to reach for the captives, to cut their bonds, to pull them into safety. Ishkatini's whisper cut through her chest like a blade.

You cannot bear the world's chains. Carry only your people, or all will be lost. She clenched her fists, the shame of restraint burning her cheeks. To turn away felt like betrayal. Yet she knew the truth. They were surrounded by soldiers, traders, buyers. To free one meant death for all. Even so, the memory would never leave her.

The image of children sold by their fathers seared itself into her, a mark no distance would erase. When they left the market, the Yowani moved in silence. The road west lay ahead, but the stain of Natchez clung to them. And Margaret knew it would cling forever.

CHAPTER 17

THE RIVERBOAT

Captain Green waited at the dock, a stout man with shar eyes and a measured smile. His boat was no raft, no flatboat scraped from the forest. It was a steamer, broad-decked and iron-braced, its paddlewheel looming like a turning mill. Smoke puffed from its stack, and guards leaned at the rail, rifles on their shoulders. This was a vessel built for both commerce and danger, and it wore its readiness plainly.

The Yowani gathered near, their wagons tight. Margaret watched as Green strode down the gangplank, his coat buttoned, his boots polished despite the mud. He spoke of terms with James the price for passage, the rules aboard, the dangers of the river. He was candid: pirates haunted bends, storms rose without warning, and no man with sense left his guard behind. Yet he did not flinch from their numbers. He had carried more, and heavier, and he would carry them. It was Green who brought forward two boys, lean and watchful, their wrists raw from rope.

He had bought them at the market Chiksa and Chata, he named them, with a quick smile that said he knew their worth. Good hands for the boat, he said. But better hands for you. They'll fetch buckets, tend the fires, sit with your young ones.

Safer here than there. Margaret saw the truth of it. These were not slaves now, not truly. They were shielded, for a time, by Green's coin and the Yowanis' circle. At dawn, fog lay thick on the water. Green ordered the gangplank raised before the sun touched the bluff. Better unseen, he said, than watched.

The paddle wheel churned, and the steamer pulled from the dock, its bulk sliding into the current like a beast into deep water. The river swallowed them whole, the fog closing like a curtain. On shore, Natchez vanished. Life aboard was cramped and constant. Margaret moved among the families, setting order. Food was portioned, waste was carried to the rail, children were kept close. Guards watched from the upper deck, their rifles never far.

Gamblers and women of the captain's company stayed in their cabins, glimpsed only in passing. The Yowani kept to the lower deck, their circle unbroken even on the water. One night, as rain swept the deck and thunder rolled, Green stood beside James at the rail. The river's no kinder than the road, he said. But it's faster. And sometimes faster is all that matters.

William stood near, rifle slung, eyes searching the mist. The wheel horse stamped in its traces, uneasy with the storm. Green nodded toward him. Best keep him close. A steady hand up front can mean the difference between landing safe and sinking deep. The river carried them south, toward the bend where the Red would meet. And every turn, every shadowed bank, carried the promise of danger.

CHAPTER 18

LOUISIANA MUD

Louisiana greeted them with swamp and silence. The river narrowed, twisting through black water that stretched into shadow. Cypress trees rose on either side, their roots knotted, their branches heavy with moss. The air smelled of rot and damp earth. Fog clung low, rising in curls from the warm water.

Every splash carried weight a fish, a snake, an alligator sliding unseen. The wagons creaked along the raised road when they left the boat, each wheel threatening to slip into the mire. The earthworks rose only a few feet above the swamp, a narrow ribbon of survival cut through death.

The beasts strained, their hooves sliding in the muck. Men walked with whips and poles, guiding the teams, keeping them from panic. No one dared fire a gun. A shot could spook the teams, send a wagon tumbling into the black water. Knives and poles were their weapons here. Children were kept inside the wagons, hidden beneath canvas. Older boys stood at the fronts and backs, knives fixed to poles, ready to strike if a snake fell from the branches above.

Women, too, kept their blades close, hands steady on hilts worn smooth with use. Margaret moved from wagon to wagon, her voice low, her eyes sharp, her every step measured against the mud's hunger. William led at the head, astride the wheel horse. His limp was hidden by the saddle, his back stiff but his rifle steady across his shoulders. He was more than a guard now. He was a leader of the riders, older men who took the lead horses, steadying the teams when the road grew slick. They watched him, and they obeyed him, his veteran's calm binding them tighter than command. At dusk, they camped on a rare patch of high ground. Fires were small, smoke lost in the fog.

The swamp pressed close, its silence broken only by the drip of water and the occasional splash that made every child shiver. Margaret sat with the mothers, reminding them of the water they had caught in skins, precious and clear. They drank sparingly, guarding it as though it were gold. The swamp water, black and foul, could not be trusted. In the dark, Ishkatini's whisper came to Margaret again. Every step forward is a step bought with fear. But forward is the only way. She looked at William, a dark shape astride his horse, his rifle a shadow against the stars. He did not falter.

And neither could she.

CHAPTER 19

THE FERRY

The Sabine lay ahead, its brown waters rolling slow but wide. Gaines' Ferry waited there, the last gate between Louisiana mud and Texas soil.

The Yowani wagons creaked into the clearing at dawn, the air sharp and clear after so many days of fog and storm. For the first time in weeks, the sky was cloudless. The sun cut hard shadows, and the people could see for miles.

Captain Green had sent them with a letter, sealed and pressed into Margaret's hand. She did not know its contents, only that Green had said it would smooth their way. James carried it to the ferry master, who broke the seal and read. His eyes narrowed, then he nodded. Passage would be given. The price had already been paid. The soldiers at the fort watched closely. Their duty was clear: guard the border, watch the river, and catch runaways.

Two of them eyed Chiksa™ and Chata, the boys Green had placed in their care. They saw only slaves. Questions rose whose property, whose papers? Margaret stepped forward before James could speak. Her voice was calm, her eyes steady. They are ours. Servants. Not runaways.

The soldiers hesitated, then let the matter drop. Margaret felt the weight of her words, the lie that bound her now. To shield the boys, she had named herself a slaveholder. The burden pressed deep, but she bore it. Ishkatini's voice whispered within her: Sin is a garment you wear for your people.

Carry it, and walk on. She closed her eyes, and for a moment she saw Red Shoes, Pushmataha, the line of chiefs and mothers before her. Their faces blurred into one, the weight of all their choices resting on her shoulders. She drew breath and stood taller. The ferry groaned under the weight of wagons, beasts, and people. The river carried them across, the current tugging but the ropes holding fast.

Children clung to their mothers, eyes wide at the water's reach. William stood at the prow, rifle slung, his figure a sentinel against the far shore. James held the reins tight, his jaw set. On the Texas side, the land spread wide, bright beneath the rising sun. Waiting at the bank stood a man, tall and spare, his face shadowed by a broad hat. He raised his hand in greeting, his voice carrying across the water. Ishkatini, he called. Margaret's breath caught.

The name was her whisper made flesh. Her ancestor, her guide, now a man of earth and bone. The ferry touched shore. Wheels rolled onto new soil. Margaret stepped down, the weight of the crossing behind her, the promise of more trials ahead. But for this moment, her people stood on Texas ground. They had come together.

They would go on together.

CHAPTER 20

THE FAR SHORE

Margaret studied him, her heart caught between awe and dread. You are here, truly here. But why? Why would you leave the world of the ancestors and walk beside us in flesh, not feather?

Ishkatini's gaze swept the line of wagons easing up the bank. Because words alone will not shield you. This land is a crucible. You must see, not only hear, what dangers lie ahead. Flesh can take the blows that whispers cannot.

She lowered her voice. And yet– the others treat you as though you are only a man. They bow, they listen, but they do not see. Why? Because they must not, Ishkatini said softly. They see a leader who does not age, and they whisper of medicine, or witchcraft. If they knew the truth, their faith would twist into fear. Better that they believe me a stubborn old chieftain who refuses to die. Better that they never learn what I am. Margaret shivered. But you cannot hold that disguise forever. No, Ishkatini admitted. Already my face has not changed in their lifetime. Soon I must step aside, before suspicion curdles into hatred.

That is why you must prepare to move again. In three or four years, you cannot remain here. You must lead them on. Margaret's breath caught. Lead them where? Must we uproot again, after all this? Ishkatini's eyes darkened. Texas will not hold you. Already I see it...war rising. The Anglos will lift the banner of liberty, but their cause will be chains. They will make Texas into a house of slavery, and you will be trapped between Mexico's soldiers and the planters' whips. Stay here, and the fire will consume you. He stepped closer, his voice low and fierce.

Do not think the Choctaw Nation will be safer. The chiefs bargain away land, and some bind Africans in bondage. If the United States ever breaks with slavery, the Nation may cling to it harder, making itself a last refuge for masters. A Nation of chains is no Nation at all. Haiti taught the world that the earth itself will not bear such weight forever. Margaret's hand went to her mouth.

Then where, Ishkatini Where can we stand? Perhaps further south Ishkatini said. Mexico does not want slaves. It binds Indians in missions, yes another cage but at least the children are not sold lik calves. Some of our cousins have gone there already, deeper than the Sabine, into the old provinces. If there is a refuge, it may be beyond Texas. Margaret's voice shook.

You ask too much. I have carried them from the treaty ground, across rivers, through swamps, onto this foreign shore. Must I promise them still more wandering? You carry the blood of chiefs, Margaret said, his voice like flint. Your burden is never finished. You will always lead them from one fire into another, until the last fire consumes you. She looked at him, her throat raw. And if I cannot endure? Then your people perish, Ishkatini said simply.

That is why I walk beside you now not as a whisper, but with hands and voice. So you do not bear this alone. Margaret closed her eyes. The smell of pine and damp earth pressed in on her senses. When she opened them again, Ishkatini was still there solid, breathing, unshaken. She lifted her chin. Then we go forward. Forward,

Ishkatini agreed. But never blind

CHAPTER 21
THE ROAD TO ST AUGUSTINE

The wagons groaned as they left the soft ground near Gaines Ferry and began the slow climb up the sandy trail. The Sabine River faded behind them, its swirling waters still heavy in Margaret's mind. She glanced back once, knowing that the crossing marked more than a boundary between Louisiana and Texas. It was the edge of one world and the uneasy beginning of another.

Ahead, Ishkatini rode with an easy grace, his pony weaving between ruts as though he knew the road as well as he knew his own breath. He had joined them just the evening before, his presence quiet but commanding. The others quickly deferred to him, for he seemed to know every twist of the path, every hollow where water might be found, every turn that might shelter a wagon train from storms." Keep the wheels steady," he called back in Choctaw, then in English for those who needed it. "This road is long, and your flour sacks will not refill themselves. If the oxen stumble or we linger too often, your provisions will be gone before Saint Augustine."

Margaret caught his words clearly. "How many days do you think?" she asked, riding alongside for a time." Four, perhaps five," he replied. "If the weather holds and if no wagons break an axle. You must press on. Always press on. Every hour we delay, we cut into the margin that will carry you to the town."

His warning carried more weight than the simple tally of days. She heard in it the truth of a man who had seen too many parties falter on this road, who knew what hunger could do when the nearest mill was a hundred miles behind. The trail narrowed between pines. In the distance, the rhythmic clatter of hooves announced riders. Margaret stiffened, her hands tightening around the reins. A file of Mexican soldiers appeared, their uniforms patched, muskets slung over shoulders, horses weary but purposeful. They were not hostile, but neither were they blind. The officer raised a hand and slowed the column as they passed. His eyes swept the wagons, pausing on the darker faces among the group. He said nothing. One of his men scribbled in a leather-bound book before nudging his horse forward. No one moved until the patrol had vanished behind the trees. Only then did the children breathe again." They saw us," Margaret murmured." They marked you," Ishkatini answered. "They are under orders to watch for runaways, and for smugglers who think the Sabine hides their crossings. They will not strike today, but your names may already be carried to their officers at Nacogdoches. Best you remember that."

That night, camped in a clearing, Margaret joined him by the fire. Sparks drifted into the dark, catching for a heartbeat before vanishing. "You know these people we are going to," she said. "Tell me what awaits us."Iannini leaned on his knee, silent for a long while. "Once, when your father Atahobiah lived, there was order. The clans spoke, and the Deer Clan still held respect enough to guide decisions. But after his death, that order faded. Now they hold councils like the white men — everyone's voice the same, no matter their clan or their place. They think it is fair, but I tell you, it is dangerous.

A tree without roots will topple in the first hard wind." "And what of me?" Margaret asked quietly. "Do they still honor blood?" He met her gaze steadily. "Some will see you as your father's daughter. Others will see only another mouth at the table. If you expect respect, you may find disappointment. And yet ..." His voice softened. "There is still strength in remembering who you are, even if others forget." The fire cracked between them. Margaret wrapped her shawl tighter and felt the weight of his words settle in her bones. Ahead lay St Augustine, where provisions and rest could be bought if coin and luck allowed.

Beyond that, the land between the rivers — and with it, the test of whether her people still had a place in this fractured country.

***

The Law of April 6, 1830
In 1830, the Mexican government passed the Law of April 6, designed to halt the flood of Anglo-American immigration into Texas. The law banned further settlement from the United States, canceled empresario land grants, and ordered the establishment of forts to enforce customs duties. Mexican patrols like the one

Margaret's party encountered were tasked with stopping smuggling and noting the presence of suspected runaways. For settlers on the road, this meant constant surveillance and the risk of being reported — a reminder that their journey through Texas was neither invisible nor without danger.

CHAPTER 22
THE COMMUNITY GATHERING

The journey to the land between the rivers had been long and uneasy, but as the wagon train finally entered the clearing where the Choctaw community gathered, Margaret felt a wave of anticipation. Ishkatini, walking confidently ahead, had promised her that this gathering would be unlike anything she had yet experienced. The clearing was alive with activity. Fires had already been lit, and the smell of roasting meats mingled with the sweetness of maize cakes.

Women moved in small groups, arranging food and drink, while children darted through the crowd. Men stood in circles, speaking quietly or laughing aloud. Margaret could see that this was no ordinary meeting—it was both a celebration and a council. Ishkatini led Margaret's group to the edge of the gathering space. "Here," he said, gesturing toward a place where they might rest. "Tonight you will meet the elders, and the people will see that you have come in peace." His voice carried both pride and caution, as though he knew the importance of these first impressions. Margaret soon found herself introduced to a man of great dignity—an elder of the Deer Clan. Though his voice was calm, his words carried weight. "We once held leadership in this land," he told her. "But the clan ways are fading. Now councils rule by the voice of many, and the authority of the clans is no longer respected."

He looked at Margaret with searching eyes. "Do not expect the power of your lineage to give you place here. That time is passing." Margaret nodded, humbled but not discouraged. Nearby, Ishkatini added his own quiet warning: without the balance of the clan structure, the people risked falling into the habits of the Anglos—chasing wealth and neglecting the bonds that had once held the community together. As the night wore on, food was shared freely, and Margaret watched William find his own place among the hunters. He spoke with them eagerly, and soon plans were made for a deer hunt that would provide venison for the winter.

Margaret was struck by how quickly her brother had gained their respect. His skill with the rifle, already known from their journey, would make him an asset. Yet even in the joy of the gathering, Margaret sensed an undercurrent of unease. The laughter was loud, but the shadows between the fires seemed longer. She wondered how long this fragile peace could last—and whether she and her people truly had a place in it.

CHAPTER 23

THE DISAPPEARANCE OF CHATA AND CHICKSA

The winter settled over the land between the rivers with a chill that seeped into the walls of the cabins. Margaret's small band had grown used to the rhythms of life here: the fields that lay fallow, the chopping of wood for the fires, the gathering of dried corn from the storehouses. William, restless as always, spent much of his time scouting the edges of the settlement, his sharp eyes always on the lookout for any sign of trouble.

Two of their greatest helps were Chata and Chicksaw. Strong, steady, and skilled in the work of the fields, they had earned the respect of nearly everyone in the camp. Margaret often said they were worth two men each, and William quietly agreed. Neighbors noticed too—their labor was admired and, perhaps, envied.

Then, one morning in the early spring, they were gone.

Margaret searched the cabin and the yard, William scoured the fields, and others fanned out along the road. No trace. No broken branches, no hurried prints in the soft ground. Just silence. Rumors spread quickly, each one darker than the last. Some whispered that neighbors, coveting their skill and strength, had stolen them away, hidden on a distant field and chained at night so they could not run again. Others said a jealous family, resentful of Margaret's claim that they were servants rather than slaves, had turned them over to the Mexican authorities in exchange for favor. And still others believed the two had slipped away of their own accord, seizing freedom in the uncertainty of the times and pressing deeper into Mexico.

William took the disappearance hard. He asked questions at every farmstead, rode out to distant clearings, and watched for signs on the road. But no answers came. Each possibility—stolen, betrayed, or self-emancipated—remained just that: a possibility. No certainty, no closure.

For Margaret, the loss struck deeper still. Chata and Chicksa had been with her since Mississippi, shadows of her own family's long journey. Their absence left an emptiness not only in the fields but in her heart. And so the story of Chata and Chicksa ended in silence, a mystery carried on the wind. Were they victims of envy, or the bravest souls of them all—two men who slipped the bonds of the old world and found freedom where no one could follow?

The answer would never be known.

CHAPTER 24
THE DECISION TO LEAVE TEXAS

The harvest had come and gone, and though the storehouses were full, the air around the settlement was heavy with unease. News filtered in from the south—Santa Anna's army advancing, the Alamo falling, and the talk of war stretching like smoke across the land. Yet it was not only the Mexican forces that troubled them. Word reached James that Mirabeau Lamar's men, fueled by suspicion and fear, had struck at Nacogdoches, killing a number of Yowani Choctaw.

The message was unmistakable: those who would not join the Texian cause might soon be seen as enemies .James spoke quietly with Margaret by the fire one evening, the embers casting long shadows on the cabin walls. He told her of Lamar's growing hostility toward Native peoples, of the Cherokee leader Chicken Trotter whose actions had given the Texans an excuse to strike, and of the townsfolk who now prowled the countryside in search of Indians to punish.

Margaret listened, her face drawn with the same worry that pressed upon them all."If they will not distinguish between Cherokee and Yowani," James said, "then it is only a matter of time before they come for us. Lamar does not want us here. To him, we are squatters on land he intends for others. Margaret nodded slowly. The decision was not hers alone, yet she bore the weight of it all the same. The land between the rivers had given them shelter, but it could no longer promise safety. She thought of the kinship bonds that had frayed, the clan structure that once guided them now fading into the noise of councils and the ambitions of men. It was time to move on.At the end of the Green Corn Festival, she gathered her family and those who would follow.

Some had chosen to remain, bound by marriage, good fortune, or stubbornness. But many more loaded their wagons, tying down what few possessions they had. They would take the northward road, aiming for the Red River and beyond to the Choctaw Nation. The morning they left, the mist hung low over the fields. Margaret climbed into the wagon, William seated beside her, and James riding ahead as guide. She did not look back. Whatever the future held—uncertainty, hardship, or hope—it lay before them now.

Behind them, Texas closed like a door. Ahead, the Red River waited.

***

The wagons rolled slowly, their canvas tops streaked with dust from the long road. Margaret felt every mile in her bones, yet when the walls of the post rose into view, she straightened in her seat. They had reached the decision, though not the final one for all time. The wind carried the smell of wood smoke and the distant voices of soldiers, and with it came the first breath of safety in many years. Distant kin would come forward to greet them. Giles Thompson, broad of shoulder and gray at the temples, would offer them shelter near his place at Boggy Depot. His welcome would not be warm, but it was steady, and that was enough. Land and food would be found; cabins would be mended or built anew.

For the first time since leaving Mississippi, Margaret allowed herself to think not only of surviving the day, but of living into the next season. At night, by the fire, she turned her thoughts back along the road. The faces of the lost rose up before her: Chata and Chicksa, carried away into mystery; her father, Atahobiah, whose steady hand had once kept the people in order; James, whose quiet strength had steadied her own. Each loss was a wound, yet each mile gained had been bought by her choices. She had sinned, if sin meant to bargain and bend in ways her ancestors never would have dreamed. Yet she had kept her people alive. Was that not the greater commandment?

Word had drifted northward of what was happening in Texas. The Alamo had fallen. Santa Anna's banners had swept across the land they had only just left behind. Margaret sat long with the news, her heart heavy with the thought of those were still caught in that maelstrom. Ishkatini, seated across the fire, spoke softly: "Sometimes survival is the greatest victory. You turned your back before the storm broke, and that saved your people."

Margaret knew he was right. Their leaving had been providence, or perhaps the whisper of ancestors steering her feet. In the weeks that followed, life steadied. William rode out with hunters, his skill with the rifle marking him as a man to be reckoned with. The young ones planted fields beside the storehouses of kin. They were no longer wanderers, though they were not yet rooted. Margaret watched them, knowing that the work ahead belonged more to them than to her. She had carried them here; they would carry the name forward. On a cool evening, when the fire cracked low, Ishkatini rose.

His eyes gleamed in the half-light, ageless, both weary and eternal. "I have walked with you in flesh," he said, "but my path is not bound to yours. When you are old, I will return. Or perhaps you will see that I never left." Then... he was gone into the night, leaving only the stir of wind in the trees. Margaret felt no fear. She understood now: he was all her ancestors, every voice from the dawn, and he would never forsake her. She lifted her gaze to the stars wheeling above. The road of the Wind Clan stretched on into lands unknown. But for now, her people had endured. Now, they would cross the wilderness.

She had reached this decision. Her destiny was at hand.

CHAPTER 25
RUMORS OF REBELLION

James had been listening carefully to every scrap of news that drifted along the roads and through the settlements. One evening, as the family gathered in the cabin, he leaned toward Margaret and began to tell her what he had learned.

"There's been fighting near Nacogdoches," he said, his voice low but steady. "Not open war, but skirmishes between settlers and the Cherokee, sometimes with Choctaw caught in between. Some of it comes down to hotheads. A Cherokee named John Benge led one raid, and there are whispers about John Bowles' people too. The Anglos see it all as one great conspiracy — to them, every Indian is part of the same band." Margaret frowned. "But we've kept clear of it. We've done nothing to raise suspicion." James nodded. "That's the trouble. It might not matter. To an angry settler, the difference between Cherokee, Choctaw, or Creek is nothing. They see us as one and the same. William even heard a man say outright, 'The only good Indian is a dead one.'"

The words hung heavy in the room. Margaret thought of the long years since they had left Mississippi. All that time, they had worked to plant fields, to raise children, to stay clear of trouble. Yet suspicion followed them still.

William, seated near the fire, shifted uneasily. "I keep wondering whether they'll mistake us for one of the raiding parties. If they do, there won't be questions asked. We'll just be targets."

No one contradicted him. Outside, the night sounds seemed to press against the cabin walls, and every gust of wind felt like the whisper of danger approaching. The family knew then that their time in Texas was running short, whether they wished it or not.

CHAPTER 26
THE SUMMER COUNCIL

By midsummer, the fields were thriving, and for a moment it seemed possible that life in Texas might finally bring stability. Rows of corn stood tall, beans wrapped their vines upward, and even the pecan trees, planted years before, began to yield their first crops. For many, this was proof that the land could indeed sustain them.

Still, Margaret called a council. The elders and families gathered in the open clearing, shaded by trees that had stood long before their arrival. The talk that evening was heavy with doubt and longing.

Some spoke firmly of staying. "We've put too many years into these farms," one man argued. "The soil is giving back now. We have blackberries growing wild, pecans ripening, and good water close at hand. Why should we leave just when it begins to pay?"

Others shook their heads. "The settlers grow restless. The Mexicans are at odds with them, and we're caught in the middle. It's only a matter of time before their anger falls on us."

James stood and turned to Margaret. "Sister, the choice falls to you, as it always has. We can remain and hope for peace, or we can move on before the storm breaks. But if we stay, we must be ready to live as Anglos do — take deeds, pay taxes, and risk being swallowed whole."

Margaret let her eyes pass over the crowd. Some faces were worn from years of labor, others marked with the hope that this land might finally be home. She knew then that her people would divide. Those determined to stay would be remembered as the Thompson Choctaws, blending their lives into Texas soil. The rest — her part of the band — would move north when the time was right.

The decision was not final that night, but the seed had been planted. Everyone knew the journey would begin again after the next Green Corn Festival, when the stores were full and the roads were still passable. For now, all they could do was tend their crops and prepare for the path ahead.

CHAPTER 27

CAPTAINS AND CORN

By spring's end the earth between the rivers had proved itself—lean but willing. The rows we set in March came up in modest, tidy bands of green, and Ishkatini's storehouse took on the quiet weight of safety: sacks of meal, strings of dried venison, baskets of beans. It would carry his household, and ours, if need be, through a hard winter. For the first time since Natchez, Margaret allowed herself one breath that was not held.

But the same breezes that cooled the fields carried new talk along the roads. Word passed that men were riding out from Nacogdoches and along the Neches—a certain kind of man, the sort who owned a ledger and a big house and could be called "captain" if he bought enough powder and promised enough glory. They went door to door and fence to fence, saying Texas would be free and asking who would stand in their company against the Mexicans.

They did not ask our people so much as measure us. When a recruiter's party stopped at Ishkanini's yard one hot afternoon, their leader—gold watch, riding whip, smile too wide—tossed a look over our women and boys as if counting sacks. He spoke to James as though to a foreman

"You've stout fellows here," he said. "A man who wishes to be welcome in this country proves it. We ride in three days."

James's answer was courteous and even. "We have fields to tend and families to keep. We will not take up this quarrel."

The captain's smile thinned. "Those who won't go along," he said, "often find they fit poorly among neighbors who will." He turned his horse, the recruiters' laughter trailing him down the lane like dust.

William watched until the riders went out of sight. "That's a line drawn," he murmured.

Margaret said nothing then, but she felt the furrow open inside her, as sharp and straight as any plow could cut. She had seen this look on men before—the one that weighed people in coin and counted their silence as consent. It was the look that had taken the boys Chata and Chicksa, whether by betrayal or by rumor or by their own brave feet south. Since their disappearance, William had ridden the back paths each evening, eyes flicking to remote fields and cabins where a pair of hands might be hidden by day and chained by night. He found nothing but closed faces and the kind of quiet that meant too much was known and no one would say it.

As summer pressed on, the recruiters returned with new stories—Santa Anna marching, San Antonio bracing, little companies forming, muskets promised at discount if a man signed his name. Around us, some neighbors drilled in a pasture and called each other "lieutenant" and "sergeant" and shouted until their voices grew hoarse. Others kept to their fields but wore the look of men who had chosen a side. Among the scattered Choctaw here, the councils had grown louder and shorter. Cotton had a vote. Slaves did too, but only through the mouths of those who owned them.

That night Margaret sat with James outside the cabin, the air holding the day's heat like a hand. Fireflies stitched small lights between the pines, and somewhere far off a drum marked steady time for a dance we could not se"We have done what we came to do," she said, low. "We proved we could stand on our own feet here. But this soil will not hold us. The clan is broken in this place. Men who own cotton will soon own the councils outright, and men who will not fight their war will be pressed until they break. Ishkatini's stores are full. If we are to move, it must be when the green corn is in and the wagons can carry it fresh."

James nodded. "If we wait until the captains own the road, we'll be asked to pay a toll we cannot pay." He was quiet a time, and then: "How many will come, do you think?"

Margaret's gaze went to the cabins scattered along the tree line. "We left Mississippi a hundred and fifty souls," she said. "Half have drifted to other places—Mexico, San Antonio, westward with cousins. Of those left... some have married into farms here, some have found their luck with cotton and will not leave it. Perhaps a third—maybe less—will follow us to the Red River."

She did not say that part of her heart had hoped for more. She did not say she understood them—the ones who stayed. Prosperity could be a tether stronger than kinship, especially where the Ishkatini held no sway. In the town she had heard talk of Thompson kin—relatives by her husband's line—who had done well in the timber and store trade. The land could make a man rich if he agreed to forget what the land had taken from others

The next day she called the households together by the storehouse door. Ishkatini stood at her side. She laid it plain: they would depart after the Green Corn, when the fields had given and the stores were heavy, when the roads were still dry and the teams could pull strong. Any family who wished to come would be counted and provisioned. Any who wished to stay would have her blessing and a share of seed and tools. There was no anger in her voice, only the steady cadence of a woman who knew the weight of choosing.

Voices rose, some with relief, some with fear. A few men asked whether the recruiters would make trouble if we left. James answered that a people on the road with their own wagons and their own food made a poor mark for extortion, and that William and the riders would keep a long, quiet watch around the column. William only touched the rifle at his shoulder and said, "We'll move like we did before: early, tight, and with our eyes up."

By evening the tally stood: perhaps thirty families, more women and children than men. Those who remained pressed food on us and offered to mend what needed mending—wheels, harness, shoes—because even where councils were bought and sold, kindness could still be given freely. Margaret thanked each one by name. She did not ask them again to come.

In the weeks that followed, the fields ripened, the green corn festival near enough to taste in the air. We cured meat, packed meal, sealed baskets with pitch. The wagons were set in order; fresh axles greased, tongues checked for soundness, wheel horses trained to the trace. Children learned once more how to sleep on the move, women how to portion food for miles instead of days. At night the distant drums grew fewer, replaced by the rattle of men drilling in pastures and the dull thud of hammers as someone somewhere built a gallows for a different kind of test.

On the last evening before the festival, Margaret stood with Ishkanini at the edge of the field. The corn leaves hissed in a light wind. "When we step off," she said, "we step away from what small ease we found here."

Ishkatini's eyes were on the road north. "Ease is a poor master," he said. "We step toward our name."

Behind them, the storehouse door stood open, the bins full and waiting. Ahead, the old habit of the road lifted its head like a horse eager for the trace.

CHAPTER 28
THE GATHERING OF VOICES

The council fire burned low, its light flickering against faces worn by years of work and worry. Margaret sat beside James, listening as the voices of the community rose and fell like the wind in the pines. For months they had managed to keep their distance from the quarrels of the Anglos and Mexicans, but now those quarrels were pressing close to their door.

An older man—one of the traders who carried news from Nacogdoches and beyond—stood and raised his hand for silence.

"You've all heard the name Sam Houston," he began. "He has been a friend to us. When the Republic of Texas was born, he urged peace with the tribes. He knew our ways. Grew up with the Cherokee, took a Cherokee wife, and the people called him the Raven. Houston kept his hand over us, and while he sat in the president's chair, there was hope the Texans might leave us be."

James leaned toward Margaret and whispered, "I've heard the same from travelers on the road. They say Houston's heart was softer toward us than most."

The speaker nodded grimly, as though answering James. "But Houston's days are nearly done. The law says he cannot stand again for president, and he will not. His enemies in the Congress fight him at every turn, and he has grown weary. The new man, Lamar, is no friend of ours. He speaks of Texas as a land for Anglos alone. If he has his way, the tribes will be driven out—or worse."

Murmurs rippled around the circle. Some shifted uneasily; others clenched their fists. Margaret felt the weight of their fear settling in her chest.

Another voice broke in, sharp with bitterness. "And you think Houston will lift a hand for us now, when he is already stepping down? No. His words of friendship are fading like smoke. What good is a raven with broken wings?"

The room grew tense. Margaret searched James's face and saw the same thought she carried: if Houston's protection was gone, then the people had little left to shield them.

William spoke next, his voice steady. "If Lamar comes, if the settlers harden their hearts, then we will be marked. They do not care to tell Choctaw from Cherokee or Creek. To them we are all the same—an obstacle to be cleared." He let his gaze linger on Margaret. "We cannot stay here forever. We must think of the road beyond."

The council fell silent, the fire's crackle filling the space between them. Houston's name lingered in the air like an echo of better days, but the shadow of the future was already stretching long across their camp.

Margaret folded her hands in her lap, steadying herself. She knew now that the question was not whether to leave, but only when.

CHAPTER 29
WRECKAGE ON THE TRAIL

The air was heavy with the smell of pecan smoke and late-summer dust as the families gathered around the clearing.

Margaret sat on a split log while James and William moved among the wagons, checking every musket, every horn of powder,
every bag of lead shot.

It was the last evening before their departure northward, and no one doubted the dangers waiting
beyond the Sabine country.

"They don't care who you are," William said firmly, holding a ramrod up to the light. "Comanche don't stop to ask if you're
Choctaw or white.

If you've got wagons and horses, you look like prey. That's how it is."

The words rippled through the group like a cold wind. Mothers pulled children closer; young men straightened their shoulders.

James raised his voice so all could hear. "We'll be crossing their hunting country, and they won't spare us because we've been here near twenty years. We'll go in formation. Wagons together. Guards posted every night. Powder dry and shot close at hand. You will obey the watch."

Margaret watched him speak with pride. He had become the hard voice of caution, while she remained the steady heart that held them together.
Beside her, Ishkatini leaned close. "The Comanche call us all settlers. To them, we are no different from the Anglos who take their rivers. Your wagons carry your lives—and they will come for them if they think they can." Margaret nodded.
"Then we must make it plain they cannot."

That afternoon, coin from the sale of corn and pecans had changed hands. A few families, determined to remain, had purchased the harvest
of those who would depart. The silver pesos jingled now in James's pouch, spent almost at once on powder, lead, and two rough-looking
frontiersmen who lounged near the edge of camp with their rifles across their knees.

One of them, a scarred veteran of San Jacinto, spat into the dust and grinned. "Ain't no war party gonna get through me for what you're
paying, lady," he told Margaret. She gave him a long look—measuring whether courage or desperation drove his boast—but said nothing.

As dusk fell, the wagons creaked into position, forming a circle around the fire. Families carried bedding and provisions inside the ring, while the men posted the first guard watch. The sound of flints snapping in lock checks echoed like a solemn prayer.

Margaret stood last, gazing at the embers of their long East Texas sojourn. "We came here seeking shelter," she murmured,
"but now the road leads north. May it lead us home."

The night swallowed her words. Beyond the circle, the dark prairie stretched toward the Red River, where no law but strength held sway.

CHAPTER 30
THE AMBUSH AND THE RECKONING

They saw the dust first—thin veils rising from the prairie grass and sliding sideways with the heat shimmer. Then the hawks turned all at once, and the hired rifleman with the San Jacinto scar said, too softly, "Riders."

William's hand lifted and chiseled three short signals in the air. The column flexed without panic. Canvas covers were thrown back and tied halfway, making low pale walls. Wagons locked hub to hub in a staggered chevron that gave every shooter a lane. Oxen were unyoked from the lead pairs and backed under the wagon bellies, broad bodies made into living bulwarks. Children and the elderly were pulled to the innermost wagons; water kegs were rolled along the ring; powder horns uncapped, flints checked.

"Under, not atop," James called. "Women to the right flank with the shotguns—two paces apart. Boys with squirrel rifles keep low and aim for horses' chests. No one fires alone. On my count."

The Comanche came in crescent formation—paint bright as summer fruit, hair feathers lifting in the wind, a sound like bees: bowstrings, pony hooves, death in a body. The first volley from the Yowani did not seek heads; it took legs. Ponies folded. The crescent broke on the wagons like a wave on pilings. Arrows rattled against canvas and pinwheeled into earth. A lance skated along a tailgate; a woman's shotgun cracked back, and the lancer tumbled, foot twisted in the rawhide loop as his pony bolted.

"Two! Now!" James shouted.

The second volley was slower and meaner, measured from shaded spaces beneath the wagons. Smoke flattened under the canvas, drifting out through the tied flaps. Women racked fresh charges with hands that had dressed deer and birthed children; the motions were the same: practiced, necessary, precise.

A handful of Comanche tried to leap from the saddle inside the ring—light as cats, brave as fire. That was where William lived. He lay on his side behind a wheel, cheek against the warm dirt, rifle braced in the V of the spokes. He did not seek faces; he cut at the space where man separates from horse. The first leaper spun and fell. The second, too. The third made it across a tailboard and landed on a flour barrel that split in a white puff; Margaret drove a trade knife up under his ribs, turning him into a hard weight that slid to the ground.

They came twice more, each pass shorter, angrier, less certain. When a gust of wind peeled back a canvas edge, Ishkanini dropped his hat and pushed the flap down with the crown, then fired blind at shadow and hoof. A pony screamed and vanished from the gap, and the hat came back to his head as if it had grown there.

Then the sound changed. It always does. The bees thinned. The crescents uncurled and became strings, then beads, then nothing at all but heat and far-off thunder where hooves rolled away into distance.

James waited, counting quiet, until the last echo left the grass. "Hold," he said. "No one stands. Listen."

Silence had a taste: sulfur and canvas and hot iron. A single ox coughed. A child hiccuped twice and stopped, as if afraid the sound might bring the riders back.

Inventory came next. It always did. Powder? Charges? Water? Wounds? They had been cut, but not gutted. One boy had an arrow groove along his forearm; an older man's cheek wore a shallow furrow where a bullet had glanced. A hired guard's boot heel was gone and his big toe purple as a plum. Only one life lost—a young husband whose head had risen at the wrong moment, curiosity stronger than doctrine. Margaret folded his hands and covered his face with his own scarf before the flies learned his name.

They did not move again until the sun tilted west. Oxen must live to pull, and that takes rest. They drove again at dusk and camped late, in a draw cut by a trickle of water that smelled of iron and leaves. No fire larger than a handful of coals. No talk louder than a murmur. The animals stood with their heads low, steam drifting from flanks as the heat unwound from the day.

"How long for the teams?" Margaret asked, keeping her voice for the small circle—James, William, Ishkanini, and the two riflemen.

James answered first. "For travel like this, at this pace, oxen need near half the day to do the next half. Two hours to cool, another to drink and chew. Then they give you ten, twelve miles. If we push them, they'll give us fifteen—but only if we pay it back with longer rest come night."

The scarred rifleman nodded. "Stock don't run on courage. You get a bolt, you lose a wagon. You lose a wagon, you lose a family."

Margaret looked toward the dark. "We stop enough to spare them. We move enough to spare us."

William rolled a cartridge between his fingers, listening to the paper crackle. "I keep thinking on the other train," he said. "They were brave. Maybe they were loud. Maybe they weren't ready to be small." He tapped the wagon bed. "We hid and made the wagons into a fort. We let them break on wood instead of flesh."

"They meant us to be afraid," Margaret said.

"They succeeded," James answered. "And it saved us."

A long quiet settled. Crickets started up in the rank grass. Somewhere a night bird made a sound like a hinge.

At last Ishkanini spoke, and when he did, the others listened with the attention people give to water in dry places. "You are thinking a thought that has no good end," he said to William gently. "If the Choctaw, the Chickasaw, the Cherokee had fought like the Comanche, would the white river have turned back?"

William didn't look away. "I am."

Ishkatini rubbed the heel of his hand along the wood of the tailgate, as though polishing a memory. "The Comanche ride a wide country—grass and sky, far between towns. To hunt them is to chase wind. The land you and I come from is tight with fields, water, roads, towns. It can be fenced and counted. That is a different hunger."

"So it was always coming," James said, not as a question.

It was always coming," Ishkatini said. "But paths change for those who walk them. If all the southern nations had made one fire, if their councils had been one council, the river might have taken longer to rise. But it would still have risen."

Margaret's eyes were on the children asleep under the wagon, two heads pressed together like seeds in a pod. "He"—she meant Jackson, and she did not say his name—"offered paper safety and brought iron."

"Paper burns," Ishkanini said. "Iron cools, and men forget its heat. What does not die is the story, if you carry it." William blew out a slow breath. "Then we carry it. And we live to deliver it."

The scarred man scratched his jaw. "I fought at San Jacinto and I'll tell you straight: a stand-up fight only works when you pick the ground and the clock. Those folks today—they didn't have either. You did. You made yourselves into a thing that was hard to kill. That's how you win against folks who can outride you."

"Then we keep doing it," James said. "No heroics. Tight circle, low fire, ready guns, small steps. We don't get drawn out. We don't chase."

Margaret's voice was firm. "And we do not leave the road of the living for the pride of the dead."

They parceled the night into watches. Powder stayed under oilcloth. Shot was counted and put into hands that would not waste it. Water kegs were cribbed so a stray hoof wouldn't crack a stave. The oxen lay, finally, with their heads turned sideways, chewing, the slow machinery of survival. The guards moved like clock hands, unhurried, on time.

Near midnight, a wind came down from the north, thin and almost cool, and the canvas breathed in and out like a living thing. Margaret lay on her side and listened to the small sounds that prove a camp is still a camp: a child's murmur, a man's cough, the whisper of a stone under a boot. Somewhere beyond the circle, coyotes tested the edge of courage and hunger and found it wanting.

Before first light, James and William moved the wagons again, leaving nothing but pressed grass and a smear of ash so faint it might have been a shadow. When the dawn finally took hold, it showed them what the night had preserved: a train that could be killed but had chosen not to be.

They went North.

CHAPTER 31

A PLACE TO REST

The wagon train rolled at last into the shadow of Fort Washington, its rough log palisades standing watch on the Red River. For Margaret and James, it marked the end of a long and perilous road. They had brought their people through — battered, fewer in number, but alive. Choctaw families already established here remembered the name of Atahobiah, and in that memory Margaret and James found welcome.

A cabin was made available for her household, little more than a single room with a hearth and bark thatch, but it was sound against the weather. Here, at least, the people could draw breath and feel that the ground beneath them might serve as home.

In the weeks that followed, word filtered north of their brother, William Wayne Thompson. He and his wife had taken another path, pressing on beyond the safety of Fort Washington toward Fort Towson, farther downriver. There, fever had struck — typhoid and malaria spreading mercilessly. The news was grim: William and his wife had perished.

Their deaths left behind an infant son. Margaret felt the weight of it immediately. She began to prepare herself for a journey to Fort Towson, determined that if the stories were true, she would return with the boy, William Clyde Thompson, and raise him in her household at Fort Washington.

It was a thought that carried both sorrow and resolve: that after all the miles and all the losses, she would now bear the responsibility for the next generation. The boy would carry their name, and with it, a fragile continuation of everything they had endured.

CHAPTER 32
A PARTING OF THE WAYS

The Yowani had scarcely settled near Fort Towson when William began to grow restless. The wagons were safe, the cabins were taking shape, and for the first time in many years, the people had a chance to breathe. But William's eyes were already fixed on the south.

Word had reached him that other families, straggling and uncertain, still hoped to make the journey north from Texas. Some were Choctaw, some mixed families, and all in danger of being swept up in the storms that were gathering. William knew what they would face on the road. He had survived it himself. Now he felt a duty to return and lead them north.

Margaret pleaded with him not to go. 'We've lost too much already,' she said, clutching his arm. 'Stay here with us, William. The Nation is large enough—you can find your peace here.'

But William shook his head. 'If I can bring even one more family through what we endured, it will be worth the risk. I can't sit idle while they face that road alone.'

James listened in silence, then nodded. 'It is your choice, brother. You've always been the strongest of us. But take care. The rivers run both ways, and danger runs with them.'

Arrangements were quickly made. A riverboat bound south would carry William down the Red River. His horse was led aboard, tethered safely near the rail, and his rifle rested across his knees. At dawn the boat's whistle shrieked, echoing against the trees, and the great paddlewheel churned the water to foam.

The family gathered on the landing. Margaret stood apart, her hands clenched tight. She waved as the boat pulled into the current, her brother's figure framed in the rising mist. He raised his hand once, then turned his gaze downstream. The paddlewheel thumped steadily, carrying him away. Soon, the river swallowed the boat in fog. Margaret's arm lowered. In her heart she knew this was a farewell not just for a season, but for all time. They would not see their brave brother again.

CHAPTER 33
MARGARET'S BLESSING

Margaret had lived long enough to see her people safely across the rivers, through the prairies, and into the new land that was promised but never truly theirs. The years had carved their lines upon her face, but her will remained unbroken. With James by her side and the boy, William Clyde Thompson, now under her care, she found a measure of peace she had scarcely imagined on the long road from Mississippi. Neighbors came and went, some Choctaw, some Chickasaw, and some of the new settlers who never quite knew how to address her. To most, she was simply the matriarch—stern, deliberate, and watchful, her presence a reminder of the old ways. To William Clyde, she was more: the guardian of stories, the keeper of memory, the one who stood between him and the uncertainties of the world.

Evenings were given to teaching. Margaret would sit by the fire with the boy, telling him of rivers and trails, of councils and broken treaties, of kin left behind and of kin who carried on. William listened, wide-eyed, his small hands clutching the quilt she had mended from scraps of Mississippi cloth. She spoke of duty, of kinship, of never forgetting who he was or where he came from. She spoke of courage, and of choosing the harder road when the easy one meant surrender.

Her health, though, began to fail. The winters were harsh, and each season seemed to weigh more heavily upon her. By the spring of the 1840s, she knew her journey was nearly done. One evening, when the sun had slipped low and painted the sky with fire, she called James and William close. Her words were plain, her voice steady though thin.

"James, you must see him through. He is young yet, but there is strength in him. He will need it, for this world has little mercy. And William Clyde—" She laid her hand gently on the boy's head. "Remember who you are. Remember your people. Carry them forward, even when others forget. The boy nodded solemnly, too young to grasp the full weight of her charge but old enough to feel its power. In that moment, Margaret's story, and the story of those who had gone before, passed into his keeping.

Not long after, Margaret's chair by the fire sat empty. Yet her presence lingered in every word William carried, in every memory James preserved, and in the unbroken chain of kinship that no distance, nor removal, nor death itself could sever.

Her blessing was not an ending. It was a beginning.

THE LONG STRUGGLE

What follows is no part of invention. *It is gathered from the record prepared by P. J. Hurley, attorney for the Choctaw Nation, and laid before Congress in 1916: a long account of promises made and broken, of names written and erased, of a people's endurance written in the margins of law. These words are taken from the Nation's own testimony, and though the tone is plain, the truth behind them carries the weight of lives and generations. It is from that history that this final chapter is drawn.*

***

In the early autumn of 1830, the Choctaw chiefs placed their marks upon the Treaty of Dancing Rabbit Creek. The treaty was meant to settle the matter once and for all: their homeland in Mississippi was ceded, their people were to move west, and in exchange, the United States gave promises—land in perpetuity, compensation for what was left behind, and, for those who would not go, the right to remain as citizens where they were born. The words were ink upon parchment, binding in law and solemn in tone. Yet even as the signatures dried, the breach began. Surveyors carved up the soil before families could gather their belongings.

White settlers poured into fields that were not yet theirs, pressing the Choctaws off the very acres the treaty said were theirs to hold a little longer. Those who set their faces westward bore the weight of the march, the Red River at last marking the edge of their new ground. Those who stayed behind—the Mississippi Choctaws—clung to the promise that the treaty's Article XIV would shield them, granting them citizenship and the right to register their lands.

But officials delayed, confused, or simply refused. Deeds were not issued, rolls were not kept, and the citizen-Choctaws found themselves adrift in a system that welcomed their labor but not their names. The Yowani, like others, were divided by this line. Some went on, their path a true odyssey across forests and rivers.

Some remained, caught in the tightening net of encroachment. All were bound, whether east or west, by the same broken treaty that had promised stability and delivered turmoil.

Those who crossed westward carried little more than what their hands could hold. They went in family groups, in scattered bands, along muddy roads and through swollen streams. Wagons broke down, children sickened, the old fell behind. Yet still they pressed on, guided by the vague assurance that somewhere beyond the Red River lay ground of their own, untroubled by the endless press of settlers. The Yowani were among them, though not in one body. Their name, like so many others, was scattered by circumstance. Some settled at the fringes of the new Nation, folding themselves into Choctaw towns already established.

Others drifted further, seeking refuge among allies or kindred in Texas, their identity kept alive not by formal rolls but by memory, kinship, and the stories told around evening fires. Those who stayed in Mississippi bore another fate. They trusted the government's word that they might hold their fields as citizens, their lands surveyed and recorded. But surveyors came and went without delivering title. Clerks lost or destroyed records. Local officials looked on them not as citizens but as intruders to be dispossessed.

One by one, farms were stripped away. Families who had been promised security awoke to find strangers plowing their cornfields, their own names erased from ledgers as though they had never existed. For decades after, the two groups—the migrants and the stayers—were bound together by a common wound. In Indian Territory, the Choctaw Nation worked to build a government, a system of laws, schools, and councils. In Mississippi, the remnants endured as best they could, caught in an endless cycle of petitions and appeals, pressing the government to honor its own ink. Each group looked across the divide and saw in the other a mirror: loss dressed in different clothing, but loss all the same.

By the latter half of the nineteenth century, the struggle had moved from the forests and rivers into the chambers of law. The Choctaws had been driven west, their Nation rebuilt in Indian Territory, but the promises that were meant to secure them had become ammunition for endless disputes. Every word of the Treaty of Dancing Rabbit Creek was pulled apart, interpreted and reinterpreted, not in the councils of chiefs but in courtrooms and congressional hearings.

The question of who was Choctaw became the fulcrum. Names were written onto rolls and struck off again, each decision carrying with it claims to land, to funds held in trust, to the very right to belong. Thousands pressed petitions, some with honest blood ties, others with forged affidavits and hired lawyers. Each petition meant delay, investigation, appeal. What should have been the settled body of a Nation became instead a battlefield of paper. Into this paper war came an army of attorneys, lobbyists, and speculators.

They haunted the halls of Washington, fanning out across the territories, promising hopeful claimants that for a fee their citizenship could be secured. False witnesses were hired, genealogies invented, records twisted. For every Choctaw family already settled upon their allotment, there loomed the danger that new claimants would be added to the rolls, thinning out the Nation's share of land and funds. The Choctaw leadership resisted as best they could.

Chiefs sent delegates to Congress, attorneys were hired to defend the Nation's sovereignty, investigators were dispatched to expose fraud. But the process itself was tilted. Each time the rolls were reopened, it was as if the ground shifted under their feet.

Cases dragged on year after year. Commissions sat, issued reports, dissolved, only for new commissions to be appointed. With every round, the certainty of citizenship became less a birthright and more a matter of legal survival. What had begun as promises written in 1830 had become a tangle of briefs, affidavits, hearings, and rulings.

The Nation had been forced into a posture of constant defense, its energy spent not on building a future but on guarding the narrow rights that remained from erosion.

In the midst of this storm of petitions and papers, the Choctaw Nation did not stand silent. Chiefs and councilors rose to the defense of their people, appointing attorneys to carry the Nation's cause into the courts of Washington. Letters crossed the miles from Indian Territory to the capital, setting out in patient detail the frauds uncovered, the false genealogies exposed, the danger to the Nation if rolls were allowed to swell unchecked.

Men like Green McCurtain and Victor Locke bore the weight of office in a time when the very definition of citizenship was under siege.

They faced delegations of claimants, some honest but many driven by promises of land that had never been theirs. They faced Congressmen willing to listen more closely to the lobbyist's coin than to the testimony of Choctaw leaders.

They faced attorneys who saw in the Nation's treasury not the survival of a people but a lucrative prize. Yet still they fought. They demanded hearings, pressed for investigations, submitted volumes of testimony that stretched on for years.

In these documents—the very papers from which this chapter is drawn—the tone is weary but unbending. "We are not opposed to citizenship," one delegate declared, "but to fraud." Page after page records the same insistence: that the Nation's identity must not be diluted, that its resources must not be stolen under cover of law. At times, victories were won. Fraudulent rolls were struck down. Spurious claims were dismissed. Yet for every battle gained, another loomed.

The machinery of appeals and commissions never ceased. The Nation was compelled to spend its strength not in building schools or farms, but in keeping watch against the endless press of paper claimants. Even so, this defense was itself an act of survival. By standing before Congress and the courts, the Choctaw Nation proclaimed its own sovereignty, its right to define itself against outsiders. In every petition resisted, in every fraudulent witness exposed, there was a declaration that the Nation still lived, still governed, still endured.

By the early years of the new century, the Choctaw Nation had spent decades in defense, its leaders worn by the endless grind of commissions, hearings, and appeals. The struggle had become generational: fathers began cases that sons would finish, if they were ever finished at all. Attorneys came and went, each promising closure, each leaving behind only heavier stacks of papers.In 1916, a kind of weary settlement was reached. The report laid before Congress by P. J. Hurley, attorney for the Nation, was not a triumph but a reckoning. It catalogued the frauds, the betrayals, the countless attempts to break down the Nation's identity by flooding its rolls with claimants who had no rightful place. It showed, in sober lines, the price of survival. What had been lost could not be measured only in acres or dollars, though these were vast.

More grievous was the time itself—the energy spent in fending off predation when it might have been used in building stronger schools, cultivating richer fields, raising the next generation in security. The Choctaw people had endured, but always with one eye turned to Washington, one hand busy in defense. Yet they had endured. The settlement did not erase the betrayals, but it did close a chapter. The rolls were fixed at last; the flood of false claimants was stemmed, if never entirely ended.

The Nation still stood, still governed itself, still carried the memory of its treaties and the determination to outlast those who would erase them. This was not victory in the bright sense of the word. It was survival—a Nation worn thin but still alive. The paper war had not broken the Choctaws, though it had scarred them. Against the weight of courts and Congress, they had managed to keep something that could not be measured in ledgers: their identity, their persistence, the unbroken thread of a people who refused to vanish.

The Red River had marked the end of the Yowani's odyssey, the border crossed after hunger and hardship, the line where the promise of a new life was meant to begin. Yet as the generations passed, that river proved only another threshold. Beyond it lay not peace, but the long attrition of hearings and commissions, a battle waged not with rifles or soldiers but with paper and pens.

***

One of my First Cousins, William Clyde Thompson, is an example of the injustice visited on the individual Yowani. William's life embodies both the resilience and the injustices endured by the Yowani Choctaw in the decades following removal.

Although he served with distinction during the Civil War—first in Mississippi 6th Infantry and later as a Captain in the Army of Tennessee under General Hood—his loyalty, his heritage, and contributions brought him no tangible reward from the Choctaw Nation. For decades, the Yowani were excluded from tribal citizenship as punishment for their departure from the Nation in the 1830s. This exclusion meant that William Clyde was never enrolled as a citizen during his lifetime, denying him the political rights, land access, and public benefits available to other Choctaw citizens.

By the time the Choctaw Council reversed its stance in 1909 and restored Yowani citizenship, the Dawes Commission allotment process had already concluded. The Nation's lands had been divided and assigned to enrolled citizens between 1899 and 1906, leaving nothing to distribute to the reinstated Yowani. The restoration was purely symbolic, offering no land, back payments, or grazing rights.

Evidence suggests that William Clyde had already passed away by 1909, eliminating even the possibility of a late enrollment. Without children or heirs to press a claim, his name did not appear among those reinstated, and no posthumous allotment was ever made on his behalf.

His story is a clear example of the broader injustice faced by the Yowani—loyalty to the Nation and years of survival on its contested frontiers were met with recognition too late to change lives. In William Clyde's case, the reward for a lifetime of service was not land or security, but the fading memory of his name among the descendants of those he fought to protect.

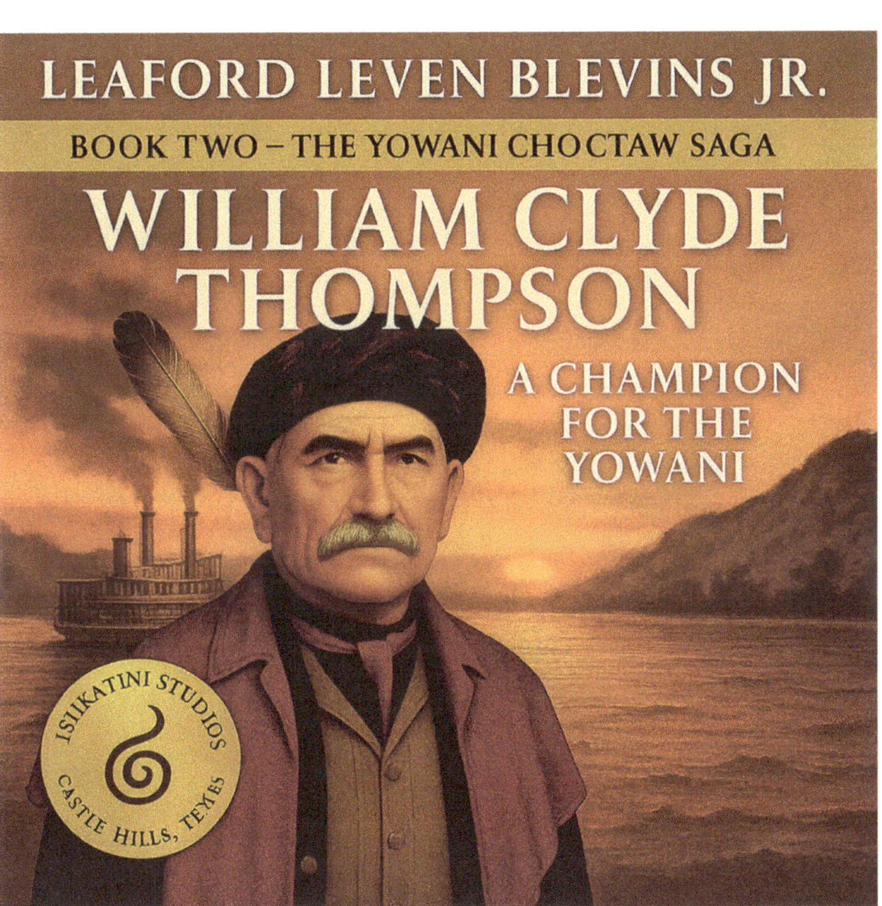

LEAFORD LEVEN BLEVINS JR.
BOOK TWO – THE YOWANI CHOCTAW SAGA
WILLIAM CLYDE THOMPSON
A CHAMPION FOR THE YOWANI
ISTIKATINI STUDIOS
CASTLE HILLS, TEXES

PART I

This book began as a search for memory. My ancestor, William Clyde Thompson, lived through one of the most violent and uncertain times in our nation's history. He was not a general whose name filled the newspapers, nor a politician whose words shaped the course of events. He was instead one of the thousands of young men swept into the Civil War — and like so many, his story nearly vanished into silence.

William Clyde was my first cousin, many times removed. His survival did not shape my own family line, but it shaped the destiny of thousands of others. Without his persistence and legal acumen in the years that followed the war, countless descendants of the Yowani Choctaw would have been denied citizenship in one of the greatest Indian Nations of this country. Their ancestors had been part of the tribe for centuries, long before removal, yet only through his determination did their rights endure.

For that, each of us owes him a great debt of gratitude. Had he not survived the war, his fight in the courts could never have been waged, and the doors of opportunity and belonging might have remained closed.

In these pages, I have tried to balance history with narrative, fact with imagination. Where the records are clear, I have followed them. Where silence reigns, I have written what might have been — always guided by the character of the man and the people who shaped him.

This is not only a story of war. It is a story of the Choctaw, of resilience, of injustice, and of endurance. It is offered as both a family remembrance and a contribution to the larger history of the Yowani Choctaw, whose voices deserve to be heard.

PART ONE

Before the legal battles and before the struggle for recognition, there was the war. This first part of the story follows William Clyde Thompson through his youth in Mississippi, his induction into the Confederate army, and his survival through some of the bloodiest campaigns of the Civil War.

Though he was not destined to be a general or a figure whose name would appear in schoolbooks, his endurance mattered. Without surviving the war, he would never have been able to carry forward the legal fight that preserved the Yowani line within the Choctaw Nation. Thousands of descendants alive today owe their standing to the persistence and survival of this one man.

HARDENING RESOLVE

CHAPTER I

THE STENCH OF DEATH

In the 1830s and 1840s, knowledge of disease was limited. Malaria and typhoid fever were common in Indian Territory, but their causes were not understood. People believed in the 'miasma theory'—that sickness spread through bad air, especially the stench of decay from swamps, stagnant water, or unburied corpses. Quinine was sometimes used against fevers, but most families relied on flight, fire, or prayer. At Fort Towson, when fever struck, bodies often outnumbered coffins, and the air itself was feared as deadly.

***

Fort Towson, Late August 1839

They smelled it long before they saw it.

The air thickened as the wagon drew closer to Fort Towson, the scent of pine and smoke giving way to something sour, rancid, and suffocating. Margaret pulled her shawl tighter over her nose and mouth, but it did little to blunt the reek. James said nothing, but his eyes narrowed, his jaw set hard against the wave of stench rolling toward them.

The fort's palisade came into view — and beyond it, disorder. Bodies lay in rows beside the rough cabins and barracks, covered with quilts, coats, or nothing at all. Too many for the shallow graves being hacked into the red clay. Dogs prowled the edges, driven back with curses and thrown stones.

"Lord have mercy," Margaret whispered.

A woman staggered past them, face pale, her eyes wild with exhaustion. She clutched a child to her chest, the little one listless, head lolling. "Don't stop here," she rasped. "The air will take you, same as the rest."

James guided the wagon forward, his voice low. "We cannot linger. We take the boy, and we leave."

The smell pressed into their throats, sickly sweet and rotting. Every breath felt like swallowing poison. People believed it was—that the stench itself carried the fever, creeping into the lungs, seeding death. Men held cloths soaked in spirits to their faces. Women burned sage and pine knots to drive the air back, but nothing masked the corruption of so many dead.

Margaret's hand trembled as she reached for the quilt folded beside her. "He will not stay here," she said, more to herself than to James. "Not one more night."

They found the cabin at the edge of the settlement, where the child had been left with neighbors who looked more frightened than sick. The baby lay in a wooden cradle, his breath shallow, his skin pale but not yet fevered. Margaret bent and gathered him swiftly, wrapping him in her quilt, holding him close as though her embrace could shield him from the air itself.

"Go," she said to James. "Now."

James swung the wagon about, the mules straining as if they too longed to escape the reek that clung to every board and stone. Behind them, Fort Towson sank back into the haze of smoke and decay, the cries of the living mingling with the silence of the dead.

Only when the trees closed around them again, muffling the smell, did Margaret breathe without shuddering. She kissed the child's forehead and whispered, "Issi hullo, aiittvtoba. You are not alone."

CHAPTER 2

THE ROAD HOME

Margaret cradles the baby while James drives. Smoke from distant brush fires lingers. The fever country falls away behind them.James: "Tell me plain, sister — what are you, really? Creek blood in your veins, Choctaw on your tongue, living under Chickasaw roofs. Are you Creek, masquerading as a Choctaw, in Chickasaw land?"Margaret looks down at the child, draws the quilt higher, and answers without heat.Margaret: "I am what duty has made me. Our mother's mother carried Wind Clan blood, yes.

But I was not raised in their towns. I married Henry Butts Thompson and took up the Yowani road. That is Choctaw work, James. I have lived it."James: "And yet you wear McCoy like armor. Here, the name opens doors. Colbert blood still buys a hearing. Call yourself Thompson all you like, but these hills remember you as McCoy."Margaret: "Names are tools. I will use the one that keeps this child safe. But hear me: the house I build in his heart is Choctaw."The wagon jolts; the baby stirs, then settles. Pines seam the horizon; ash hangs in the air like sifted flour.James: "You talk of houses, but land is what holds a house up. The Chickasaw are carving their own ground now.

The Colberts make certain of it — George, Levi, Holmes... big fish in a smaller pond. With them, we are first among families. With the Choctaw, we are only one voice among many — the Joneses on the Red, the Garvins, the Fraziers — all with louder claims."Margaret: "Loudness is not greatness. The Thompsons are not a small name among the Choctaw. Not the loudest, no — but steady. I married into a line that keeps its promises. This boy will learn that first."James: "Promises don't fill a belly or win a council vote. You've seen it: the Choctaw guard the chief's chair for full-blood men. The Chickasaw judge a man by his skill. Governor Johnston will send whomever serves the Nation best — even a son-in-law like Murray, if need be. That is a wide door, sister."Margaret: "Then walk through it, brother. Be the judge you were made to be. Rule our people well. But do not tell me this child is anything but Choctaw. I will not choose a smaller river just to hear our name echo off both banks."They ride a while with only harness and wheel-noise between them. A hawk rings high above the pines.James: "You know what the Doaksville men have made — purchase here, boundaries there. Paper fences.

Today Choctaw, tomorrow Chickasaw, and a U.S. agent counting posts. Where will the boy stand when the lines harden?"Margaret: "On his feet. On the ground I teach him to know. He will understand the Chickasaw law from your mouth and the Choctaw heart from mine. If paper fences move, he will still know his name."James: "Names are not enough. Men will ask him to prove it."Margaret: "Then he will prove it. He will say: I am Yowani. I am Thompson by my mother's vow and my father's blood. I am Choctaw though I live under Chickasaw trees. And when they laugh, he will not bend."James glances over; something like admiration crosses his face, then slips away.James: "You wager much on a small boy."Margaret: "I wager on what I can hold. My sons are gone to Texas. Their children are far. This child is here — mine to teach. I will pour every truth I have into him until his bones ring with it."James: "Truths in the night are easy. Daylight brings the counters. The Yowani are few — today only a handful of families. Tomorrow the councils will ask, 'Who are you among so many?'"Margaret: "Few multiply. What we save today will be thousands tomorrow. They will look back and ask how the line held. Let the answer be this: a grandmother would not let it go."The baby wakes and fusses.

Margaret loosens the quilt, hums a low tune, then speaks softly in Choctaw. Margaret: "Issi hullo, aiittvtoba — little deer, be brave. The road is long, but it leads home."James: "If he hunts with me, he will learn these valleys, the laws, the men who write them. He will know the Colberts by deed if not by dinner. He will see how a small Nation keeps its balance when big boots cross its floor."Margaret: "Teach him. Give him your law and your woods. I will give him a spine that does not bend when men with papers say he is not what he is."James: "One day he will stand before councils. They will say, 'You live in Chickasaw land. Your grandmother calls herself McCoy. Your blood is Creek by the old stories. Why do you claim Choctaw?'"

Margaret: "And he will answer: 'Because my mother taught me to carry the fire. Because the Yowani carried me. Because a name is not where you sleep, but what you keep when you wake.'"

The road lifts; a breeze carries the last sour edge of Fort Towson from their clothes. For a moment, the air is clean.

James: "Very well, sister. Let him be Choctaw in his heart. I will see that he speaks Chickasaw in the courthouse, and English to the agents. He'll need all three."

Margaret: "Then we are agreed. They ride on. Behind them, the dead lie quiet. Before them, the living wait — and a boy who will one day learn to name himself against the wind.

CHAPTER 3

THE RETURN AND THE DISTANCE

Late August 1839, returning to their settlement. Margaret holds the child close while James drives the wagon. They have survived the fever country, but their neighbors watch warily as they arrive.

The wagon creaked back into the settlement at dusk, shadows long across the clearing. Margaret held the baby close, his breath steady against her breast. James flicked the reins, eyes fixed on the cabins ahead, where smoke drifted from chimneys and dogs barked.

People came out to see them return. Dickson Frazier, his wife, and a few others stood at the edges of their yards. But no one stepped forward.

"Did you go?" someone called, voice sharp. "To Towson?"

James nodded once.

A murmur rippled through the gathering. Feet shuffled backward. Hands went to mouths and noses. The space between wagon and neighbor grew wider, as if an invisible fence had been raised.

Margaret lifted her chin. "We brought him home. He will be raised among his kin."

Dickson's wife shook her head. "We warned you not to go. Fever clings to the clothes, to the hair. Best not come near till we see if it's taken hold of you."

James's jaw tightened, but he gave a short nod. "We understand."

"Not yet sick," someone muttered. "But best wait and see."

The baby stirred, gave a weak cry. Margaret rocked him gently, but the sound seemed to only deepen the neighbors' caution.

"We will bring food," Dickson said at last. "We'll leave it at your fence. No one here wishes you harm, but we must mind our families."

James raised a hand in acknowledgment. "That will do. We will keep apart until the danger passes."

The neighbors withdrew, doors closing, leaving the road empty once more.

For a long moment James and Margaret sat in silence, the child the only sound between them. Finally, James clucked to the mules, steering toward their own cabin.

Margaret whispered into the quilt: "Issi hullo — little deer. This is the welcome the world gives. But you will endure."

Behind them, the settlement settled back into its wary quiet. Ahead of them, night gathered — and with it, the long work of survival.

CHAPTER 4

INTERLUDE

The decade before the war was a time of building and of testing, when the Choctaw and Chickasaw Nations strove to shape a future for their children amid constant uncertainty. The dust of removal had not yet settled, but schools had risen from the raw clearings of the new country, and councils met in log houses and stone halls to speak of constitutions, laws, and the rights of free people.

For William Clyde, boyhood blurred into youth under the weight of these changes. His world was no longer just the salt works at Boggy Depot or the scattered farms near Fort Towson; it was a nation in the making, with teachers, ministers, and lawmakers intent on giving shape to something permanent. The schools were the most visible sign of that ambition. At Spencer Academy, Choctaw boys bent over books of Latin and Greek; at Bloomfield, Chickasaw girls were taught music and scripture beside their English letters. Missionaries from the East praised their students' diligence, while elders debated whether too much learning of the white man's kind would dull the memory of their own people's ways.

The Chickasaws, having gained formal separation from the Choctaws in 1856, moved swiftly to assert themselves as a sovereign people. A constitution was written, modeled in part on the American system but stamped with Chickasaw identity. Tishomingo became the capital, its courthouse and council hall small but proud symbols of order and legitimacy. Men like James McCoy — Margaret's brother — took part in the labor of framing laws and balancing the delicate line between tradition and survival in a white man's world.

To a young man like William Clyde, the air was thick with the promise of opportunity. Schooling opened doors; politics beckoned ambitious voices; the very act of nation-building offered a sense that destiny might yet be steered. And yet the pull of Mississippi, where his family's roots lay, lingered. Stories of kin still there, of lands once theirs, of prospects brighter than the hard soil of Indian Territory — these whispers worked on his mind as steadily as the sermons of the teachers.

Margaret did not trust it. She had lived long enough to know what Mississippi could mean for a Choctaw boy grown tall. She had seen treaties broken, families torn, promises twisted to the Nation's harm. "Do not go back," she would have told him, her voice sharpened by memory. "There is nothing there but sorrow for our people. Your place is here, where we have rebuilt, where we are shaping something new."

But youth does not always heed the cautions of age. William Clyde's eyes turned eastward, beyond the Red River, toward the land that had once been home to his mother's clan. To him it seemed not a place of sorrow but of possibility — of study, of self-making, perhaps even of fortune. Against Margaret's better judgment, he began to imagine his road leading back into Mississippi.

This was the tension of his time: between what was safe and what was possible, between the lessons of elders and the restless hope of youth. It was a choice that would shape the years ahead, as the shadow of war crept steadily across both Nations, and as William Clyde's path bent toward conflict that neither schools nor constitutions could shield him from.

CHAPTER 5

THE JOURNEY EAST

The boat that carried William Clyde down the Red River pushed through muddy waters thick with the commerce of the South. Cotton bales, whiskey barrels, crates of tools — all stacked on deck beside the trunks of travelers like himself. By the time the vessel nosed into Natchez, smoke curled across the bluffs and the docks rang with shouts of stevedores. The town was alive, proud, and restless, its wealth gleaming in brick facades and fine carriages drawn up near the port.

But the true measure of Natchez's prosperity lay just beyond the wharf.

William Clyde had heard Margaret's warnings all his life — of markets where men and women were sold like livestock, of families broken and bloodlines scattered. Yet it was one thing to hear a grandmother's grief, another to step into the dim interior of a slave mart in the year of 1855.

The hall smelled of sweat and cigar smoke, its air heavy with the sweet bite of spirits. Benches lined the floor, where planters leaned forward with canes resting between their knees, their eyes sharp and appraising. In the center stood a narrow wooden platform, polished smooth by countless feet. Upon it, a boy was made to open his mouth so that buyers could count his teeth. A girl, barely past childhood, endured the rough touch of strangers measuring hips and shoulders. A man, broad-shouldered and in his prime, was prodded like a horse at auction, his price already whispered in the corner — fifteen hundred dollars, perhaps more, the equivalent of more than fifty thousand dollars in modern reckoning.

An older woman was led up next, her back bent from years of labor. The room quieted, the value of her womb past, her hands worn. She would be sold for less than half the sum of the younger man, perhaps six or seven hundred dollars

— twenty-five thousand today, a "discounted" life measured in coin. Behind her waited a young mother with an infant clutched to her breast. She fetched more than the elder, though not because of mercy. Buyers spoke of "double value" — the mother's labor and the child's future, twelve hundred dollars or more, near forty-five thousand in today's wealth.

Injuries told their own cruel arithmetic. A man limping from an old wound was held back, the auctioneer murmuring that he might be "brought forward once mended." Others bore scars, their value marked down like bruised cattle. Skill could lift the price: a seamstress, a cook, a blacksmith — each carried a different sum in the ledgers of men who saw no souls, only capital.

William Clyde stood at the door, his breath caught between fascination and revulsion. He was young enough to be drawn by the sheer energy of the place, yet old enough to sense the rot beneath its clamor. Margaret's stories had been true, and worse: here was the proof, living flesh appraised with the coldness of coin.

Outside, the city bustled as though nothing were amiss. Cotton still rolled in from the hinterlands, carriages rattled along the bluff, laughter echoed from taverns. Yet William Clyde carried the scene with him as he set out eastward along the Natchez Trace. Where Margaret had once led wagons through a gauntlet of danger and hunger, he found a road now broadened, cleared, and settled. Inns and farmhouses offered rest, the shadows of ambush long since driven away. His journey was steady, almost uneventful, a mirror-image of Margaret's desperate westward flight.

But the safety of the road only disguised the greater peril ahead. Mississippi, rich and proud, thrived on the very trade he had just witnessed. Its fields grew fat with cotton, its planters fat with power, its future bound to a system already straining at the seams. The laughter in the auction hall was the laughter of men standing on the edge of fire, blind to the spark that would soon set their world ablaze.

William Clyde pressed onward toward Clarke County and the kin who awaited him there, unaware that he had walked into the heart of a storm.

CHAPTER 6

CLARKE COUNTY AND THE MARKHAMS

The road eastward from Natchez brought William Clyde into Clarke County, a land of broad fields and rich soil, greener than anything he had known in the Choctaw Nation. The Chickasawhay River wound through the countryside, its waters slow and brown, nourishing farms and carrying timber downstream. Near Shubuta, where Margaret had once lived and raised her family, he found the home of his Markham kin.

The Markham house was no crude cabin. Built a decade or more after the Choctaw removal, it stood solid by frontier standards, a frame of pine and oak resting on stout stilts that lifted it above the damp earth. Wide porches wrapped around its sides, shaded by the sweep of tall trees. Brick chimneys, their clay drawn from the riverbanks, rose at either end, and smoke curled from them in the evenings when the air grew cool. Inside, the walls were whitewashed, the floors of polished pine, the rooms filled with furniture

By the measure of Mississippi, the house was modest prosperity. But to William Clyde, fresh from the rough clearings of Indian Territory, it seemed impressive: a home of permanence, its confidence written in every timber and brick. Chickens scratched in the yard; a smokehouse and barn stood nearby; children's voices drifted across the fields.

He walked the land with quiet awe. It was beautiful country — fertile, well-watered, alive with promise. He knew that Margaret had once lived here, that his own father had been born not far away. Standing in the Markham fields, he felt a surge of belonging, as though he had stepped into the pages of his family's past.

And yet he could not ignore the tension beneath the beauty. Margaret had told him all his life that this land was taken at gunpoint, that Choctaw families were forced from their homes so that settlers like the Markhams could claim it. He had never doubted her. He had seen the respect she commanded in Indian Territory, and the authority his uncle James McCoy carried in tribal councils. Their words were truth.

But the Markhams told another story: of hard labor and clearing, of survival and enterprise. They did not speak of dispossession, only of what they had built. To them, the land was rightfully theirs, defended by sweat and vigilance. William Clyde could not call them liars, yet he could not dismiss what Margaret had told him. The contradiction pressed on him, leaving him unsettled — torn between admiration for their home and suspicion of its foundation.

Here, in Clarke County, the land itself carried two truths, and he stood in the middle of them.

CHAPTER 7

BLOODLINES AND BARGAINS

In Clarke County, surrounded by the Markham home and the fertile fields of the Chickasawhay bottomland, William Clyde found himself thinking often of the parents he had never known. His father, William Wayne, existed only in stories: a boy who had grown up under Margaret's care, then a young man gone too soon. His mother, Sarah Markham, was little more than a name. He had no memories of her face, no voice to recall, only the knowledge that she too had passed while he was still a child.

Yet in the very walls of the Markham house, he could feel their presence. Here was the land his mother's family had claimed, land that had been Choctaw not so long ago. Here were the fields that had passed from one people to another, not by war alone but by marriage — a union that bound a white settler and a Choctaw woman in a compact that still shaped his life.

What had that marriage been?

Some said it was a bargain. A Choctaw father, determined to keep his Article 14 land, knew that only by joining his family with a white man's name could he protect it from seizure or fraud. So he gave his daughter in marriage, young as she was, so that the title would be safe. The settler gained property he could never have otherwise afforded; the Choctaw gained security against dispossession. It was a contract written not on paper but in flesh.

But others believed there was more. Perhaps there had been affection between the two. The Markham man may have seen not only the chance for land but also a woman he could value as wife and partner. Perhaps, too, the Choctaw father was not merely a calculating patriarch but a man who believed his daughter's future might be secured in this new world, where treaties erased borders and mixed families often fared better than those who stood alone.

William Clyde could not know. He could only imagine the permutations. He pictured his grandmother Margaret, debating with this other Choctaw woman back in 1830. Margaret chose removal, believing survival lay in the west. The other woman chose to stay, trusting Article 14 to secure her ground. One left, one remained. And now, years later, Margaret's grandson stood in Clarke County — descended from both women, carrying in his blood the story of departure and the story of remaining.

The question of agency haunted him most. Margaret had married at fourteen; was it not likely that Sarah's mother had, too? A girl with little say, her future decided by fathers and husbands, her body and children bound to bargains she did not choose. Was she loved? Was she honored? Or was she traded like the acres her marriage secured?

And yet, among the Choctaw as among the Chickasaw, intermarriage was not always shameful. It was sometimes embraced as alliance, as peace, as practical wisdom. There had been good men and bad men, good motives and bad motives, on both sides. It was too simple to say the white man exploited and the Choctaw suffered, or that the Choctaw schemed and the white man was blameless. The truth was muddled, as truth often is.

All William Clyde knew was this: from such a union he was born. A father and a mother he never knew, their choices — or the choices made for them — had shaped the very ground beneath his feet. He was the living bridge between two decisions made a generation earlier, between two women who had chosen different paths. And now he walked those paths, searching for a place where both truths could be borne in a single life.

CHAPTER 8

QUITMAN, BOOKS, AND THE MASTER'S WORD

At the Markham place, William Clyde quickly saw what made their comfort possible. The house was fine, the fields green, the family well-fed and secure — and all of it rested on the steady labor of enslaved men and women. Cabins lined the edge of the fields, smoke rising from their chimneys, children playing in the dirt while their mothers cooked over open fires. It was not destitution; compared to some frontier whites William Clyde had known, these people were clothed, sheltered, and provisioned. But the situation was very sad and hopeless. One morning word came that another field hand was needed. The three boys — William Clyde and his two Markham cousins — were sent into Quitman to see what could be had at the market.

The road into town jolted beneath the wagon wheels, dust rising behind them. The older cousin talked constantly of Mississippi's destiny. "The governor's right — we won't let the North rule us. If it comes to war, we'll show 'em. Six Mississippi was glorious in Mexico, and we'll be glorious again." The younger cousin, not much older than William Clyde, chimed in with equal fire: "It'll be like riding for King Richard in Ivanhoe — only better, because this time it's for our own country. Yankees will have hell to pay if they cross us."

William Clyde listened, unsettled. He had read Scott's words, felt the pull of knightly honor, but he could not reconcile that glory with the weary men and women he had seen in Natchez.

In Quitman the market was thin. A few older men with bent backs, a woman coughing so hard she had to steady herself on the block, two boys with hollow eyes. Prices were high for poor stock. The cousins examined them, but all were deemed unsuitable. "Uncle won't pay for this lot," the older said. "Not worth the feed." They turned back empty-handed.

But the younger cousin had another errand in mind. Whispering, he tugged at William Clyde's sleeve: "There's a shop here that has a copy of Uncle Tom's Cabin. We can buy it for a dime, maybe less. I want to see what the fuss is about." The three of them slipped into a narrow shop where the bookseller, glancing around, produced a battered copy from beneath the counter. The paper was cheap, the cover torn, its pages already smudged by many hands. The cousins pooled coins, and soon the forbidden book was hidden beneath William Clyde's coat.

Back at the plantation, they smuggled it into the library. At night, by lamplight, they took turns reading passages, whispering of Eliza crossing the ice, of Uncle Tom's quiet endurance. For William Clyde, the words struck deep — not because they were new, but because they echoed what he had already seen with his own eyes.

It did not last. One afternoon the master of the house entered the library and found the book lying out. His face darkened as he turned its pages.

"Who brought this trash here?" he thundered. The cousins stood silent, eyes downcast. William Clyde stepped forward. "I did."

The master's gaze burned into him. "Boy, this will fill your head with lies. Abolitionist poison. Do you think you can understand our ways from a Yankee book? These people are mine, and I treat them as my own. They are safer here than they would ever be free. Out there, they'd starve, or be hunted down by men with no care for them. Here, they are fed, clothed, and protected. I sell no one — not one. They live as my children... for they are my children."

The words hung heavy. To the cousins, it was a proud defense. But William Clyde heard the undertone. He had seen the children in the quarters, their faces bearing the master's jaw, his eyes. He realized then what "breeding" meant — not only among slaves paired for labor, but in the master's own shadow across his flock. Protection and possession were one. His claim to fatherhood was both metaphor and fact.

That night, William Clyde lay awake, turning the master's words in his mind. He did not doubt the man's sincerity — he truly believed he was protecting his people. Yet it was protection rooted in ownership, affection tangled with power, bloodlines blurred by coercion. Which was worse? Freedom with hunger and struggle, or bondage with bread and shelter?

No answer came, only the weight of contradiction. He was caught between Margaret's truth and the Markhams' truth, between Ivanhoe's dream of glory and Uncle Tom's cry of suffering. And in that tension, his path toward manhood and war began to take shape.

CHAPTER 9

UNDER THE PREACHER'S WORD

The Markhams never missed a Wednesday night prayer meeting. The little clapboard Baptist church, whitewashed and plain, stood at the crossroads outside of Quitman. Oil lamps burned in the windows, and the benches were filled with families—men in shirtsleeves, women with fans, children restless but hushed by the weight of worship.

That evening the preacher opened his Bible and read with booming voice: "Servants, obey in all things your masters according to the flesh; not with eyeservice, as men pleasers; but in singleness of heart, fearing God." He closed the book, looking out across the room with stern conviction. "Brethren, the Lord has spoken. Our institution is no sin, but His design. Those who labor in our fields are entrusted to our care, just as surely as our own children. To free them is to abandon them—to deliver them to hunger, cruelty, and ruin."

Heads nodded all through the pews. William Clyde felt his cousins shifting beside him, straight-backed with pride. The preacher pressed harder. "There are agitators abroad, sowing lies, poisoning the mind with tales of cruelty. Pay them no heed. We stand on God's Word, and if the North threatens our peace, Mississippi shall stand as she always has—firm and unshaken."

The congregation sang a hymn, voices rising like thunder through the rafters. When the service ended, men spilled out into the yard, where the night air was heavy with summer heat. An old oak spread its limbs over the churchyard, and there they gathered—cigars lit, smoke curling under the stars.

William Clyde's uncle was among them, his cousins close by, listening as the older men spoke. "Governor McWillie will not yield," one planter said, his cigar glowing in the dark. "He'll hold Jackson steady if it comes to secession." Another added, "South Carolina won't stand alone. Mississippi's ready. We'll fight, and we'll win."

The cousins laughed, brash and eager. "Let the Yankees try," said the older. "They'll have hell to pay." The younger, his head filled with Ivanhoe's knights, declared, "It will be like riding into glory—defending our rights, our honor, our land."

The men nodded, satisfied. They spoke of railroads, of levees, of the legislature in Jackson, but always the talk returned to secession. The war they imagined was swift and righteous, a test of Southern steel against Northern weakness.

William Clyde stood at the edge of the circle, the cigar smoke stinging his eyes. The preacher's voice still rang in his ears, laced with scripture. The men's talk of glory pressed on him like a drumbeat. And yet, behind it all, he heard Margaret's warning, saw the faces on the auction block in Natchez, remembered the forbidden book hidden in the library. God's Word, the planter's pride, the cousin's bravado—all braided into a knot he could not untangle.

As the meeting broke apart and families mounted their wagons, William Clyde felt the pull of two worlds: one that claimed divine sanction for bondage, and another, quieter voice that whispered of freedom and sorrow. Between them, he walked the dusty road home, carrying the weight of both truths into the darkness.

CHAPTER 10

REFLECTIONS ON SLAVERY AND GLORY

William Clyde carried the words of the preacher, the bravado of his cousins, and the memory of Natchez with him like stones in his pocket—heavy, pressing, but never easy to set down. He found himself thinking often of Margaret, of her pride in the fact that their Yowani kin had owned few, if any, slaves. She had spoken of it not with bitterness, but with a kind of dignity, as though it marked them as different, freer in spirit, less entangled in the white man's ways.

Yet he could not ignore the contradictions. He had heard stories of the great Chickasaw and Choctaw leaders who held hundreds of enslaved people—Greenville Folsom, the Jones family, others whose names were spoken with awe. Their wealth and power had come from the same soil that Margaret's family once walked. Cotton thrived in Mississippi; it made men rich. Why then had the Yowani not followed that path? Was it simply poverty that kept them from it, or was there some quiet objection, some cultural reluctance they never named?

The Markham fields gave him one answer. Here, slavery was the foundation of comfort. The cabins were sturdy, the rations steady, and the people in them looked stronger than many poor whites he had seen in Indian Territory. His uncle said they were family, and in truth many of them bore his features. To the Markhams, slavery was not wickedness but order—an institution sanctioned by God, confirmed by Scripture, and defended as essential to the Southern way of life.

And yet Natchez lingered. The market hall, the smoke and laughter, the bodies handled like cattle. That vision sat uneasily against the sermons and the plantation calm. Margaret's scorn for that place had been absolute, and William Clyde felt its echo every time he recalled the block.

His cousins gave him no pause. They saw no contradiction. To them, Mississippi's destiny was glory—war, honor, and victory. They spoke as knights of old, their heads filled with Ivanhoe's battles, their hearts eager for the test. William Clyde, younger, impressionable, could not help but be drawn to it. There was a thrill in their certainty, a power in their pride.

And so he found himself caught between two truths: Margaret's quiet pride in abstention and the Markhams' loud defense of mastery. He did not reject slavery outright, nor did he embrace it with the fervor of his cousins. His thoughts were clouded, uncertain, ambiguous. What stirred him most was not bondage or freedom, but the promise of glory—the chance to fight for a cause, to prove himself a man, to stand among his kin with honor.

If slavery was bound up in that cause, then so be it. He could not untangle it; he could only march with the current of his time, carrying both doubt and desire in equal measure. In that gray space, his future was being written.

CHAPTER II

THE CALL TO ORDER

By 1855 William Clyde was sixteen, old enough at last to be noticed by the men of standing in Clarke County. His uncle had long been a member of the Shubuta Lodge, chartered in January of 1849, and it was through that circle of influence that William Clyde's path into manhood was to be marked. One warm evening he lingered outside the lodge hall, the lamps glowing behind shuttered windows while his uncle and the others conducted their work inside. When the meeting broke, a planter friend of his uncle's laid an offer on the table.

The honor was not lost on him. To be asked meant he was being counted among men. He accepted, and soon enough he was led through the solemn rituals that bound him to the fraternity. When it was done, he emerged not only as his uncle's nephew but as a brother of the lodge, a "made man" in the eyes of the town.

With membership came fellowship. Once a month the lodge hosted a supper, the tables spread with roasted chicken, corn bread, and pies. After the plates were cleared and cigars lit, the talk turned from food to forming a militia.

The idea found quick support. Men nodded, voices rising in agreement. A company would give the community pride, discipline, and readiness should Mississippi call. It would also give the younger generation a sense of purpose. Before long, the plan was settled: a Shubuta Rifle Company would be raised, its nucleus drawn from the very sons of the lodge.

The Markham boys were eager, their eyes alight with visions of drill and honor. William Clyde felt the same stirring. He had read of knights and causes in the Markham's library.

So it began. After lodge nights, the young men gathered in the fields to practice. They shouldered rifles, learned to keep step, drilled in formation until the rhythm of the drumbeat became second nature. Targets were set against tree stumps, shots cracked through the air, and the smell of powder mingled with sweat and pride. They were not soldiers yet, but they carried themselves as if they were.

Week by week, the company grew steadier, their lines straighter, their volleys sharper. They became a fixture in the militia.

By the time 1861 approached, the pattern was set. The lodge still met in secrecy and ritual, but the wider world pressed closer with every month. Talk of secession grew louder, news from Jackson carried rumors of war. When the governor's call finally came, the men of the Shubuta Rifle Company would be ready—citizen soldiers, sworn to Mississippi, marching toward the storm.

CHAPTER 12
INTO THE RANKS

Through 1860 the rhythm of life in Clarke County continued, but always with an undercurrent of tension. The Markham plantation carried on its work, the lodge met each month, and after each gathering the young men of the Shubuta Rifles drilled in the fields. William Clyde marched with his cousins, musket on shoulder, sweat running down his back as the drumbeat set their cadence. They practiced volleys, took aim at crude targets pinned against stumps, and dreamed aloud of the glory that might await. It was an exciting thing to imagine..

In January of 1861 Mississippi made its choice. The news spread quickly—secession had been declared, and Governor Pettus called upon the militia companies to muster in Jackson. The quiet drilling of evenings was now to be tested in earnest. Clarke County men packed their kits, embraced their families, and prepared for the long road north.

The Markham household held a supper before departure. Pride and anxiety mingled around the table. The elder men spoke of honor and duty; the women busied themselves with food and whispered prayers. William Clyde felt the weight of their eyes, knowing that he, too, was expected to prove himself.

The journey to Jackson was crowded and chaotic. Wagons creaked along muddy roads, men in mismatched uniforms marched in uneven lines, and church and lodge banners fluttered above the crowds. Every county had its own contingent, and the capital swelled with the sound of drums, shouts, and hymns. Companies were being folded together, consolidated into regiments that could be ordered into the field.

It was there that William Clyde's path shifted. Amid the confusion of mustering, he was approached by a lieutenant whose name carried weight in his mother's memory—Markham. The officer looked him over and, recognizing the family tie, spoke plainly: "We could use another strong back in the Simpson Fencibles. You'll march with us."

And so it was decided. Though he had drilled with the Shubuta Rifles, William Clyde was placed into Company H of the 6th Mississippi Infantry. His cousins went elsewhere, absorbed into other companies, but kinship bound him here. He shouldered his musket with the men of Simpson County, strangers yet bound by common cause.

The next days passed in a blur of drill and oath-taking. Officers barked orders, rolls were called, and the raw collection of county companies became a regiment. The 6th Mississippi Infantry was born, and William Clyde Thompson was among its ranks. He was no longer merely a nephew under his uncle's roof or a lodge boy learning to march. He was now a soldier of Mississippi, sworn to a cause that promised both honor and trial.

As the regiment prepared to move, William Clyde felt the shift within himself. The drills of home were behind him. Before him stretched the road of war, uncertain and immense, yet lined with the promise of glory. With musket in hand and doubt in his heart, he stepped into the ranks, one young man carried forward by the current of history.

CHAPTER 13
THE COST OF ALLEGIANCE

In July of 1861 the Simpson Fencibles called their first full roll. A lieutenant read aloud what each man must bring for the march to Jackson—blanket, canteen, shirts enough to last, a musket or rifle fit for field use. Cartridge boxes would be provided in time, but the rest was to be furnished by each man and his household. The words fell heavy on William Clyde. He had no father to supply him, no family fortune to outfit him as the Markham boys had. His uncle could cover what coin might buy, but much else had to be provided by the hands of the household.

The household rallied to the task. Shirts were cut and stitched, pants mended, a haversack fashioned from coarse cloth. His uncle purchased a musket and powder, and the older women of the house oversaw the packing of bread, salt pork, and dried fruit. The enslaved seamstresses worked by lamplight, their hands deft, their faces expressionless as they sewed straps, patched coats, and pieced together a blanket roll. Their labor made his departure possible. William Clyde felt the irony keenly: the very women whose bondage this war would seek to preserve were the ones outfitting him to fight it.

Among the free women of the household there was also kindness. One, quiet in her ways, pressed a small gift into his hands—a cap stitched anew, its lining discreetly embroidered with a verse from the Psalms: "Be strong, and let your heart take courage, all you who hope in the Lord." She said nothing more, only smiled, but William Clyde knew it was meant to steady him. Later, as he tried on the cap, he traced the hidden words with his finger. It marked the piece as his, and it marked him as belonging, if only in this household, to a circle of care.

He thought often in those days of his place. He had not been born in Mississippi, nor raised in its fields. His heart carried as much allegiance to the Choctaw Nation as to any state. The Choctaw, officially neutral, sought to avoid this war, though later history would twist their role and charge them falsely with rebellion, a pretext to strip away still more of their sovereignty. By heritage he owed Mississippi nothing. He could have walked away, returned to the Choctaw country, and washed his hands of the struggle.

Yet he did not. Mississippi exacted a high price for his short stay. For the modest shelter, education, and fellowship given him, he was now to march into war. It was no fair trade. Yet loyalty bound him—to his uncle who fed him, to his cousins who drilled beside him, to the lodge brothers who welcomed him, and to the church that blessed his duty. He marched not out of fervent belief, but out of gratitude, obligation, and the quiet fear of being left behind.

When the day came to depart, his gear was ready. The musket rested on his shoulder, the haversack hung at his side, and the cap with its secret verse shaded his eyes. Behind him the women who had prepared his kit stood silent in the yard. Ahead lay Jackson, Grenada, and the road of war. With each step he felt the weight of Mississippi's claim upon him—and the heavier weight of all he might lose in giving himself to it.

CHAPTER 14
THE RIBBON IN THE CAP

The depot at Shubuta was crowded that morning, the platform thick with families and wagons. Women carried baskets of food, children clung to fathers' hands, and the hiss of the locomotive echoed against the low hills. It was here that William Clyde was to leave home behind, bound north for Grenada where the regiment would be formally mustered. He shifted his musket on his shoulder and touched the brim of his new cap. The cap carried a secret, one that pressed softly against his brow as if whispering a vow.

The night before, by lamplight, the women of the household had prepared his final gift. With red and black thread—the colors of the Choctaw Nation—they embroidered a ribbon with the words: "The best service is that which is done in peril of life." Quietly, one of them sewed it to the inner surface of the sweatband in his cap. There it would be hidden from sight, protected from sweat, invisible unless someone looked for it. Only William Clyde knew it was there, the motto resting against his skin, a talisman of glory stitched in secret.

He had tried on the cap in the dim light of his room, adjusting the band until it sat snugly. As his fingers traced the unseen ribbon, he felt both pride and unease. Pride in the glory it promised, the chivalric call that echoed from the pages of Ivanhoe; unease because he knew he had no real obligation to Mississippi. He could have turned back to the Choctaw Nation, to his grandparents who needed him, to the people who expected his survival, not his sacrifice. And yet here he stood, driven by the desire to prove himself and bring honor to his family, even if that honor came at terrible cost.

At the depot, goodbyes were brief. His younger cousins helped him carry his gear, then turned their horses back toward the plantation. Women pressed food into his hands, murmured blessings, and wiped at their eyes. The locomotive gave a long whistle, and the soldiers began to climb aboard. William Clyde stepped up with them, the platform falling away behind him.

As the train lurched forward, he raised his hand in farewell. The cap shaded his eyes, the hidden ribbon pressed firm against his brow. Ahead lay Grenada, the muster, and the road of war. Behind him, the life he might have chosen slipped quietly into the distance. The words inside his cap were his alone, a vow stitched in Choctaw colors, binding him to glory even as he carried the weight of responsibility on his shoulders.

CHAPTER 15
THE MUSTER AT GRENADA

The train steamed northward, the whistle echoing across pine ridges and fields. At each stop new boys clambered aboard, cheered on by families, while others slipped quietly away into the crowd, too nervous to ride further. Fear was the invisible passenger, louder with every mile, thinning the ranks despite the show of bravado.

William Clyde rode with three cousins, pressed shoulder to shoulder on a hard wooden bench. The youngest, the same cousin whose book had once caused trouble, spoke often of reasons not to go on. He muttered about Lincoln, about how Mississippi was not their true home, about how the Choctaw should stay out of the white man's quarrel. But everyone knew his real burden was fear. William Clyde pitied him, remembering how he had once taken the blame for that book. He could not carry him now.

By the time the train pulled into Grenada, the air was thick with smoke, music, and shouting. Campfires dotted the fields, wagons rattled, drums beat out cadences. Women—wives, sweethearts, and those who followed the soldiers—moved among the recruits. For boys barely grown, it was a heady night of liquor, laughter, and nervous bravado.

The cousins joined the swirl. Bottles passed hand to hand, the youngest drinking hardest, as though to drown the fear he could not name. He slipped away with a woman, but soon returned pale and stumbling, too sick, too ashamed. Later, he lay down near the fire, clutching a bottle that smelled of both spirits and laudanum. No one thought much of it; many men drank themselves to sleep. But when the sun rose, he did not wake.

The news spread quickly through the camp—one boy gone before muster. Some whispered it was an accident, too much drink and laudanum for a body untested. Others muttered darker things—that he had chosen not to face the line at all. No one could be sure. His parents would be told he died before the roll, sparing them the weight of disgrace.

For William Clyde, the loss cut deep. He saw how fear could claim a man before the enemy ever fired a shot. He felt pity, but also a grim resolve. When the officers called the men to muster, he stepped forward. The oath was spoken, and in that instant his life was no longer his own. The ribbon pressed against his brow, unseen but present, binding him to a path from which there was no return.

CHAPTER 16
WINTER CAMP AT CORINTH

The winter of 1861 settled heavy upon the Confederate camps in northern Mississippi. At Corinth, the fields turned to mud, tents sagged beneath steady rains, and smoke from damp wood drifted low across the encampment. Disease stalked the rows of canvas like an enemy more constant than the Federals. Men coughed, shivered, and cursed their luck, while others slipped away on leave or simply deserted.

William Clyde had nowhere to go. He watched men come and go, called home to sick wives or the birth of children. But for him there was no summons, no farm to tend, no family waiting in Mississippi. His roots were in the Choctaw Nation, far from this muddy gathering, and so he remained—becoming a fixture in the camp by sheer constancy. His presence, his accent, and the stories he carried from the Nation marked him as different, and in that difference many found curiosity and eventually respect. Around the campfires, men asked him to tell of the lands west, of Margaret McCoy, of the Council House. He answered carefully, revealing little but enough to satisfy their curiosity. They began to call him "Billy Clyde," the name rolling easily from their tongues. It carried a warmth that made him feel both included and apart.

In January, after a day of drill in the frozen mud, the company sergeant paused before dismissing the line. "Billy Clyde," he called. The men turned. "You've a knack for keeping these boys steady. From now on, you'll serve as corporal for this squad." The words were plain, but the effect was not. A murmur ran through the men—agreement, approval. William Clyde felt the weight settle upon him at once. He was no longer invisible. Now a handful of lives were his to mind.

The lieutenant with the Markham name took notice as well. Young, eager, and anxious, he seemed to find reassurance in William Clyde's steadiness. More and more often, he placed him close by in formation or assigned him to carry messages. Billy Clyde understood. It was not just trust; it was a shield. The lieutenant wanted reliable men at his elbow, and William Clyde had become one of them.

At night, alone in his tent, William Clyde touched the inner band of his cap and felt the ribbon stitched there in Choctaw red and black. "The best service is that which is done in peril of life." He had thought of it as a challenge to his courage. Now it bound him to others. He was no longer free to think only of survival. His steadiness had become a promise to those who looked to him, a weight he bore with pride and with a quiet, gathering resolve.

Rumors of a coming battle stirred the camp as spring approached. The men spoke of moving north, of Grant's army on the Tennessee River. William Clyde listened in silence, the ribbon pressing against his brow. Whatever lay ahead, his path was no longer his own.

CHAPTER 17

THE ROAD TO SHILOH

The march north from Corinth began in cold rain and sucking mud. Spring had come to Mississippi, but its warmth had not yet reached the soldiers' tents and thin blankets. The men of the Sixth Mississippi Infantry bent their heads against the drizzle and trudged mile after mile, their shoes ruined within days. At night, they huddled in shallow camps along the roadside, smoke from damp fires clinging to their lungs, the coughs of the sick echoing in the dark.

By the end of the first week, William Clyde could not tell whether the days were harder than the nights. His clothes were never dry, his belly never full, and his body ached with the relentless pace of the march. Disease spread among the ranks—colds, fevers, the flux—and men fell out by the roadside, too weak to continue. There were no camp followers now. The women and merchants who had clung to the regiment at Corinth had melted away. Only the soldiers remained, bound to one another by misery and silence.

William Clyde felt the absence of comfort keenly. The illusions of Ivanhoe seemed a distant mockery—knights in bright armor replaced by mud-smeared boys with hollow eyes. Glory felt like a word invented to persuade fools. He wondered more than once if he had been a fool to come this far. In the Choctaw Nation, his grandparents needed him. No oath had bound him to Mississippi. He could have gone home. Yet here he was, trapped by pride and loyalty to cousins who could not know the depth of his doubts.

At night, he and the two remaining Markham cousins pressed close beneath a single oilcloth, sharing what warmth they could. They did not speak of the cousin who had fallen, though his absence weighed heavier than the wet blankets. Instead, their talk circled the same desperate theme—how to survive what was coming. One swore he would always keep low when the firing began. Another practiced loading his musket by touch in the dark. William Clyde listened, then offered what he could: *"We watch each other's backs. If one falls, the others don't leave him."*

As April approached, rumors hardened into orders. The Federals under Grant were camped near Pittsburg Landing, just north of a country church called Shiloh. The Confederate army would strike at dawn. On the evening of April 5th, the regiment bivouacked in the woods south of that church. The rain fell harder, soaking the earth into black mud. The men lay in their clothes, clutching their muskets, listening to the restless murmur of thousands of voices and the drum of rain on canvas.

William Clyde lay awake long after his cousins slept, the ribbon in his cap pressing against his forehead. Its black and red thread bore words that had once thrilled him—*"The best service is that which is done in peril of life."* Now the phrase was heavy with dread. He touched it and whispered a prayer, not for glory, but for survival. And for the first time, he admitted to himself that courage was not the absence of fear but the will to keep walking forward through it.

CHAPTER 18

SHILOH: BAPTIZED IN BLOOD

The woods were gray with mist when the Confederates moved forward at dawn. William Clyde had expected banners, trumpet calls, something from the tales of Ivanhoe. Instead, they crept through wet leaves and cold fog like hunters stalking prey. Ahead, Union camps were just stirring—men frying bacon, water steaming in tin cups. When the first volley shattered the silence, it felt less like battle and more like murder. William Clyde's stomach twisted. This was not honor. This was ambush.

The Union lines collapsed in shock, blue-coated men running half-dressed through the smoke. Tents burned, horses screamed, and for a brief moment the Confederates drove everything before them. William Clyde fired, reloaded, and fired again, but with each shot his disquiet grew. Glory, he thought, did not look like this.

By afternoon the chaos hardened into resistance. The Union artillery had been brought forward and dug in along the ridges behind a sunken road. The Hornet's Nest, they called it, though William Clyde did not yet know the name. Cannon mouths gaped through the smoke, waiting. He and his two cousins pressed close together as their regiment charged again and again into the storm. The air was thick with shrieking metal. Grape and canister tore the woods to pieces. Then came the moment that would burn itself into William Clyde's soul forever.

A Federal gun belched smoke and thunder straight into their line. His cousins were at his shoulders—one to the left, one to the right. At that very instant, a single tree trunk stood between William Clyde and the cannon's muzzle. The chain shot struck home. Both cousins were cut down in an instant—one nearly torn in two, the other's leg sheared away, blood fountaining into the mud. They fell against him as they died, their life pouring out over his uniform, soaking him until he dripped red.

He lay with them, keeping the vow they had sworn never to abandon one another. Around him the battle raged on, but he did not move. His cousins' breaths rattled, slowed, and ceased, their bodies growing cold against him. When at last he rose, he was staggering, his face and coat so covered in blood that comrades thought he had been mortally wounded. But not a scratch was on him. The tree had spared him. His cousins had not.

In that moment, William Clyde felt something shift. Honor was no longer banners or charges, not the glory of Ivanhoe's knights. Honor was this: to keep faith beside the dying, to rise again when the living were gone. His bravery, he realized, would forever be marked not by his own wounds, but by the blood of those he loved.

As the sun set on Shiloh's first day, William Clyde walked forward alone. The ribbon in his cap pressed against his brow, and his coat bore the crimson memory of his kin. From that day forward, he knew his life was borrowed time—every hour a gift taken at the cost of theirs.

CHAPTER 19

AFTER SHILOH

The smoke of Shiloh lingered long after the guns fell silent. William Clyde walked among the wreckage of the battlefield, the cries of the wounded still echoing through the woods. The Sixth Mississippi was a shadow of itself—what had begun as ranks of proud boys and men was now little more than a handful of battered survivors. His cousins lay among the fallen, their blood still dried stiff on his coat. There would be no letters home from them, no witnesses to what they had endured together.

Word spread quickly through the Confederate lines: General Albert Sidney Johnston was dead, struck down by a stray bullet to the leg. Jefferson Davis had called him the South's greatest hope. Around the campfires, men spoke of the loss in hushed tones, their faces lined with fear. In his place, General P.G.T. Beauregard assumed command. Some called him brilliant, others whispered of his past as a speculator and slave dealer, a man more showman than soldier. Whatever his talents, he was not Johnston, and the men felt the difference.

Across the field, the Federals rejoiced. Grant's name was already rising, though his methods earned him the bitter title of butcher. The North could afford the butcher's bill. The South could not. The numbers alone told the story: the Confederacy bled too heavily to survive many more days like these.

For William Clyde, the dream of Ivanhoe had ended in the mud at Shiloh. Honor was no longer measured in charges or banners. It was counted in the keeping of a vow beside dying kin. Now even that witness was gone. His cousins could tell no tales of his courage or his shame. Whatever he did from this day forward would be his alone. He was free, in the loneliest sense of the word.

The regiment regrouped, but their laughter was hollow. "Next time," one man said, "we'll spend more time digging than fighting." The words drew a few grim smiles. William Clyde did not laugh. He knew it was no joke. Ahead lay not glory, but the trenches and starvation of places like Vicksburg. The war would not be won—it would only be endured.

CHAPTER 20
VICKSBURG

By the time William Clyde reached Vicksburg, he wore an officer's insignia. The path from Shiloh to this hilltop city had been marked not by glory but by attrition, and his new rank carried with it a burden far heavier than his musket. The cousins who once walked beside him were gone. In their place stood a handful of gaunt boys who looked to him for food, for protection, and for the strength to endure. The siege was a misery without end. Union guns rained shells into the city day and night. Civilians and soldiers alike dug caves into the hillsides, hiding like burrowed animals. William Clyde's men carved out their own hole, deeper and deeper, the earth cool but stifling. Their world shrank to mud walls, smoke, and the constant hunger that gnawed them hollow.

Food became his torment. The rations dwindled to scraps of mule meat, peas ground with corn, and finally whatever could be caught or scavenged. He watched his men's faces grow thinner, eyes sinking into shadows, lips cracking from thirst. He bartered, scrounged, pleaded with quartermasters, but there was never enough. Each night he lay awake, asking the same question: *How do I keep them alive one more day?*

When at last the order came to surrender, the men of the Sixth Mississippi stood in silence. On July 4, 1863, they marched out of the trenches, stacked their arms, and signed their names on slips of paper that promised they would never take up arms again until exchanged. William Clyde's hand did not tremble as he wrote. He had learned long ago that words on paper did not stop bullets, and oaths did not feed starving men.

The Union officers believed they had ended the fight for thirty thousand Confederates in one stroke. But in the ragged silence after the surrender, William

Clyde knew better. His men looked to him still, and survival was not yet certain. He told himself the paroles were a formality, a trick of lawyers and politicians. If duty called again, he would march. Honor had bled away long ago—at Shiloh with his cousins, in the caves of Vicksburg with his starving soldiers. What remained was only the will to endure.

When the men dispersed, many drifted home, their war ended. William Clyde did not. He rose from the earth of Vicksburg, thinner, harder, and carrying no illusions. Glory was gone. His word was broken. What remained was the simple, brutal truth of survival.

CHAPTER 21

AFTER VICKSBURG

The surrender at Vicksburg left William Clyde hollow. He had survived hunger and bombardment, only to sit in a line with thousands of others while Union clerks recorded his name. A parole slip was pressed into his hand — a piece of paper binding his honor as tightly as any chain. He had promised not to take up arms until exchanged.

For a while, that promise seemed like a release. He could have walked away. The river was there, broad and dark, and beyond it the Choctaw Nation — his grandmother's land, his true home. With every mile the army trudged, he thought of it: a raft lashed together, a skiff borrowed under cover of night, a chance to turn west instead of north But the exchange system churned on, indifferent to his doubts. Officer for officer, man for man, his name was eventually called. Suddenly the paper he had signed at Vicksburg no longer held him. He was free to fight again — or free to run. He chose to return. Whether it was loyalty to his uncle's kin, the weight of his Masonic brothers, or simply the shame of breaking away, he never fully knew.

The Mississippi regiments re-formed, ragged but determined. His survival at Shiloh and endurance at Vicksburg had marked him in the eyes of superiors. By the time he rejoined the line, he carried a lieutenant's responsibility — men looked to him for rations, orders, and a sense that the cause still mattered. He was no longer a boy trailing cousins; he was a leader bound to strangers who now trusted him.

Yet he carried a private disquiet. In his cap, hidden beneath the sweatband, the red and black ribbon with its embroidered verse still reminded him of Ivanhoe's code of honor. But what honor was left in parole, in exchange, in trudging back into a war he already knew could not be won? Every step north toward Tennessee was a step away from the freedom that still beckoned across the river — a freedom he had once again denied himself.

CHAPTER 22

FRANKLIN (A CODA)

The march north ended at Franklin, Tennessee, on a cold November day in 1864. The men of Hood's army had been driven to exhaustion, and William Clyde knew in his bones that no good could come of the fight.

The battle itself was chaos. Confederate ranks charged into fortified Union positions, swept by cannon and musket fire. William Clyde went forward with his men, as duty required, though his heart was already west across the Mississippi.

Somewhere in the smoke he felt the blast, a tearing heat along his side. He staggered but did not fall until the wave of soldiers broke around him. By nightfall he was a prisoner, carried into the Union lines with hundreds of others.

In that moment he discovered a strange truth: he was freer in defeat than he had ever been in Hood's army. The march was over. The prison gates were real this time, but they promised certainty — no more forced campaigns, no more doomed charges.

Weeks passed in northern prison camps. Cold, hunger, and boredom filled the days, but no bullets. In the winter he was exchanged as an officer. By the spring of 1865, the war itself collapsed. His parole was final.

William Clyde turned west at last. Across Arkansas and into the Choctaw Nation he went, carrying scars that never quite healed and memories he seldom spoke aloud. He returned not as a hero crowned with glory, but as a survivor who had carried others as far as he could, and who now carried only himself back to the people who had raised him.

PART ONE

William Clyde Thompson survived the war, but survival brought no guarantee of justice. Like the rest of the Choctaw people, the Yowani were deprived of their land, excluded from allotments, and denied the restitution that was their due. They were as entitled as any other Choctaw citizen—yet they were left outside the circle of benefit. His survival meant that the fight would not end on the battlefield, but would continue in courts and councils, where the struggle for recognition and fairness proved just as long and bitter.

RESOLUTION TO WIN

PART 2

The story of the Yowani did not end with the return from war. If anything, the war only sharpened the contrast between the sacrifice of men like William Clyde Thompson and the treatment his people received afterward. Like every other Choctaw family, the Yowani had already endured removal, dispersal, and the loss of their homeland. They were citizens by blood, heritage, and law—yet when the time came for allotments, they were denied what was rightfully theirs. This injustice cannot be understated. The Yowani were not outsiders pressing for undeserved privilege; they were as entitled as any other member of the Choctaw Nation. Their exclusion was not an accident of paperwork, but the final act in a long chain of displacements. William Clyde's survival after the war made it possible for him to champion his people through this trial, but the fight ahead would prove as consuming and as costly as any battle he faced in uniform. It was in courtrooms, not on battlefields, that the fate of his people would now be decided.

CHAPTER 23

THE RIVER HOME

The sergeant spotted the bars before he said a word.

He was a big man, weathered and careful, the kind of soldier who had learned that lowering your voice got you farther than raising it. He studied the frayed gray coat on William Clyde's arm, then the faint, dried maroon on the sleeve that wasn't dust at all.

"Beggin' your pardon, sir," the sergeant said. "You'll want to stow that." His eyes flicked to the captain's insignia—still sewn, still proud. "Around here, folks see the color before they see the man."

William Clyde met his gaze. "It's my coat," he said. "And those are my bars."

"Yes, sir," the sergeant answered. "And you've got your papers." He nodded at the folded parole tucked in William Clyde's pocket. "That'll do for the law. But men are quicker than the law, especially at the landing." He let the warning hang. Then, softer: "I mean no offense. I was a sergeant when I took mine off. Hurt like the devil. But I took 'em off."

William Clyde looked down at the coat, the cloth heavier in summer heat, the blood his cousins' and some that might've been his. He didn't argue. He folded the garment with care and slid it into his duffel, bars intact, stitching unbroken. He would not unmake what he had been. But he could put it away.

"Thank you," he said.

The sergeant only dipped his head. "Good day to you, Captain."

***

Memphis received him in heat and river stink—the sweet rot of summer and the steady groan of steamboats tied two and three deep. He made his way along the landing to a warehouse office where a clerk said the name "Colbert" with enough respect to fetch a private room and a pitcher of water.

His kin arrived before the hour was out: a man of middle years with the kind of grooming that comes from knowing your name opens doors, and a younger woman whose eyes were quicker than her smile. The man embraced him like a nephew, not like a stranger.

"You've your grandmother's cheekbones," he said, stepping back to look. "And your grandfather's stubbornness, if what I hear is true."

"I'm told both are curses," William Clyde said.

"Blessings when they serve you. Curses when they don't. Sit." The man gestured to a chair. "We'll make you fit to travel proper."

Bundles appeared: a clean white shirt with firm collar, a lighter coat suited to July, trousers without a stain. The woman laid them out as if dressing a mannequin—the old uniform was accepted without comment and set aside.

"In civilian clothes," the man said, "you are a gentleman among gentlemen. On these boats, the first thing they see is the cut of your lapels. The second thing is the way you carry yourself." "He already carries himself like an officer," the woman said. She met William Clyde's eyes. "That doesn't wash off."

He felt it then—the posture war had put into him, the habit of looking directly into a man, the sense that rooms parted, however slightly, when he entered because someone had once taught him to expect it. Respect had become a kind of muscle. He hadn't noticed until she said it.

They ate a simple meal. Conversation moved uncertainly at first—how was the passage east, was the parole honored, what news from Richmond—and then the man cleared his throat and squared the papers on the table.

"There's another matter," he said. "I'm afraid we learned of it only the day before yesterday." His voice grew gentle in that practiced way men have when they cannot soften the blow. "Margaret is gone."

The words were a gate closing. He had known the war could take anything, yet some part of him had counted on a day after all of this when he would sit at her fire and tell her he had made it home. Now the fire would be coals, and the chair beside it empty.

"When?" he asked.

"Early summer," the man said. "Peacefully. You were in the field. No fault in that."

He nodded, that soldier's nod that stands in for grief when tears are unwise.

The woman reached and put two fingers lightly against his wrist—not a comfort exactly, but an acknowledgment.

"We'll see you home," she said. "That's the thing that matters."

They gave him a small roll of banknotes, a watch with a firm spring, and a letter sealed with a careful hand.

"Carry this to those who ask," the man said. "It will speak for you in the Nation. And this—" He tapped the money. "—will speak for you on the river."

"You honor me," William Clyde said.

"We honor ourselves," the man replied. "You are Thompson and you are Colbert. That is enough."

***

He boarded an Arkansas River boat two days later, a packet smaller than the deep-bellied Mississippians, nimble in the brown water. On deck, under the awning, there were merchants with ledgers, a Methodist minister with a valise of tracts, two federal men in broadcloth loosening their ties against the heat. The crewmen glanced at William Clyde's clothes and made space for him on a bench without asking his name.

He sat quiet, the Colbert letter in his inside pocket, the parole folded against it like a thinner heart. The captain's coat lay in the duffel at his feet. He did not put his hand on it, but he felt its weight, the way a man knows where his knife is even when he isn't reaching for it.

The river ran fast for July, shouldering at its banks, the pilot favoring the outside of bends to avoid hidden snags. Sandbars shifted like rumor. At certain landings, planks were splintered where freshet had pushed driftwood through. The pilot cursed softly when an eddy shoved them off a landing just as the gangplank went down, then laughed and tried again. The river taught patience by threatening those who hurried.

In that restless quiet where passengers watch the water and pretend not to watch each other, the federal men grew careless. They spoke in the relaxed tones of men who have talked business long enough to forget the walls have ears.

"Fort Smith by September," one said. "Get the preliminaries laid and the treaties drawn by spring."

"Rails are the hinge," the other replied. "Coal's nothing in the ground. But tie it to iron and you've got heat in Chicago and profit in St. Louis."

"And the chiefs?"

"They'll sign. They'll call it friendship. We'll call it progress. Same paper."

They chuckled, not unkindly, not like villains—more like men admiring a plan well laid. Then one of them, the older, let the mask slip.

"They're not a people anymore," he said, almost reflective. "Not like they were. Not after this war. You'll see. They'll be citizens and tenants and customers. Good for business." The words slid into William Clyde like a thin knife. He kept his face polite, his posture easy, exactly as a gentleman does when he overhears something that isn't meant for him. No one looked twice at him. He had the right coat, the right bearing, the right indifference.

A deckhand came by with a pot of coffee and nodded to him respectfully. "Top you off, sir?"

"Thank you," William Clyde said. He let the man pour.

The day wore on. The minister offered a tract to anyone who'd take one, blessing all equally and meaning it as far as a man can see into another man's soul. A child cried in the heat and slept with her head against her mother's arm. The pilot edged past a snag so sudden and black it seemed like the river had thrown a spear.

Toward evening, when the heat lost interest in tormenting the living and gave them back their breath, William Clyde stood at the rail and watched the light shiver on the water. He thought of his grandmother's hands, red from soap, moving over a shirt just this color once, in a different home, with a different future. He thought of the coat folded in his bag, the bars stitched where a needle had once gone in and come out and left a tiny pucker in the wool. He thought of the men across the deck making tidy plans out of lives not theirs.

He was a soldier who had laid down his visible arms. But he had not surrendered. The world had given him a different battlefield. He felt the shaping of it in his chest the way he'd once felt a line dress forward on command.

A crewman he had barely noticed earlier drifted near him—sunburnt, river-lean, eyes quick. He had the look of a man who hears much and repeats little.

"Beggin' your pardon," the man said. "You headin' for Fort Smith?" "I am."

The crewman nodded toward the federal men. "Plenty like them ahead. Plenty behind. Best to know you're walkin' into a room where the deal was struck on the porch."

"Thank you," William Clyde said. "I appreciate the warning."

"Not warning, sir," the man said. "Just the weather." He tipped his cap and moved on.

***

They made Fort Smith near sundown two days later. The landing was mud and sawdust, boards laid like a promise over the worst of it. Soldiers on the bluff above—blue coats this time—watched the boat tie up. A small crowd had gathered, drawn by the reliable entertainment of arrival.

As he stepped off the gangplank, a young corporal glanced at his duffel, then at his collar and cuffs, reading the fabric and the fit as if they were documents. Whatever he saw satisfied him. He nodded. "Evenin', sir."

"Evening," William Clyde said.

On the bulletin board near the warehouse door, fresh notices were tacked at clean angles. He did not need to read them to know what they were. A clerk with tidy hair and ink on his fingers saw him looking.

"Council in September," the clerk said, almost cheerfully. "Government men to meet with the tribes. Set things back to rights."

William Clyde gave a small, polite smile—the sort given by men who know that arguing with a clerk accomplishes less than nothing. He touched the inside pocket where the letter from his kin lay warm, and the other pocket where the parole rested against his ribs. Then he adjusted his hat and went to find a room.

By habit, he set his bag on a table and opened it first. The coat lay there like a folded memory—the bars bright even in the dim light of a boarding room, the sleeve stiff where blood had dried and no one had thought to wash it clean. He didn't take it out. He didn't look at it long. The thing he needed from it had already moved into his bones.

He sat, then, and stared at the window until the glass reflected him back. The man in the pane was tidy, respectable, anonymous. The man in the room was Yowani. Both were true. Both would be necessary.

Tomorrow, he would carry the letter to the men who needed to see it. He would speak to those who would listen. He would tell what he had heard on the water—that rails had already been laid in men's minds, that coal had already been spent in their counting rooms, that paper had already been folded around the future of his people like a shroud.

He had come by the river, as his grandmother once had, from a world that could no longer keep him. He had returned not to glory but to work.

Outside, the Arkansas breathed against its banks. In September, men would gather to call what they did progress. He would be there, without his bars and without his coat, and he would not be blind.

CHAPTER 24

THE QUIET MEETING

The steamboat left him at the landing below Fort Smith in the fading heat of an August day. By now, William Clyde carried himself with the bearing of an officer, though his coat with its captain's bars lay carefully folded and hidden deep in a leather satchel. He had taken care to have it cleaned and pressed in Memphis—no longer a tattered relic of the battlefield but a memento he dared not display. In its place, he wore plain southern clothes given to him by his Colbert kin, garments that allowed him to move without drawing suspicion.

Even so, he felt every question in the eyes of strangers. His accent betrayed him as southern. His bearing marked him as one who had worn rank. If any Union official asked about his service, his answer was prepared: "I was paroled at Vicksburg and sent home. I gave my word not to fight again, and I have kept it." It was not a lie, not exactly. It was a shield—one that protected him from entanglements that could ruin both him and those he had come to help.

That evening, under the cover of lamplight, he was guided to a modest house near the edge of town. The meeting had been arranged quietly; names were not spoken aloud in public. Winchester Colbert was already inside, seated at a plain oak table with another of his kin. They greeted William Clyde not as a stranger but as a blood relation, a grandson of the Wind Clan through Margaret McCoy, and one who had survived the fire that consumed so many others.

"You have heard things on the river," Winchester said, his voice low but steady. "Men talk when they think no one is listening."

William Clyde nodded. "They talk of land as if it were already theirs. Coal and timber, rails to carry it north. They laugh at what will be taken, as if the treaties are nothing but paper ash. I heard it with my own ears."

The older men exchanged glances, neither surprised nor comforted. They had expected treachery; now they had confirmation. "You did well to bring this to us," Winchester said. "It gives us time to prepare our words. The Chickasaw cannot be seen as fools at this council."

William Clyde felt the weight of the moment. All his years of being shaped by others—by his uncle's household in Mississippi, by the Markhams' example of southern gentility, by the Confederacy's brutal crucible—seemed to converge here. His great-uncle James McCoy had once imagined a generation able to walk in both worlds, to speak as equals with white officials while holding firm to Choctaw and Chickasaw identity. William Clyde realized, with a start, that he was fulfilling that vision. He was the messenger between two languages, two truths.

They spoke for an hour, voices hushed, the shutters drawn tight. Plans were made, names weighed, strategies considered. William Clyde offered what he had overheard, careful not to claim more knowledge than he had, but firm in the details he knew to be true. When at last he left the house, the night air felt heavy, charged with consequence.

For the first time since leaving Franklin, he felt that his survival might have meaning beyond himself.

CHAPTER 25

COVER OF RESPECTABILITY

William Clyde quickly learned that in Fort Smith, survival depended as much upon perception as truth. His Chickasaw and Choctaw lineage, his Confederate service, even his captain's bars—all of it could either lift him into circles of trust or brand him with suspicion. What mattered most now was the story he carried. When questioned by curious eyes in the hotel lobby or on the wharf, his accent marked him as Southern, and his bearing marked him as a man who had been respected. Yet he never admitted to soldiering beyond the vague words, "I was with Mississippi men until the parole at Vicksburg." That answer was tidy, believable, and above reproach. It implied loyalty to the South, but also honor in keeping his word to the Union.

With his uniform coat pressed and hidden in a leather satchel, he appeared as any young gentleman planter's son might—travel-worn, but decent. The Colberts had seen to that in Memphis, outfitting him with proper civilian clothes, a letter of introduction, and stern advice to carry himself as if nothing in his past were worth inquiry.

It worked. A Union sergeant on the Arkansas packet boat had warned him quietly: "Sir, best keep your bars hidden. You'll get farther with manners than with metal." William Clyde had nodded, slipping his coat away without protest. He would not discard it, for it had become part keepsake, part relic, soaked in blood not his own. But he would not wear it again in public.

At Fort Smith, his evenings were spent quietly at the hotel, where federal negotiators gathered in the parlor. There, over cigars and whiskey, they spoke freely, assuming the well-dressed young man in the corner was no more than another planter's son awaiting news of cotton prices. He heard enough to know their designs: coal, timber, land leases, and the slow erosion of tribal sovereignty, all to be forced upon the tribes under the guise of new treaties.

When he met privately with Winchester Colbert and James McCoy, William Clyde relayed every overheard phrase. The Colberts understood immediately the value of this information. Here was a young man who could move between two worlds—the officers' parlor and the tribal council fire—and not betray himself in either.

It was exactly the skill James McCoy had once prayed the Yowani line would produce: a man who could listen in one language, then speak in another, without losing respect on either side.

CHAPTER 26

THE BRIDGE HE WAS MEANT TO BE

By the second night in Fort Smith, William Clyde understood that the safest room was the one no one knew he had entered. A boy no older than sixteen met him at the back of a grocer's and led him down a narrow alley where wash water leaked from eaves and the boards smelled of soap and summer rot. They slipped through a side door into a parlor kept dim on purpose—shutters cracked just enough to let the lamp smoke climb.

Winchester Colbert rose from a straight-backed chair. Another kinsman sat in the corner, half in shadow, listening the way old hunters listen. No names were exchanged. It was the kind of discretion that felt like prayer. "You heard them again tonight?" Winchester asked.

"I did," William Clyde said. "They speak of the western lands as a foregone thing. Rails first—north and east. Coal leases to follow. Timber as 'incidental' once the right-of-way is cut."

Winchester's mouth bent—neither a smile nor a frown. "Incidental," he repeated softly, tasting the word like something gone sour. "What else?"

"They do not expect resistance in the courts," William Clyde said. "One said, 'Their courts won't stand long.' Another said, 'Congress will fix the rest.' They mean to weaken our law before they take the rest of the land."

The kinsman in the corner shifted, the chair creaking. "They'll promise friendship on the page," he murmured, "and then change the page."

Winchester gestured for William Clyde to sit. "Tell me, nephew—if they press you in the hotel or in the street, what do you say of the war?"

"That I was paroled at Vicksburg and kept my word," William Clyde answered. The sentence felt practiced now, smooth as a coin. "I tell them I am traveling to settle family business, and I let them decide what that is."

Winchester nodded once. "Good. It is enough truth to hold." He studied the young man in the lamplight—the clean collar, the steady posture, the patient eyes. "James McCoy told me, years before the war, that we would need men who could sit at a white man's table without forgetting the council fire. He hoped one of Margaret's grandsons would grow into that task."

William Clyde felt the words land in his chest. James was not in Fort Smith; he was back at Boggy Depot, where the talk was straighter and the roads muddier. But his voice seemed to cross the miles anyway: Learn their manners, their law, their confidence—use it to keep our people whole.

"I can carry what I hear," William Clyde said. "And I can keep my own counsel while I do it."

"That is the work," Winchester replied. He leaned forward, elbows on knees. "There is more you should know. They do not speak only of rails and coal. They speak of mouths to feed and votes to gather. They would make us citizens while taking away the house a citizen should own. They would give a man a paper and call it freedom, then take the ground from under his feet. In a few years' time they will call for allotment—split the Nation into pieces so small a surveyor can't find the heart of it."

The lamp popped. Outside, a wagon rattled by, iron tires bumping over knots in the street. William Clyde thought of the coat folded in his leather satchel—bars bright, sleeve stiff where blood had dried; of the riverboat men laughing about progress; of Margaret's hands, red from lye and work, and the stories she told by firelight. Honor had changed clothes on him, that was all.

"What would you have me do, sir?" he asked.

"Listen. Remember. Carry this." Winchester produced a sealed letter and tapped it against his palm. "When the council breaks, you will go south by the stage road until Poteau, then turn toward Boggy Depot. Give this to James. Tell him what you have told me—exact words where you can. He will know how to lay it before our lawmakers."

William Clyde took the letter. The seal was clean, impressed by a familiar hand. "Yes, sir."

Winchester sat back. "If any man asks you your business, you are a merchant's agent, returning home with prices and news. If a soldier presses you, you were paroled at Vicksburg and have kept your word. And if you begin to doubt what you are"—he paused, letting the quiet thicken—"you are Yowani, and that is enough."

The kinsman in the corner finally spoke up, voice dry as cedar. "There's talk they'll claim the western prairie was never truly ours because few lived upon it. Remind James: pasture leased is not pasture lost. A grazing fence can be mended; a broken court cannot."

William Clyde nodded, storing the phrasing exactly. "Pasture leased is not pasture lost," he repeated. They ended as they had begun—without ceremony. The handclasp was brief. The boy who had led him in reappeared from the darkness like a thought and guided him back through the side door to the alley. The night had cooled. Somewhere a dog barked twice and stopped.

He walked to the hotel with the quiet confidence of a man used to being saluted, and yet no one turned their head. He had learned invisibility with a captain's posture; it was a rare skill, and dangerously useful. In the upstairs hall, a federal officer he recognized from the boat narrowed his eyes, searching his memory, then seemed to place him.

"Vicksburg, was it?" the officer asked.

"Yes, sir," William Clyde said. "Paroled."

The man's shoulders loosened. "You kept your word?"

"I did."

"Then you'll do all right," the officer said, almost kindly. "The country needs men who can keep their word." He tipped his hat and moved on.

In his room, William Clyde set the sealed letter inside his satchel, beside the folded coat. Two artifacts of different kinds of allegiance. He poured a little water into the basin and washed his hands, watching the lamplight tremble in the bowl as if the surface were a second river. From the street below came a fragment of laughter, a burst of piano from the saloon, the stop-and-start clatter of a buggy turning uphill.

He lay back on the bed without taking off his boots. Sleep came in small waves. Each time he drifted, he saw rails crossing a prairie and a clerk stamping a form; each time he woke, he felt the weight of the satchel beside him and the plain truth waiting down the road. He had survived the war to arrive at this—work without glory, danger without banners, and a fight conducted in rooms with shutters cracked to let the smoke out.

Between two worlds, he had found the narrow bridge James McCoy envisioned. Now he had to walk it.

CHAPTER 27

TOWARD TUSKAHOMA

William Clyde disembarks at Fort Smith with Winchester Colbert's letter in his possession, his Confederate coat folded neatly away. The summer air is heavy with the smell of the river, but his thoughts are already turning south and west, toward the Choctaw Nation.

He hears talk in the hotel halls and the tavern corners of the Fort Smith meeting — words sharp with ambition, dripping with disdain for the tribes' future. He takes mental notes, remembering every phrase, every hint of intent. These overheard words will not vanish; they will travel with him.

The path that stretches before him is both familiar and foreign. This is Choctaw country, and yet after the war, the ground feels unsettled. William Clyde knows that soon he will have to choose where to carry his loyalty and what role he must play in the tribe's precarious future.

It is then that talk of Tuskahoma reaches him. A new seat of Choctaw political life, nestled in the foothills, already whispered of as the gathering place of leaders and visionaries. And there, among them, lives John Duncan Thompson — his cousin, born in 1838, a man whose voice is already carrying weight in the councils of the Nation.

For William Clyde, the thought is both anchor and summons. To Tuskahoma he will go, with Winchester's sealed words as his introduction and his own war-worn bearing as proof of endurance.

As he gathers his belongings — the pressed civilian clothes gifted to him in Memphis, the leather bag concealing his bloodstained coat — he realizes he is leaving behind more than the river. He is stepping into the role his great-uncle James McCoy once envisioned for him: the bridge between two worlds.

The road south and west from Fort Smith promises uncertainty, but also destiny. And at its end, waiting in Tuskahoma, is family — and the beginning of the next fight.

CHAPTER 28

HILLS OF TOMORROW

The hills above Nanih Waiya went copper at dusk, then bruised purple as the light slid away. Oaks crowded the slopes with their late-season reds and golds; clusters of medium pines darkened the ridgelines and salted the air with sap. Off to the northwest, Buffalo Mountain shouldered up against the sky, and further east the Potato Hills knuckled the horizon in a broken chain. Below the cabin, a shallow creek worried its banks and wandered toward broader water. Cattle lowed somewhere beyond the trees, and a dog answered once and fell quiet.

William Clyde Thompson came in slow, letting the mare choose her footing on the red earth. The road behind him ran all the way to Fort Smith in his mind—names, faces, hard talk. He felt the weight of it in his shoulders. All he wanted now was the simple grammar of kin: a door, firelight, the first exchange of eyes that said, You are home among your own.

John Duncan Thompson met him on the porch, broad-shouldered and steady, only a year older but already wearing the land like a fitted coat. Their hands locked at the forearm the way their uncles had taught them. Neither spoke at first. The war, and all the things a man cannot say about it, sat between them like another guest.

Inside, the cabin held heat and the comfortable disorder of a place being lived in: stacked wood, a scatter of tools, a cradle of horse tack near the door. John set out cornbread and beans with a mason jar of milk, and they ate as men do who have done this together since boyhood, the pauses in conversation easy and familiar.

"It feels strange," John said finally, leaning back. "Seeing you here after... all of it. Shiloh, Vicksburg. I didn't count on it."

William Clyde put down his spoon. "I lived when others didn't. That's the sum I can carry." He settled his gaze on the fire. "I don't care to tell the rest. Men cut

down like stalks of cane. Ground slick and red. No sense in those pictures."
John nodded. "I figured as much. Folks will ask you. I'll turn them aside."
A log shifted; sparks climbed the flue. William Clyde reached to the sideboard and broke the cornbread in half again, more for the movement than the hunger. "I'll tell them one thing," he said. "In Mississippi, I saw plantations enough to fill a man's nightmares. Slavery doesn't belong to us. Not here. Our hills won't bend to a cotton empire. Maybe down on the Red you can coax a field, but not in these uplands. And they've got machines coming—gins and pickers that eat labor for breakfast. Soon the enslaved will be more burden than strength. Washington talks like slavery is civilization, but I call it a curse."

John's mouth twitched toward a smile that didn't quite come. "You won't find argument from me. I look south of here and see pasture rolling out to the horizon. Horses, cattle. Timber where the ground rises, water enough if you know the draws. That's a life a man can make and keep."

William Clyde breathed out through his nose, a small admission that the talk had loosened a knot inside him. "I've had my fill of blood," he said. "Give me fences and calves, arguments over a bull, a broken gate, a neighbor who returned a borrowed chisel. I could live in such arguments and be content."

John rubbed a palm over his jaw. "You came from Fort Smith," he said softly, making the words a question. "They say Winchester Colbert was there."

William Clyde's eyes stayed on the fire, but the rest of him stilled. When he spoke, it was nearer a whisper than his voice had been all evening.

"I did more than see him. I listened in places where my face was not invited. I was no delegate. Call it spying if you like. I watched who stood close to whom. I counted who went into what tent and came out with what expression. And once, by chance or Providence, I spoke to Colbert—a few sentences only. He asked after our grandmother Margaret. Said he remembered the strength of her will. Of politics, he would not say much, only this: that the United States has a long memory and little mercy."
John's hand dropped from his jaw and closed around his knee. "He's right," he said. "Already the talk is hard—emancipation, ceding the Leased District, rails to cross our land. Agents who say they come friendly and carry maps rolled tight

under their arms."

"They rolled them out," William Clyde said, eyes narrowing as if the paper were still on the table in front of him. "Lines and boxes. Men with rulers where no man lived, measuring what they do not feel." He lifted his gaze. "There's more, John. They talk of distributing the Nation's land—taking what we hold in common and giving every man and woman a piece to claim as his own. Allotment, some called it. It was quiet talk, careful. But it was there. And if that day comes, the question of who is Choctaw will become everything."

John blinked, once, as if to clear grit. "Allotment," he said, tasting the word. "You mean to cut the Nation into parcels like they do in Arkansas—fences from one creek to the next and a title in a drawer?"

"That very thing," William Clyde said. "They called it civilization, progress. I call it another kind of removal. You can drive a people off their land by force, or you can slice the land under their feet into pieces so small they can be bought and lost."

John shook his head. "That can't be the way here."

William Clyde's voice was steady and low. "I hope not. But I saw the way those men looked at a map—like surveyors seeing a harvest. They asked for names. They wanted lists. Blood, family, place. If your name isn't on those papers when the time comes, you may be told you are nothing. Not in insult—by law."

John stared into the red heart of the fire. "You mean my children, our children, could be questioned."

"Yes," William Clyde said. "If we do not stand and be counted among our own. If we let our belonging live only in stories and not on paper. One day men who never smelled these oaks after rain will claim the right to say we are or are not Choctaw."

Silence held for a moment, thick as wool. Outside, the dog woofed once and lay back down.

John spoke first. "Then we make certain of the rolls," he said. "We take no chances."

"We do more than that," William Clyde answered. "We go to Council. We speak when we can, where we can. I was there when they spoke of the Freedmen—free now in law, unfree in the habits of men. If we do not take them in as citizens, they will drift and be used. If we do, some will rage. There's no path without hard ground. But whatever we choose, we must choose as a Nation and write it with care, because the paper will outlive our voices."

John lifted his eyes. "There's talk here already—men threatening to walk out of meetings if rations are to be shared, others who say adoption is right. Families divided at their own tables." He made a small, helpless motion with his hands. "I don't want our future written by anger."

"That's why the rolls matter," William Clyde said. "Not as a weapon, but as an anchor. The paper must match the truth—that we were here, are here, belong here. Our grandmother didn't pull us across the border and lay us in these hills so that one day a clerk in a room a thousand miles away could decide we were strangers."

John gave a short, grim laugh. "God save us from clerks. "They won't come as soldiers," William Clyde said. "They'll come as clerks and commissioners. They'll set up tables and ask questions like prayers. What blood are you? Where were you born? Who was your mother's mother? And if a line in a ledger doesn't match their notion, they will put a mark by your name that no amount of truth will rub off."

John looked past the fire toward the black window where their own faces dimly hovered. "You really think they mean to cut it up so neat?"

"I think they mean to change us into something they understand," William Clyde said. "A people whose land can be valued on a page. When the day comes—and it will, if what I heard holds true—the ones on the roll will be given a piece. Those off the roll will be told to pay to sit on the ground they stand on or to move along."

John's brow furrowed. "Pay? You mean some kind of rent?"

"Call it a fee, a tax, a permit—whatever word the paper likes. But not for those who are recognized as citizens. We live on the Nation's land as the Nation itself, without fee to our own. Outsiders pay to be here. That's right and just. But if a clerk can erase you with a stroke, he can turn you into an outsider in your own home."

John's hand made a fist on his knee. "My children will not pay rent to live where I put themNor yours."

"Then we see that the rolls are true," William Clyde said. "We make certain of it now, while our elders still breathe and can lay out the lines of kin. We keep our names where they should be."

He reached to the mantle and took down a small, smoke-darkened frame. Inside, a scrap of paper in a careful old hand: names, a date, a place near Doaksville. Their grandmother's work, recorded when a visitor from Mississippi had once demanded to know who they were. John had kept it there for years, a talisman against forgetting.

"Margaret knew," John said softly, returning the frame. "She always knew the day would come when paper would be made to carry what should live in the bones."

They fell quiet then, each turning the same wheel of thought: how a life made in hills and creeks and seasons could be forced into ledgers; how the warmth of this room could be translated, coldly, into a parcel and a number.

After a time, John leaned forward, elbows on knees. "You'll stay a while?" he asked. "Put your hand to some fencing, help me mend the roofline. We can see what these pastures will bear. If I set cattle here and you set cattle down toward Boggy, we'll be neighbors in more than talk."

"I'll stay long enough to make the place proof against the first hard freeze," William Clyde said. "I've ridden enough for one season. And I mean to ride for a different reason next—into Council, not into war."

John's grin came now, genuine and boyish, the face William Clyde knew from creek days and salt-works errands. "I'd pay money to watch you take a strip off a commissioner with your quiet voice," he said. "You make a man hear himself and not like what he hears."

"I'll settle for making him listen," William Clyde said. "And for writing down what is true while we still can."

Wind pressed around the corners of the cabin and then relented. The fire sank a little. John stood and added a split of oak. Outside, the darkness held the shapes of the hills as surely as daylight, just with different edges.

"You remember that trail over Winding Stair?" John asked, voice drifting as if to himself. "The one the old men showed us when we were boys—the path east toward Arkansas, where our people came on foot."

"I remember," William Clyde said. "I remember how the elders spoke of it like a scar that had become a road."

"Maybe this allotment you fear will be a different sort of scar," John said. "One we cannot see from the ridge but feel when we step wrong."

"Maybe," William Clyde said. "But scars tell us where we've been cut. They don't tell us we're finished."

John nodded at that, pleased by the shape of the words. "Then we'll make plans," he said. "We'll put our names where they cannot be missed. We'll see about cattle. We'll find a place for the Freedmen that does not shame us. We'll be citizens not because a paper says it, but because our lives say it—and then we'll make the paper agree."

William Clyde stood and stretched, joints answering with small complaints. He went to the door and opened it to the night. The air was cool and clean.

Somewhere across the draw a calf bawled twice, found what it wanted, and went silent. The stars had their winter sharpness already.

"Tomorrow," he said, not turning. "We'll start tomorrow."

"Tomorrow," John echoed. He blew out the lantern by the table; the room leaned into firelight alone.

They stood a moment longer in the doorway—two young men, kin by blood and by the long, stubborn memory of a grandmother who had carried them all—looking out over the country that would try to make and unmake them. The hills did not answer. They did not have to. The ground itself held their place. For now.

CHAPTER 29

THE FIRE AT PENNINGTON

For nearly a decade after his marriage, William Clyde Thompson settled into the rhythms of Trinity County. The general store where he had begun as a clerk became his daily stage: shelves stacked with bolts of calico, barrels of flour, jars of sorghum, kegs of nails. Farmers and freedmen alike leaned on his counter, placing orders they could not yet pay for, while he jotted careful entries in the ledger.

At first it seemed the system would hold. Cotton prices rose and fell, but neighbors were honest, and their word counted as good as coin.

"Pay you after harvest," they'd say, and most did. Over time, though, the debts began to stick. Crops failed. Markets sagged. The end of the war had left more hunger than prosperity, and William Clyde found himself caught between creditors demanding payment and neighbors begging for more time.

Despite the hardship, his fairness earned him respect. By 1876, townsfolk whispered that he was the kind of man who ought to sit in the courthouse—steady, impartial, honest as the day was long. When the county seat shifted to Pennington, his name appeared on the ballot. In September, the results were tallied: Judge Thompson.

For a moment, he believed he could make a difference. The office was more administrative than judicial, but the title carried weight. He kept minutes, managed probate, oversaw small disputes. He worked by day in the store and by evening at the courthouse, where oil lamps cast his shadow long against the pine-board walls.

But not everyone welcomed his election. Some saw danger in a man who held both the books of their debts and the authority of the bench.

A handful of hard-pressed farmers muttered that "Thompson could ruin us twice over." Others resented his Choctaw blood, whispered that outsiders had no place in county power.

The tension came to a head on a damp November night. The courthouse, still new to Pennington, went up in flames.

Townsfolk would later say a lantern tipped, or that sparks from a hearth caught the timber. William Clyde knew better.

He had been in his office, ledger open, when smoke curled under the door. By the time he reached the hall, fire was already racing up the walls. His old leg wound slowed him, each step dragging. For an instant, he thought the building would be his tomb.

Shouts outside. A door forced open. He staggered into the cold air, coughing, while behind him the courthouse roared like a furnace.

The crowd gathered in silence, faces lit orange by the flames. No one said it aloud, but the thought hung heavy: the fire was no accident.

That night, Sarah wept in their small house, clutching his hand as though to anchor him. Their children, Arthur and Mary, slept in the next room, unaware of how close their father had come to death. "They'll try again," she whispered. "If they think you're in their way, they'll finish it next time."

William Clyde stared into the darkness, the ache in his leg throbbing with each heartbeat. He had survived battlefields and prisons, only to face betrayal among neighbors. He could not ask Sarah—or their children—to live with that fear.

Two months after his election, he resigned. His name slipped quietly from the county rolls, another judge sworn in to replace him. The fire had not only singed his hair and choked his lungs; it had destroyed deeds, wills, accounts—the very papers that proved who a man was and what he owned. In the ashes, families would fight over what had been lost, and some would lose everything. Clyde knew then that records were as fragile as kindling. If they could burn in Pennington, they could vanish anywhere.

He thought of his children—Arthur and Mary—and how their names might one day rest on paper that could be burned, hidden, or stolen.

Without those lines of ink, their place in the Nation could be denied as easily as a log cast into fire.

Sarah gripped his hand and said, "If the fire didn't take you, it might still take our future. Leave the courthouse, Clyde. Let others chase the smoke. We need our children's names written where they'll last."

The decision was made: they would leave Trinity County. The north called—the Chickasaw Nation, Marlow, a fresh start among people who would judge him not for ledgers or lost records, but for the work he could do with his own two hands.

As the ashes of Pennington's courthouse cooled, William Clyde turned his face toward Indian Territory once more.

The war had ended eleven years before, yet only now did he feel he was truly beginning to leave its shadow.

CHAPTER 30

REUNION IN MARLOW

The road into Marlow stretched wide under the fading light, the air carrying the smell of grass, cattle, and the dust of passing wagons.

William Clyde Thompson guided the team with Sarah beside him, Arthur and Mary in the back, their eyes wide at the new country that opened before them. It was the late 1870s, and the Chickasaw Nation was changing—some said for the better, others said for the worse.

On the edge of town, John Duncan Thompson Jr. waited. His figure was broad-shouldered, weathered by years of farm and council work, but his face lit up when he saw his cousin step down from the wagon. The men clasped forearms, pulling each other into a brief embrace.

"Clyde," John said. "By God, you've made it back."

Inside, after Sarah and the children were settled and the stew eaten, the men drew their chairs close to the fire. The air carried the sound of the wind outside, and the crackle of oak logs inside.

William Clyde began. "Texas gave me work, but little peace. The store kept men on credit until their harvests failed them, and when I thought I'd help the county, the courthouse went up in smoke. I left with my name intact but little else."

John nodded grimly. "Fires are more than wood burning. They take records, too. Deeds, wills, proof of who a man is. That's why I tell everyone: paper is as fragile as kindling."

William Clyde leaned forward. "That's why I've come. I won't have Arthur and Mary's names vanish with smoke."

John stirred the fire. "The Nation is changing, Clyde. Washington insists on counting us again and again, each roll setting cousin against cousin. It is the oldest trick of empire—divide and conquer. The British used it in India, in Africa, and the Americans use it here. Elevate a smaller group, pit them against the larger, and you have discord where unity once stood. While we quarrel, they take what they want."

William Clyde frowned. "And the people allow this?"

John shook his head. "It's not allowance—it's survival. But listen close: the paper will decide the future. Get on the roll and you exist. Miss it, and you'll spend your life proving what you already know in your blood."

The talk turned darker. John leaned close. "You've heard of McAlester?"

"I've heard the name," William Clyde said.

"He married into the Burney family and used the rights it gave him to secure coal leases. The contracts go through Washington, written so thin the Nation earns pennies for every ton mined. McAlester grows rich, and our people grow poorer. Some call it progress, others call it theft. Either way, the ground itself is slipping from under us. The same will happen with timber, with oil—whatever they can reach."

William Clyde's jaw tightened. "So the Nation is robbed with pen and ink, not just rifles."

"That's the truth," John said. "And the leases are only part of it. Freedmen's rights are another fire— the treaty freed them, but now the fight is whether to make them citizens. Some say yes, because freedom without citizenship is only half a promise. Others say no, fearing less for justice than for a smaller pot to share. Every argument splits us deeper. The government watches and smiles."

Sarah, who had listened quietly, spoke at last. "So our children's place will depend on which paper survives, and whose hand writes the names." John nodded solemnly. "Yes. The courthouse in Pennington proved that once. Lost rolls prove it again. Some vanished when Washington men came, then reappeared years later in the Capitol at Tushka Homma. Copies sit with lawyers in McAlester, hidden for safekeeping. We must guard every scrap, for without them, the Nation itself fades."

William Clyde stirred, thinking of smoke and ash. "Then I will stand for my children's names. I will not let them be lost."

John smiled, weary but firm. "That's the spine we need. There's trade here, honest work. But there is also the slow theft done on good stationery. Keep your books, Clyde, and keep copies of everything. Carry water for the fires, and carry records for the courts. It may be the only way we endure."

The cousins sat in silence, the fire's glow throwing long shadows against the wall.

Arthur listened from the doorway, and Mary, drowsy on Sarah's lap, stirred when she heard the word "ledger." "Is that the book that keeps us?" she murmured, half-asleep.

"Yes," William Clyde said softly. "And there will be more than one."

Outside, a train whistle drifted across the plains, long and mournful, reminding them all that the world was changing—and that the struggle over names, land, and memory had only begun.

CHAPTER 31
FRACTIONS AND PROMISES

The lamps burned low in John Duncan Thompson Jr.'s house at Marlow. Outside, the prairie wind pressed at the shutters, but inside the firelight drew the family close. William Clyde sat opposite his cousin, Sarah at his side with Mary drowsing against her, and Arthur listening in the doorway. Sarah Jane had joined them too, her sharp eyes watching the fire as much as the men.

They had eaten well, but the talk was heavier than the stew.

John Duncan stirred his coffee. "You've come home in a hard season, Clyde. The Nation has not been the same since the treaties of '66. They took land, forced us to give up more than we could afford, and set Freedmen among us as citizens without our consent. We are still arguing over what it means."

William Clyde nodded slowly. "I heard enough of it in Fort Smith to know the treaty was a punishment. We fought for the South, and this was the price. But it feels like more than punishment—it feels like preparation for something worse."

John Duncan leaned forward. "The Atoka agreement opened the way for railroads. They promised us it would protect our sovereignty. But a road cut through a country does more than carry trains. It carries men with ledgers. It carries eyes from Washington."

Sarah Jane spoke up, her voice quiet but clear. "I've heard the talk in town. They say we must be measured now, written down as halves, quarters, eighths. If I am called one-eighth and I marry a white man, what does that make my son? One-sixteenth? Nothing at all?"

The room stilled. William Clyde looked at her with sympathy. "That is their design, Sarah Jane. It is a clock they set ticking, counting us down until there is nothing left on paper. Even if the truth lives in our blood, the record wil say otherwise."

John Duncan nodded grimly. "You see it plain. The fractions are not for us—they are for them. Each generation weaker on the page, until a child who grows in our house is written as a stranger. And a stranger cannot claim land, or rights, or citizenship."

Sarah shifted Mary and spoke for the first time. "So our children's place depends not on who we are, but on what they choose to write. A cruel arithmetic."

"Yes," John Duncan said. "And yet, the leaders go along with it. Do you know why? Because they still speak of a promise. They say that if we comply—if we take the rolls, if we abide the treaties—one day we may have a state of our own. Not Oklahoma, but Sequoyah. A land governed under our own laws."

Sarah Jane frowned. "And if that promise is broken?"

John Duncan's gaze was hard. "Then all this measuring and dividing was never for Sequoyah. It was only for Oklahoma. But the chiefs hold to the hope, and so they bend, believing the paper will lead to freedom."

The fire popped. William Clyde stared into it, seeing the faces of men lost in war. "I cannot trust a promise written by the same hand that writes us into fractions." Sarah Jane's jaw set. "Then I will not go in. I will not be judged like cattle, measured like corn. If that means no land, then so be it. My dignity is not for them to weigh."

John Duncan sighed heavily. "Dignity feeds the spirit, cousin, but paper feeds the courts. Without a record, your children may stand with empty hands when their time comes. Sarah Jane lifted her chin. "Then they must choose for themselves. But I will not bow to it."

William Clyde looked from her to John. "Perhaps that is the trap—they force us to choose between truth and survival. Refuse, and you lose the land. Agree, and you lose the truth. But one choice at least leaves the children something to stand on when the fight comes."

Arthur shifted at the door, and even young Mary stirred, sensing the weight of words. The family sat long in silence, each turning over the cruel puzzle laid before them.

At last John Duncan spoke again. "Remember this: they count us now because they mean to end us later. These rolls, these fractions, these treaties—they are not for our preservation. They are the tools to break the Nation. When the land is divided, and the assets sold, and the government abolished, they will say we are no more. That is the plan."

"And Sequoyah?" Sarah asked softly.

John Duncan's eyes were steady, but his voice was low. "Sequoyah is the carrot they dangle. Perhaps it will come, perhaps

not. But until then, we must guard our names, our papers, and our memory. For without them, the promise is nothing."

The fire burned low, the wind pressed harder at the shutters, and the family sat together in the half-light, knowing that

the hardest fight was yet to come—not on the battlefield, but on the page.

***

Historical Note — Treaties, Atoka, and the Promise of Sequoyah The conversation in Chapter 35 reflects the tensions and uncertainties that shaped Choctaw and Chickasaw life in the decades following the Civil War.

Civil War Treaties (1866): After siding with the Confederacy, both the Choctaw and Chickasaw Nations were forced to sign punitive treaties with the United States in 1866. These treaties required emancipation of slaves, recognition of Freedmen rights, and cession of additional lands. They also set the precedent for increased federal oversight in Indian Territory.

Atoka Agreement (1866 framework, expanded later): The Atoka provisions allowed railroads to cross Choctaw and Chickasaw lands. While presented as a step toward economic progress and a guarantee of sovereignty, in practice it opened the door for deeper federal intrusion. Railroads brought commerce, but they also brought outside officials, surveyors, and speculators who mapped tribal lands with an eye to future division and sale.

Blood Quantum and Rolls: The late 19th century saw the rise of the "blood quantum" system, a colonial invention that attempted to measure Native identity in fractions (1/2, 1/4, 1/8, 1/16). This was not a traditional Choctaw way of defining belonging, which had always been rooted in clan, matrilineal descent, and community. The system was designed to reduce the number of people eligible for land, resources, and citizenship over generations, ultimately shrinking the recognized population.

The Promise of Sequoyah: In the aftermath of the war and in the decades that followed, federal officials spoke often of the possibility of a separate Native-governed state in Indian Territory. This state, to be called Sequoyah, was held out as a promise to encourage compliance with federal directives, including census-taking and al-

lotment preparations. Choctaw and Chickasaw leaders believed that cooperation might lead to true self-government under their own constitution. In reality, the promise was never fulfilled. When statehood arrived in 1907, Indian Territory was merged with Oklahoma Territory, and the dream of Sequoyah was extinguished.

The Larger Design: The system of treaties, rolls, blood quantum, and eventual allotment was aimed not at preserving tribal governments but at dismantling them. The plan was to divide communal land into private allotments, sell off "surplus" lands, and then abolish the tribal governments altogether. What remained for Native families was only what one ancestor managed to secure through enrollment — a fraction of a fraction of the original Nation.

This context makes the private family conversations in Marlow all the more poignant. They sensed, long before the Dawes Commission or the Curtis Act, that the system was designed to erase them on paper even if they endured in truth.

CHAPTER 32

THE GREEN CORN AT MARLOW

The corn stood high and tasseled, the fields around Marlow breathing out the warm, sweet smell of summer's finish. When the word went out that there would be a Green Corn at the edge of town—down by the grove where the sycamores leaned over the creek—families set aside their tools, sharpened their knives for roasting, and brought baskets that creaked with fruit and bread.

William Clyde rose early, opened the store only long enough to set out barrels of water and a sack of coffee, then closed the shutters. Sarah was already ahead of him, apron pinned, moving like a tide through the kitchen—corn dodgers cooling by the window, a kettle of beans low on the back of the stove, Arthur carrying wood in, Mary twisting willow switches into rings she would later toss for prizes.

By noon, the grove was a village: quilts spread like flags, kettles hung, children darting between shadows. Two bonfires were ringed with stone—one banked low to roast the new ears, one fed bright for the evening. A preacher from the Chickasaw side offered a prayer in English and Chickasaw; an older woman, hair braided to her waist, followed in Choctaw—short, steady words of thanks and forgiveness, the kind of speech that smooths a year's rough places.

John Duncan found William Clyde near the tables. "You've done a good thing," he said.

"It's our thing," William replied. "Green Corn belongs to everyone who's kept the seed."

"Even so," John said, "someone must say when to gather."

They walked the grove together, greeting folks as they came—Choctaw and

Chickasaw families from the bottoms, intermarried whites who'd years ago married into clans, a handful of Texas cousins from Mount Tabor testing the air like birds at the edge of a field. There were settlers too, men with sun-seamed faces and women with wash-rough hands, curious, cautious, drawn by the smell of roasting corn and the sound of a fiddle that never quite stopped.

When the meal was eaten and the children wore themselves into a happy quiet, William Clyde stepped onto a low wagon and raised a hand.

"Neighbors," he said, "this is a day for thanks and for setting things right. We have eaten, and now we can talk. If anyone wishes to speak—to ask, or warn, or say what is on the heart—come forward. I'll keep the peace and keep the order."

A murmur moved through the crowd. The first to step forward was an elder named Hattak Homma, his voice low but carrying.

"We have kept Green Corn since before these oaks were saplings," he said. "In those days we forgave debts and began again, because a people cannot go on if every quarrel lives forever. But there are quarrels now that do not live with us; they live on paper. The rolls. The fractions. I ask only this: that we remember who we are when we see our names in a stranger's hand."

A young settler named Baylor lifted his hat. "Begging no offense," he began, "I come from Kansas with my wife and two boys. We aim to do right by our neighbors. But a man hears talk. Some say there'll be allotments. Some say the land will open. We don't want trouble—we want a plot to tend, same as anybody."

A stillness ran through the grove. William nodded to him and answered plain. "Sir, this country is not Kansas. Our land is held by the Nations, not by the section lines you know. If allotments come, they will come through paper first. Paper will say who belongs. That is not set by me or you today—but I'll tell you true: every time a name is left off, someone somewhere gets a bigger share. That is an old rule of the world. See that you do no harm while you wait on your future." Baylor flushed, then dipped his head. "Fairly said."

From the Mount Tabor knot stepped a woman in a sun-faded dress—Sarah Jane, with Benjamion her hip and Walter tugging at her skirt. Her eyes were bright. "Cousin," she called, "if a woman is written as only one-eighth, and she marries outside, what becomes of her children when the counting comes? Will a son of one-sixteenth be counted at all?"

A heaviness took the air. William did not dodge it. "That is the fear," he said. "It's why I keep two ledgers for every name, one for the trade and one for the roll. The fractions are a clock set against us. But the clock has not run out yet."

The murmur grew. John climbed onto the wagon beside William "Green Corn is for mending," John said, "and for plain speech. You all know me. I will say it plain: the government talks of measuring us because it means to divide our land. They have not yet done it—but they will try. They promise that if we comply, we may govern ourselves stronger—maybe a state of our own, not Oklahoma. Some of us believe. Some of us doubt. Either way, we will keep our names, and we will keep our records, and we will keep each other."

At that moment, a man in the crowd raised a hard question. "And what of the Freedmen? The treaty said they were to be counted among us.

I see none here today. Are they to be on the rolls, or left outside?"

The question hung heavy. Eyes turned away; men shifted their boots in the dust. No one spoke first. Finally, William said, "Their absence today tells its own truth. This gathering is as much about who is here as who is not. We may argue about it in town meetings, and Washington will argue louder still. But know this—every exclusion feeds another man's share."

There was no applause, only silence, and then a shuffle as the talk moved on. Some lookerelieved, others uneasy. The matter was not settled, only marked.

From the back stepped a broad-shouldered man in a vest too fine for the dust—an attorney from the rail camps, visiting "to pay respects." He smiled the way a man does who is used to being listened to. "Gentlemen," he said, "ladies—no offense meant. Progress brings opportunities. Railroads, leases, markets. It is only sense that business be done in proper form and for fair rates."

"Fair for whom?" a voice called. Laughter, not kind.

William raised his hand. "Sir, you are welcome to roast an ear among us," he said evenly. "But you should know our memory is long. We have seen low rates written in far-off offices, and we have seen men grow rich on what belongs to many. If business comes, let it come in daylight, with terms a grandmother can read and a child can inherit."

The lawyer bowed, but his face had cooled.

A preacher spoke about forgiveness. A stockman spoke about fences. A teacher—intermarried, with a Choctaw wife—spoke about the school she kept in her kitchen on winter afternoons.

By dusk the fires were tall, and the roasted ears passed hand to hand until even the smallest child was butter-bright and content. Sarah and the other women stacked plates and laughed in that weary, triumphant way of people who have run a day to ground and found it good. The fiddle took up an old tune, and a new one answered.

Before the dance, John touched William's arm. "You told them hope and warning in one breath," he said.

"I learned hard lessons in Texas," William answered. "Encourage a man to come, but make sure he knows there is a price for every name that is missing." "And will they come?" John asked, glancing toward the Mount Tabor cousins.

"They will," William said. "But they will come with their papers, and we will make copies, and we will keep them where no fire reaches. The men with ledgers of their own will call that defiance. I call it being ready."

Night dropped gently over the grove. Sparks rose. Children fell asleep on quilts while the elders spoke in low, steady voices. The Green Corn closed the year with thanks and opened the next with a reckoning: not a fight of rifles, but of names, ledgers, and the stubborn will to belong.

From the crowd another voice rose, sharper with skepticism. "And how do they think to tell the difference? A man whose grandmother fled with the Seminoles looks no different than a man whose grandfather farmed this very creek. Yet one is written 'Indian,' the other 'Freedman.' Who among us can prove which blood runs stronger?"

William Clyde lifted his head. "That is the trick of it. They do not care for truth, only for categories. The less of us they count as Choctaw, the more land lies open. The difference is not in our faces, nor in our lives, but in the ledgers of men who never walked this soil."

The crowd murmured at that, uneasy but knowing.

***

Historical Note — Green Corn Festival, Freedmen, and Ancestry
The Green Corn Festival was one of the central communal ceremonies of the Choctaw and other Muskogean peoples, marking
renewal, thanksgiving, and the settling of disputes. In Indian Territory during the late 19th century, Choctaw families continued the practice, blending tradition with frontier realities.
The absence of Freedmen at such a festival reflects both cultural continuity and social tension. Although the Treaty of 1866 required that Freedmen emancipated from slavery in the Choctaw and Chickasaw Nations be admitted as citizens, in practice both Nations resisted. Prejudice inherited from the American South reinforced this exclusion. Freedmen often lived in separate settlements, with limited access to tribal gatherings, schools, or resources. Their absence at public celebrations

like Green Corn was as much a social statement as a practical reality.

At the same time, the boundaries were not clear. For generations, some Choctaws intermarried with Africans (enslaved or free), with Seminoles who themselves had African kin, and with runaways from Cuba, Haiti, and elsewhere. Physical distinctions were often meaningless. A person could be labeled "full-blood" or "Freedman" depending on political motives and paperwork rather than heritage. This exposed the arbitrary and self-serving nature of blood quantum categories.

By dramatizing this in dialogue, the chapter shows how identity was contested in public: some voices admitted the impossibility of drawing clean lines, while others clung to categories enforced by Washington. The system was less about truth than about control. Every exclusion meant fewer names on the rolls, and every missing name meant larger shares of land and other benefits for those who remained.

Thus, the Green Corn Festival in Marlow becomes not only a moment of thanksgiving but also a mirror of the Chocta Nation's dilemmas in the late 19th century: the endurance of cultural tradition alongside the erosion of sovereignty, the weight of prejudice, and the manipulation of ancestry for political and economic ends.

CHAPTER 33

TAKING THE BOYS IN

The evening was warm in 1897, the cicadas humming as the shadows lengthened across the yard. Sarah Jane sat on the porch, her hands restless in her lap, while her two youngest boys lingered nearby. John Henry, called Hank, was nearly ten and tried to whittle a stick into a spear. Little Charles Bradley, just five, tumbled in the dust with a worn leather ball, too young to understand the weight of the talk between his mother and her uncle.

"I cannot stomach it," Sarah Jane said at last. "To march them before strangers and let some clerk decide whether they are Choctaw. They are my sons. They are McCoys and Thompsons both. What more should anyone need?"

William Clyde leaned against the porch rail, his face lined by years of war and petition, his voice steady. "I know the insult of it, Sarah Jane. I have felt it myself. But paper holds power in this age. If their names are not written, then one day it will be as if they never lived in this Nation at all."

Sarah Jane's eyes flashed. "They would make us beg for what is already ours. It is shameful. Do they mean to measure my sons' blood as if it were cornmeal?"

William did not flinch. "Yes. And worse besides. But listen to me: if you withhold them now, their children will have no claim. If they are written down, no matter how bitter the ink tastes, that name may yet carry forward. I will take them myself. They are my blood too, and I will see that they are treated right."

She looked toward Hank, who glanced up warily, half-hearing. Then to Charlie, who laughed and tossed his ball again. Her shoulders sagged. "They are so young. Hank will not understand, and Charlie...he is still a child."

William stepped closer, lowering his voice. "That is why it must be done now. The men in Washington do not wait for children to grow. They close the books when it suits them. These boys must be entered before the books are shut forever."

Silence hung for a moment, broken only by the cicadas. Sarah Jane's hand trembled as she brushed hair from her face. "You swear to me, Clyde, that this is for their good?"

"I swear it," he said. "Land may not come. Money may not come. But their names will endure. There will come a day when men are glad their grandfather stood before the commission, even if the boys never know it themselves."

At last, Sarah Jane nodded, a tear slipping down her cheek. "Then take them. Take my boys in. I cannot bear to see it, but I trust you to see it done."

William bent and called softly. "Hank, Charlie—come along, lads. We have business in town." The boys came running, unaware of the gravity of their errand, their small feet thudding on the packed earth. Sarah Jane watched them go, her heart torn between pride and sorrow. The night closed in around her, and she whispered into the dark, "Let this not be in vain."

***

Historical Note — Enrollment and Citizenship by Blood In 1898, John Henry (Hank) Darken and Charles Bradley Darken Jr. were recorded on the Choctaw citizenship census through the efforts of their uncle, William Clyde Thompson. This was a crucial step, for the census became the foundation for later determinations of citizenship.

In 1909, following years of appeals, the Yowani Choctaws were formally reinstated and granted citizenship by blood. This decision attached roll numbers to Hank and Charlie, securing a legal recognition that their descendants could later use to establish their own citizenship.

Yet there is no evidence that either Hank or Charlie ever acted upon or acknowledged this citizenship in their lifetimes. Charles Bradley Darken Jr. died of influenza in 1919 at the age of 27, while returning from the funeral of his half-brother, Ben Welch. Hank served in France during the First World War as part of the American Expeditionary Force. Neither man left a record of claiming Choctaw rights or exercising tribal citizenship, despite their legal status on the rolls.

The irony is plain: though the paper recognition secured by William Clyde en-

dured, the boys themselves lived and died without seeming to know—or perhaps without caring—that they had been written down as citizens of the Choctaw Nation.

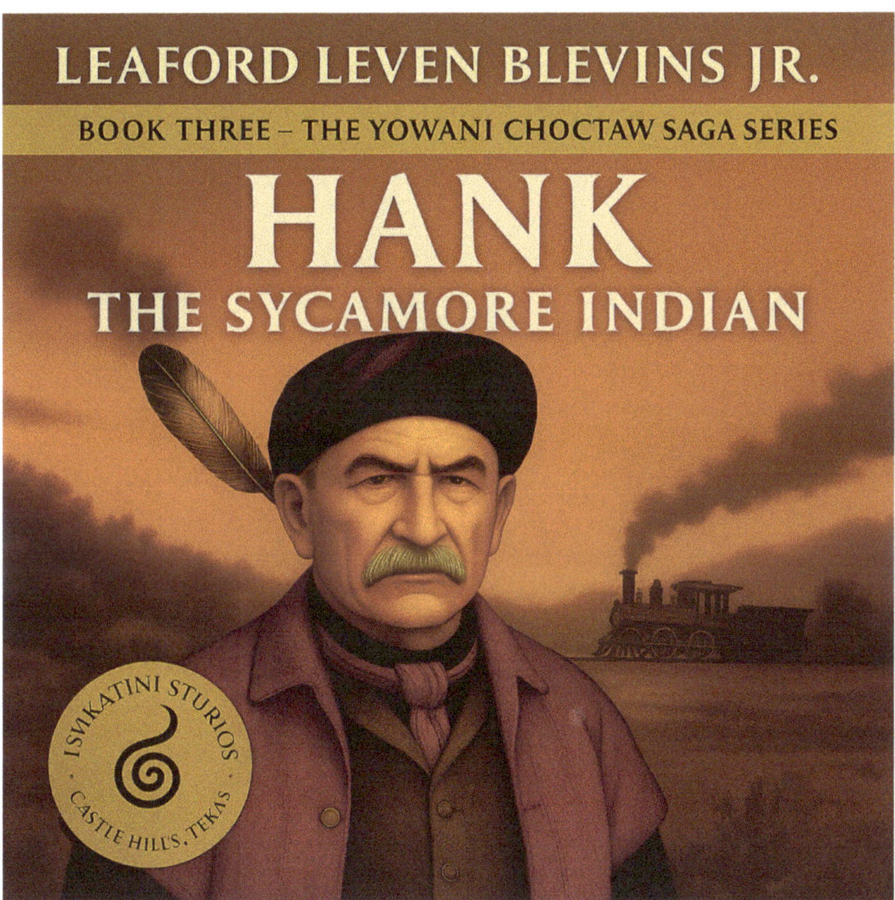

LEAFORD LEVEN BLEVINS JR.
BOOK THREE – THE YOWANI CHOCTAW SAGA SERIES
HANK
THE SYCAMORE INDIAN
ISVKATINI STURIOS
CASTLE HILLS, TEKAS

THE REINSTATEMENT ROLLS

Before we step into Hank's story, allow me to pause and speak to you directly. What follows will make little sense without first understanding the laws and decisions that shaped the world he lived in. The difference between a Choctaw with land and a Choctaw without was not a matter of luck or hard work. It was the outcome of federal policy, of the Dawes Commission, and of the bitter struggle of families who fought to be recognized. This is not background trivia—it is the ground Hank walked upon, the reason some of his neighbors thrived while he had nothing waiting at home.

The Dawes Commission was established in 1893 to break up the communal lands of the Five Tribes—Choctaw, Chickasaw, Cherokee, Creek, and Seminole—and enroll individual citizens for allotments. In theory, it promised fairness: each recognized citizen would receive a parcel of land in exchange for surrendering the old communal system. In practice, the Commission was riddled with prejudice, politics, and clerical error. Whole families were left off the rolls or denied enrollment because their paperwork was judged inadequate, their ancestry questioned, or their names lost in bureaucratic shuffle.

To address the obvious injustices, Congress authorized what became known as the Reinstatement Rolls. These were supplemental enrollment lists intended to correct mistakes and add those wrongly excluded. But the process was slow and selective. Applicants had to bring affidavits, witnesses, and proof of identity. The Commission's decisions were final unless appealed to federal court, and few appeals ever succeeded. Even when names were eventually restored, it was often too late to matter.

The result was devastating. Families were divided—one brother with land, another without. Some cousins became landowners while others became tenants or sharecroppers. A class system emerged within the Choctaw Nation itself: those with allotments were secure, those without lived as second-class citizens on their own soil. The promise of justice had been reduced to a handful of names written too late on the right piece of paper.

Hank's own family was among those caught in this net. They were placed on a reinstatement roll with about seventy names. But the recognition came so late that no land remained to be allotted. The family received citizenship in name only—without the acres that were meant to sustain them. It was a cruel irony: they were finally told they belonged, but given nothing to show for it.

Hank's cousin, William Clyde Thompson, had spent much of his life fighting for that reinstatement. He gathered evidence, pressed petitions, and refused to let the claim die. In the end, he succeeded in having the family's names restored. But his victory was hollow. Recognition came without restitution. The land was gone, allotted to others or swallowed by the timber companies and speculators who descended on Choctaw country. The family's legal identity was affirmed, but their economic future had already been stolen.

This was Hank's inheritance. He went to war as a Choctaw without land, a man whose citizenship had been recognized too late to give him any standing. His neighbors Jesse and Tinker returned from the war to farms and families. Hank returned to nothing. This difference—rooted in law, in the Reinstatement Rolls and the failures of the Dawes system—set the stage for every conversation, every moment of tension, and every flicker of jealousy that followed. For many Choctaw families, this deep sense of persecution and unfairness helped to shape a powerful faith. If the promises of earth could not be trusted, then the promises of heaven had to be. Strong belief in a better life hereafter was often the only answer to injustice in this one, and it colored Hank's own convictions as he carried them into war. The greater the sense of persecution a people endured, the deeper their faith became. This was universal, not unique to the Choctaw. Yet the same faith that sustained them also set them apart. It created a bond within, but it also formed a barrier against the world outside—a wall that both protected and imprisoned. For Hank and his people, this tension between faith and exclusion would shape every step of their journey.

The ink of the Dawes Commission had dried before Hank ever shouldered a rifle. Its shadow followed him all the way to France—and back again.

CHAPTER I

THE LOST GENERATION: JOHN HENRY "HANK" DARKEN

By the time John Henry "Hank" Darken reached his thirtieth year, there was little to show for the citizenship his cousin had fought so fiercely to secure. He was not married, had no children, and held no land of his own. There is no record of formal schooling, no property, and no recognized occupation. Whatever inheritance of land and tribal connection might once have been his was gone—swept away by allotment, taxation, and the erosion of tribal life itself.

The man who had labored to keep that inheritance alive was Hank's cousin, Captain William Clyde Thompson. Thompson had served in the Confederate Army as a young man, later devoting the long years after the war to securing recognition for the Yowani Choctaw. He argued before commissions and pressed petitions through the courts, insisting that the descendants of Margaret McCoy and her line were Choctaw by right of blood and history. In 1909, through sheer persistence, Thompson succeeded: seventy names—Darkens, Darrens, Thompsons, and others—were restored to the Choctaw Nation roll.

But what had he truly won? By then the Nation was only a shell. Its chiefs were appointed from Washington. Its council chambers stood empty. Its governance, once rooted in clan and kin, had been deliberately stripped away. All that remained was land, and even that was fragile—sold under pressure, seized for taxes, or divided into slivers so small they could no longer support a family. The recognition of 1909 was little more than a legal shadow.

Hank, born into that shadow, became the embodiment of his generation of Yowani Choctaw: a people acknowledged on paper but hollowed out in practice.

For many like him, the path of least resistance was to slip quietly into the broader society of Oklahoma. With light skin and an English surname, it was easier to pass as "just another farmer" than to claim an Indian identity that carried only prejudice and no benefit. The "full-blood" Choctaw who remained visible were often scorned by their white neighbors as lazy, dirty, and shiftless. A cruel saying followed them: their get-up-and-go had got up and went.

Hank's own life reflected the bind of that generation. He could play the guitar. He could work a team of horses beside his brother, Charles Bradley Darken Jr. He could get by. But he had no land, no property, no education, and no recognized role in a tribal community. He was, in every sense, dispossessedAnd then came the war. In 1917 the call went out for men to fight under the flag of the very United States that had destroyed his Nation and attempted to erase his heritage from the earth. Yet Hank enlisted. Whether from necessity, patriotism, or the promise of adventure, he joined the American Expeditionary Force and shipped out for France. There, as a corporal in Battery F, he bore the deepest irony of his time: fighting for a government that had all but annihilated the people to whom he truly belonged.

Yet France gave him something that Atoka County never had: movement, excitement, purpose. It lifted him out of poverty and monotony and thrust him into a world of armies, cities, and ideas. Paris showed him that life could be different. And when he returned home, he did not return unchanged. He took a wife. He began a family. Whatever impulse had been missing before—the drive to seize life as his own—had been awakened on foreign soil.

In this way Hank stands as both symbol and man: the symbol of a lost Yowani generation, adrift in the ruins of tribal life, and the man who found, in war, the unlikely spark that carried him forward into the rest of his days.

CHAPTER 2

THE FAREWELL AT ATOKA

The depot at Atoka was alive with motion that morning. The Katy line ran north and south, its tracks humming with the weight of departure. Men in uniform milled about the platform, their mothers and wives clutching them by the arm, children darting at their feet. The smell of coal smoke hung in the air, and the great engine gave a hiss as if impatient to be gone. Hank shifted the guitar case on his shoulder and looked down the track. Beyond Denison lay Fort Worth, and Camp Bowie—the place that would strip these men of their old lives and turn them into soldiers. France seemed impossibly far away, but Fort Worth was close enough to picture. The war began there, for him, in Texas.

Beside him stood his younger brother, Tuff—Charles Bradley Darken Jr.—already a husband, already a father twice over. His wife, Ona, held their little girl's hand—Dutchie, bright-eyed and restless, too young to understand what kind of leaving this was.

Tuff leaned close, his voice half a jest, half a rebuke.

"Well, big brother, looks like it's taken the Kaiser to light a fire under you. You're near thirty and no wife, no land, no babies. You can play that guitar, and you can drive a team, but that's not much to build a life on. Maybe this trip to Texas, and then across the ocean, will knock some sense into you."

Hank gave a crooked smile. "You always were the mouthy one, Tuff. Some of us take a little longer to get started."

"Started?" Tuff laughed, though his eyes stayed serious. "I was started before I was twenty-five. Married, babies crying in the night, work enough to keep food on the table. You've been drifting, Hank. Playing songs, fooling with horses. This—" he nodded toward the waiting train, "—this might be the best thing that ever happened to you. You'll come back with something to talk about besides the weather in Atoka County."

Hank looked at his brother, at Ona's quiet face, at Dutchie tugging against her mother's hand. "Maybe you're right," he said softly. "Maybe I need this. Maybe I'll come back ready for something more."

Tuff put a hand on his shoulder. "You better. Don't waste your chance, Hank. Don't come back the same as you left. Find yourself over there."

CHAPTER 3

OFF TO FIGHT THE HUN

At Denison, the cars filled. By the time the train rattled on toward Fort Worth, the journey had turned into a press of bodies, uniforms packed shoulder to shoulder, voices raised over the hiss of steam.

Segregation rode the rails with them. Black draftees who boarded along the line were pushed into separate cars, crammed in under the eye of the conductors. Even some Choctaw boys with darker skin were challenged, ordered to move until they stood their ground: "Indian. Not Negro." Hank watched the arguments play out and felt a guilty relief that no one looked twice at him. His light complexion and English surname kept him safe from those humiliations.

He thought then of Otis, a full-blood from a large family, a man whose brothers and cousins had each drawn half-sections of land in the allotment. By the time the parcels were tallied, they held ranches that stretched across whole townships—thousands of acres, some of it doubled where the surveyors judged the soil poor. Otis had land, cattle, a stake in the world. Hank had nothing.

It was the cruel arithmetic of the allotment system. For those with large families, the law had multiplied advantage, parcel after parcel, until they sat secure on enormous spreads. For men like Hank, with no allotment, there was only labor—driving teams, selling his hands where he could. Now the draft had swept them all together. Otis with his land. Hank with his empty pockets. Black sharecroppers. White boys from Oklahoma farms. Each funneled westward in crowded cars, bound for the same war.

Hank pressed his forehead against the glass, watching the prairie fields flicker by. Around him the car was thick with men, the air sour with sweat and coal smoke. Every jolt of the train rattled through his bones.

There was no pride in being Choctaw. None. To be called Choctaw was to be reminded that he was less—less than the full-bloods who sat on land, less than the whites who ran the county courthouse. It meant only that he had been cheated twice: once by Washington, once by his own Nation.

He let out a bitter laugh under his breath. "Second-class Choctaw," he muttered. That was all he had ever been.

And yet, here he was, in uniform, heading to Camp Bowie in Fort Worth to fight for the same government that had stripped the Nation bare.

CHAPTER 4

CAMP BOWIE

The train ground to a halt on the edge of Fort Worth, and the men spilled out into the dust. Camp Bowie stretched wide across the prairie, rows of barracks and tents laid out in military order. It was a city of soldiers, raised almost overnightThere was little glamour to it. The days blurred with drill after drill, marching in step until boots ached and shoulders sagged. Instructors barked the rhythm of salutes, the proper tilt of a hat, the endless courtesies of rank and chain of command. Rifles were issued, their bolts worked back and forth until the motions were second nature. For most of the boys from Oklahoma, it was familiar enough—they had been hunting since they could walk, and the crack of a rifle was no stranger.

What was new were the horses. The 131st Field Artillery would ride no trucks or tractors. Their guns were hauled on great wooden caissons pulled by teams of horses, and it was the soldier's duty to curry, feed, and harness them day after day. Hank took to it easily. He had worked horses his whole life in Atoka County, driving teams for the fields and hauling loads to town. The smell of sweat and leather, the weight of tack, the steady rhythm of hooves—this was his element.

Around him, the camp swarmed with men from every corner of Texas and Oklahoma. Among them were Choctaw boys who spoke the language freely, laughing in syllables that once had marked Hank as lesser. He caught the words in fragments, enough to know what tongue it was, but he did not join them. To him, "Choctaw" had meant only exclusion, a reminder of what he had been denied. Still, he watched, and in time he would remember that some of those same words, spoken by men not so different from himself, would be turned into an unbreakable code across the battlefields of France.

So the weeks passed—drill, salute, harness, clean, repeat. When orders finally came down to move east, the men packed their gear, shouldered rifles and cases, and marched once more to the railhead. The war would not wait on them. France lay ahead, and before France, the long ride across the South.

✳✳✳

When the order finally came down, there was no ceremony. A bugle, a shouted roll call, and then the shuffle of boots toward the siding where the trains waited. Camp Bowie faded into dust and drill behind them. Ahead lay Texarkana, Memphis, Birmingham, Atlanta—and beyond them, the ocean. Hank swung his guitar case aboard and found a place at the window. The wheels lurched, and once again he was leaving one world for another.

CHAPTER 5
THROUGH THE HOMELANDS

The train pulled out of Fort Worth with a groan of iron and steam, turning east toward Texarkana. The cars were already crowded, and at each stop more men climbed aboard—farm boys with cardboard suitcases, Black sharecroppers pressed into separate cars, Choctaw and Creek recruits who stood their ground when challenged. The hiss of steam and the shuffle of boots filled the aisles.At Texarkana, the train overflowed. Men packed shoulder to shoulder, the air sour with coal smoke and sweat. Hank pressed against the window, watching the pine forests flicker past. He thought of the irony: the government that had stripped his people of land and name now packed them into cars to fight its war overseas.

By the time the train rolled into Memphis, the great junction town, Hank felt the weight of history in every mile. The line pressed on into Mississippi, into Chickasaw country. Place-names echoed with the syllables of his ancestors. Once, his people had walked west from these hills. Now he was carried east, bound not for freedom but for France.Somewhere near Oxford, an officer in pressed khaki shifted in the aisle seat across from him, apaperback in his hand. Hank caught the name on the cover: Faulkner. The man glanced up.

"Ever read him?" he asked.

Hank shook his head. "Don't read much."

The officer smiled faintly. "He writes about this country here—these hills, these towns. Folks say he's trying to catch the soul of Mississippi.Hank looked back out the window, at fields dotted with cabins, at names that carried the cadence of Choctaw and Chickasaw. "I've got no soul here," he muttered.The officer didn't hear, or chose not to. He turned back to his book.

The whistle shrieked as the train rolled on through Birmingham, then Atlanta. The cars rattled through the night, eastward to the coast, toward Camp Mills on Long Island—"Fort Nicks," the soldiers called it. France lay just beyond the ocean, and Hank watched the landscape pass, knowing he was crossing lands his people had once held, retracing steps long broken by exile. The wheels carried him forward, away from home, into history.

CHAPTER 6

THE TRAIN EAST, JULY 1918

July, 1918. The heat on the parade ground at Camp Bowie pressed like a hand against the throat of the world. Men moved in slow, heavy shapes beneath the sun; canvas and wool and sweat blurred into the same dry smear. They filed into the troop trains as if they were being loaded for long storage — not knowing how long — and the cars snapped shut behind them with that final, small click that meant there was no turning back.

The car they shoved him into had been meant for stock. Benches nailed to rough planks ran along the sides; men sat facing in, knees nearly touching the men opposite. A bucket in the corner was the only concession to human needs — the single, reeking bucket that would stand as the car's latrine for the trip. Sweat pooled in collars. Breath hung heavy in the car, warmed and stale. The smell came first: sweat, the lingering tang of horse and manure from the corral, old tobacco, and a sourness that came from bodies that could not be washed and from the bucket that could not be emptied often enough. It was a smell that filled the mouth and made the eyes sting.

At every stop more men were hustled aboard. At Texarkana they forced a group of Black draftees into the next car and then into this one; the officers barked about keeping the companies separate, but there was nowhere to place separation when the cars were full to overflowing. In that press, every line of difference — class, color, tribe — collapsed into the single fact of being close enough to feel the other man's heat. Hank, who had measured himself by the small island of rank that "white" gave him in the world he'd come from, found that island swallowed in the steam and smell. There was no place to stand above anyone here.

Outside, Mississippi folded up against the rails as a living wall. The trees — pines and tall hardwoods — lifted like columns, so dense that they closed the sky into a band of distant blue. The sun was there, but the road moved under a green ceiling; the world looked tunneled, safe-looking and secret at once, as though it could hide whatever came through it and sudden as the dark of a room. That degree of enclosure unsettled Hank. In Oklahoma and West Texas the horizon was a wide, honest thing; you could see trouble coming a long way off. Here the woods gave no warning. You could not tell by looking whether a threat waited in those shadows or whether a friend paced just over the ridge. It made him feel fenced in by the country itself.

People began to cough. At first it was a dry hacking that could be passed off as dust and tiredness. Then someone leaned forward and could not lift his head again. They wrapped him and carried him down at the next whistle. A stretcher. A blanket. The train's doors opened and men in uniform took the still body and walked away. The next stop another stretcher. The next a quieter space left at the corner of the car where someone had not woken. Men whispered about fever; someone swore he had seen a man with a blue-lined face. The word influenza moved through the car like a bad wind.

Every stop the train slowed and the dead or the sick were taken off. Sometimes they were carried away in sheets to the little town hospitals that the rail-workers and townspeople had pushed together for the surge. Sometimes they were left to local undertakers who had no room. Hank began to count the empty places on the benches like one counts fenceposts. Twenty-four hours after a cough, men could be fevered to stillness. Two days. Three. It was fast; sometimes it was a blur from cough to the thinness of skin over bone.

Hank watched a man in the far corner who had been laughing with his friends two nights before now lie still, lips dry, hands curled like a child's. At one stop they slid him off the car on a board, and Hank watched as a town man covered him with a sheet. He realized how quickly the train could turn from a means of passage into a slow-moving ship of the dead. The car felt smaller with each empty place; the air seemed heavier as if the train carried its own weather. He began to think, without admitting it even to himself, that if the fever came, no orderly measure of bravery would spare him. Maybe the safer fate would be the line of fire—a quick, human end—rather than the hush of the influenza.

When the train eased into Corinth the name jolted him: Corinth. The memory of the older road returned like an old voice. He remembered being a boy in a buggy, riding into that town with William Clyde Thompson to register for the

Choctaw census while his mother stayed away. He could see the older man's lean face and hear, in his mind, the stories of the Confederate march, the way William Clyde had said the name Shiloh as if the syllable had a weight to it. William Clyde had gone north out of Corinth for a different cause, a different flag; Hank now sat in the uniform of the United States, headed east toward a war in a land he had never seen. The mirror made his head spin.Beside him, the Black soldier closed his book and looked straight ahead. He said nothing. In that time and place there were things one did not voice aloud; silence could be a measure of self-preservation. But Hank felt the thought in the car as if it were breathed by the timbers themselves: that places like Corinth had been gathering points for wars that betrayed people in different ways. The quiet between the two men said as much as words couldAnd yet the train kept taking men off at stops. The car grew incrementally emptier and then more crowded as replacements came in elsewhere; the number of human bodies on board did not always fall. Sometimes the ambulances and stretchers left behind a collection of husks and then other draftees filled the benches for the next leg; death did not make immediate room but only shifted the press. It made Hank think about how the numbers worked—the arithmetic of a rolling grave. He began to watch the faces of his companions less for camaraderie than to measure time: who had a cough? who kept hitting the rail of sleep with a wet, feverish head? He thought of the bucket in the corner and wished he could crawl into it and hide until the train stopped for good.

He considered the sea, too. If he passed the trains and got to Camp Mills or whatever staging point held their troopships, the thought of the Atlantic made a new pressure in his chest. Troop ships had been vectors for the influenza just as trains had been. Whole decks could be taken at once; outbreaks on board had led to hundreds being carried off. When men died at sea the navy or the transport crew often conducted burials at sea — a shrouded lowering into the dark, a closing of hands and the absence of anything like a funeral for family.

Hank imagined a man's body being slipped over the rail into black water and could not find an image small enough to comfort him. The idea of choking on illness in the dark belly of a transport, of being carried to the rail and let go, felt worse to him than an open shot in the field. At least in the field the end would have witnesses, maybe a chaplain, maybe someone to fold a uniform. At least the body might be found and a name carved in a stone. At sea, a name might be listed on a manifest and erased by salt. That thought made him hunch lower in his cloth, like a child pulling a blanket tight against the wind.

Days slid by. Men's tempers shortened; the small kindnesses that kept boredom at bay began to disappear as the coughs rose like a second tide. The slop bucket filled and overflowed before some station could manage the waste. Men went to the boards and slept in the gaps that the dead had made in the benches. Hank found his mind returning to William Clyde again and again — to the old man's laughter in the kitchen, to thinned eyes and knotted fingers as he told of camps and marches that had once seemed to belong to another century. He wondered whether the difference between then and now was only the color of the cloth on a man's back. William Clyde had gone off wearing gray to a cause his grandchildren would not defend. Hank was leaving in blue and could not say what he defended but the country's call. He felt like an instrument plucked by someone else's hand.

At a small station someone rolled a stretcher out and then another, and someone else never came back on. A boy two bunks down from Hank coughed himself thin and was carried off like a sack. Hank watched the face wrapped in the sheet as the town men took it and a dog nosed at the hand. He could not bring himself to look away; the sight burned under his eyes the way old sunburn aches when you lie down. He did not dare count how many had been taken in the last day. He only measured them in the empty space they left, and the more empty space there was, the smaller the car felt and the more isolated he felt inside a crowd.When at last the train eased toward the coast it was with the slower tread of men who had seen too many stops. Some cars were half-empty, others still packed; some men whispered prayers that were more for the moment than for God. Hank folded his hands on his knees and tried to make himself as small as the plank beneath him. He told himself false things — that if he stayed very still and did not breathe too deep maybe the fever would step over him like water around a stone. He thought of home, of the broad sky of Oklahoma, the smell of cut alfalfa, the way a storm made a clean geometry across the plains. He wanted that horizon like a cure.

The train carried them on. The world outside kept rolling in that muffled green, a place that could hide everything from view. Inside, the car counted its losses with the quiet rhythms of men being slid off on boards and blanketed and taken away. Hank kept his eyes on the people whose faces did not yet look like they were about to fold, but the list of names in his head grew anyway. At night, when the car rocked and the lanterns swung, his thoughts were a simple, repeated prayer: please not me; please not me.

CHAPTER 7

INCIDENT ON THE TRAIN TO ATLANTA

"The past is never dead. It's not even past."
*—William Faulkner, *Requiem for a Nun**

The train pulled out of Corinth, Mississippi, its cars already bursting with men. The air inside was thick with sweat and the sour breath of influenza. Hank had found a narrow seat along the wall, close to Otis—the quiet Choctaw who had boarded back in Atoka with the others. Otis kept to himself, always alert, always careful not to draw attentionAt the next whistle stop, a few more boarded. Among them was a young lieutenant, sharp as a knife. His khaki uniform was pressed to perfection, boots polished, Sam Browne belt gleaming. His drawl placed him immediately: Mississippi. His name, spoken by one of his companions, was Lieutenant Markham.

The name struck Hank with a jolt of recognition. Markham—the same family married into the Thompsons through William Wayne Thompson, father of William Clyde Thompson, Hank's own cousin. William Clyde had spoken often of the Markhams during stories of his Civil War service. The Markhams had prospered in Mississippi, inheriting and holding land that once belonged to the Choctaw. They had never left Mississippi—why would they, when they had gained so much from what others lost? And now here was one of their descendants, polished and proud, carrying forward the authority born of that legacy. Hank felt the bitter coincidence: that Otis, a Choctaw, would be singled out by a Markham, heir to the very soil his people had walked away from.

Markham's eyes swept the crowded car, hunting for a seat. They landed on Otis.

He strode down the aisle, spurs clicking against the wooden floor. 'You there, boy,' he barked. 'Get up. What are you doin' in this car? You belong back yonder with the n*****s.'

The word rang like a slap. Heads turned. Otis froze, startled, then slowly stood. The car jolted forward under steam, and with nowhere to sit, he braced himself against the wall. One of the officer's companions slid into his seat as if it had been meant for him all along.

Markham wasn't finished. 'Next stop, you get off this car and move where you belong. Ain't no place for you here.'

Otis's face burned, though he said nothing. To be mistaken for black—lowest of the low in the white man's ladder—was a wound deeper than any insult. He knew better than to answer an officer. Silence was survival. Hank felt the sting as if it were his own. He leaned forward, careful with his tone. 'Sir,' he said, 'that man is my friend from Atoka. He is a full-blood Choctaw Indian. He is not a Negro.'

Markham gave him a long, cold look. His lips curled into a sneer. 'He looks black to me.'

'He isn't, sir.' 'I don't give a damn,' the officer shot back. 'He looks black, and that's all that matters. When we stop, he moves.'

There was nothing more Hank could say without drawing trouble on himself. Otis's eyes met his for a moment, and in that brief look Hank knew his friend had seen the attempt—and the futility.

At the next stop, Otis obeyed. He stepped into the car with the black soldiers. It was even more crowded, the sickness further along there. Men coughed and collapsed in the aisles, leaving spaces only for others to fall into. Otis found a seat at last, but the air was thick with contagion and despair.

Two days later, in Atlanta, Hank saw him once more. This time, Otis was being carried out, a sheet draped over his still body. On his chest lay a Faulkner novel, as though he had drifted into sleep with a story of Mississippi in his hands.

But the story was already written. Otis was dead—killed not only by influenza, but by the long reach of prejudice. Lieutenant Markham, sharp in uniform and sharp in cruelty, was heir to the very land once held by Otis's people. The land was lost. Respect was denied. And in that denial, Otis's fate was sealed.

CHAPTER 8

CAMP GORDON

They reached Atlanta under a wet blanket of heat, the cars belching men and sickness. Camp Gordon took them in the way a depot takes freight: quick, orderly, unsentimental. The dead were counted, sheets pulled, tags tied; the sick were hauled to hospital barracks. The rest were marched to a scraped parade ground and told to stand by for orders.Hank kept a tally in his head—who was missing from Battery F, who had coughed all night and now didn't answer roll. Two cots stayed empty after the first formation; by noon, there were three. The sergeants said very little. Men learned to read the silence.

Replacements came in before sundown, dusty from other trains. Faces Hank didn't know took places in the line: a thin boy with a twitch in his eye, a joker with a mean streak, a solid farmhand who'd lost his boots to blisters and wrapped his feet in burlap. Battery F was whole on paper, hollow in the gut.

That afternoon, word spread fast enough to need no bulletin: the new section officer was the same young lieutenant from the train. Markham. Hank's breath caught when he heard the name called out—Lieutenant Markham, reporting to Battery F. He had hoped, childishly, that the uniform might make the man better than the man. But the first orders came clipped and cold, the same voice, the same eyes that had stripped Otis of his seat.

Seeing the gaps in the ranks and the new men shuffling into them, Hank felt a tug in his chest. Otis was gone. Others like him were gone too—the darker Choctaws, the ones the Army confused and classified with Negro units, pushed into the most crowded cars, left to breathe disease. Attrition did not fall evenly. Hank knew that. Everyone knew it, though no one said it aloud.

His mother's voice floated back to him: that he was a Sycamore Indian—white on the outside, all Indian on the inside. He had laughed at it once. He didn't now. The Army, and the world, paid attention to bark. He had the kind that spared him. Otis had worn his color on the outside, and it had marked him for death.

Americans loved their hyphens, Hank thought. Italian-American. Irish-American. Mexican-American. Every wave kept a piece of the old country in its name. But there was no hyphen for an Indian. You were meant to become American, or fade out. He could pass when he needed to—HALITO for greeting, YAKOKE for thanks, a handful of Choctaw curses and market words, enough to say who he was to those who needed to hear it. Enough to know who he belonged to when no one else did.

At dusk the burial detail marched past with stretchers. Markham turned their section out for equipment check, voice brisk, boots gleaming. Hank watched him the way a man watches a snake—respectful of its speed, wary of its strike. He hoped, against what he knew, that soldiering might sand the man's edges. It didn't. Not that day. Not any day he could remember after.

By morning, orders were cut. Battery F, reorganized and at strength, would reboard. Camp Gordon had done what it was built to do: bury, mend, fill the holes, and send the living on.

CHAPTER 9

BACK ON THE TRAIN EAST

By the time they were halfway up the coast, the heat and the wool and the sweat had blended into a stench so foul you could hardly tell if a man was dead or alivThey loaded out from Camp Gordon under a noonday sun. The Army had exactly one kind of uniform for summer: wool. It held heat like a stove and sweat like a sponge. The cars turned into ovens. Men slumped with their caps over their eyes, chins dark with dust, collars wilted and salt-stiff.This time the groupings were by the book—Battery F together, sections sorted, names checked and rechecked. Hank's gun crew packed in around him, the new men trying on their places like boots not yet broken. He counted heads the way he breathed. He had to.

They rattled north through Georgia pine and Carolina swamp, across the brown rivers and into tobacco country. At night the cars sweated lantern light and the low talk of rumor. Word filtered along the aisle that U-boats had torpedoed troop ships—whole decks gone in a single strike, men bobbing in oil, lifeboats sliced to splinters. No one knew how much of it was true, only that it could be.

Past Richmond the air thinned and cooled, but the smell hung on them—rancid wool and old smoke and fever. Men stank the same whether they were breathing or not. Every so often someone slumped too far and didn't move until the medic came. The train didn't stop for long; there were timetables and other trains and a war to catch.

New Jersey flashed by in a rattle of bridges and yards. Then the water appeared—broad, gray, and busy, with cranes pecking at the sky and ships at anchor. Long Island waited beyond with its camps and piers and forms to fill. The men fell quiet at the first smell of salt. Whatever they had been on the train—sweating, joking, arguing—they were bound for the ocean now.

Hank felt the crew draw nearer without moving. He looked down the aisle to where Lieutenant Markham stood braced by a window, cap squared, eyes on nothing you could see. Hank didn't pray much, but he asked for what a corporal could ask for: steady hands on the guns, fair weather, and a little luck in the dark water.

CHAPTER 10
ATLANTIC CROSSING

The Atlantic lay ahead, gray and restless. The troopship pressed eastward with its decks crammed full, the stink of wool and men still clinging after the train. Seasickness took its toll the first day out, and the aisles between bunks became rivers of misery. There was no running, no hiding, no deserting now—only waiting for the voyage to end.

The Choctaws from Atoka stayed close together. They spoke in their own tongue, quiet and steady, not for show but for comfort. Hank caught the familiar words—HALITO here, YAKOKE there. Other men noticed too, and one officer, the Captain, lingered longer than most. He said nothing at first, only listened. His eyes marked the sound the way a man marks the edge of a map, as if filing it away for use.

To pass the time, the officers and YMCA men arranged a boxing tournament. The main deck was cleared when the sea allowed, lanterns strung, a square roped off. Men crowded around, betting with coins, smokes, and IOUs. Someone jeered at the Choctaws, daring them to put up a fighter. They would have preferred to stay back, not draw eyes, but among themselves they chose Noah. Hank knew him from Atoka—a quiet man, sturdy as a mule, with a left hook like a hammer.

Noah stepped into the ring without boasting. His opponent was a mouthy replacement from Camp Gordon, a joker who laughed loud and promised to drop Noah in one round. The bell clanged, the crowd roared, and fists flew. Noah absorbed the first swings without blinking, then planted his feet and let loose that left hook. It landed square and final. The joker toppled like a felled tree, and the crowd gasped, then howled. The Choctaws exchanged quiet nods. Hank pocketed a modest winning, but more than that, he felt respect swell around Noah. The man didn't strut. He didn't need to.

Later, Hank saw the Captain speaking low with other officers, eyes still thoughtful from what he'd overheard in Choctaw. Something was turning in the man's head, though Hank could not guess what. For now, it was enough that the Captain had seen Noah fight and had noticed the tongue they spoke.One night Hank leaned on the rail and thought of Lieutenant Markham. Somewhere on land, the man was hiding, slipped away like smoke. Hank found himself hoping they never caught him. Better gone than back in command. Better gone than among them now.

The ship pressed on into rougher seas. Squalls rose out of the dark, rain lashing the decks, waves heaving the bow high and then slamming it down. The men clung to railings and cursed the Atlantic. When the storm passed, the air turned cold and the water stretched endless. France waited just beyond the horizon, and every man aboard knew the real fight was still to come.

Even then, the influenza had not quit. In the cramped bunks below decks, men continued to cough deep into the night. Some never rose again in the morning.Hank was roused before dawn one morning by an order: bodies needed to be cleared. The morgue locker was full; the stench creeping beyond the holds. A small squad was assigned—stretchers, shrouds, and the salt sea.Hank's name came up. Corporal in Battery F. He would help. He would carry men he had known—the thin ones, the coughers, the ones drifting into shadows. He wrapped the cloth shroud tight around a body, said a terse prayer, and with others tipped the plank. The body dropped into gray water and vanished into the Atlantic dawn. The ship's colors dipped, the chaplain's voice echoed in the damp airHank stood by the rail, watched the wake swallow it. He felt a hollow part in his gut, part grief and part rage. You belong to the sea now, he thought. You are not coming hoBy the time they crossed into the North Atlantic, the death tally had grown.

The new lieutenant quietly took over, organizing duty rosters, watches, disposal squads. The ship's doctor worked flat out. Each morning, fewer men answered muster.When land finally appeared—the jagged shape of France against a gray sky—Hank's bones shook with relief. But he carried salt and sorrow in his skin. The war had begun before the ship docked, and the ocean had claimed more souls than the bullets ever would.

The ship slid into Brest harbor under gray skies, gulls wheeling overhead, coal smoke hanging heavy over the water. The men disembarked, stumbling down the gangplanks into mud and rain. French stevedores shouted, American MPs barked orders, and the weary troops were herded toward staging camps outside the cityHank trudged with the others, boots sinking into wet earth. France smelled of mud, coal, and damp wool. It was not a land of glory but of labor, waiting, and uncertainty. Yet for Hank, it carried a strange weight.

His father had told him stories passed down from generation to generation—of the Darkens, once d'Arkens, who had lived in the northeast corner of France centuries ago. They had been weavers in Flanders, Protestants in a Catholic land, driven out as Huguenots. They had fled to Norwich, England, and there become builders, contractors, architects. From there the family crossed to America, changing names along the way. Now, after three hundred years, Hank Darken set foot again on French soil.

He stood in the rain outside Brest, mud on his boots, France gray all around him. He was not a weaver or a builder here, only a corporal in a muddy army, but still the first of his blood to return. And that thought stayed with him as the men settled into their sodden camp, waiting for the trains to carry them east toward the front.

CHAPTER II

THE TRAIN EAST OF PARIS

The French boxcars rattled and groaned, each painted with the words 'Hommes 40—Chevaux 8,' forty men or eight horses. Battery F filled theirs like both at once. From Brest they lurched eastward, stopping often to let priority trains pass. The journey toward Paris and beyond would take several days, though the miles themselves were not so many. The cars smelled of sweat, wool, and stale bread, and the constant swaying beat the men into a dull weariness.For Hank, there was no thought now of slipping away.

France was not Oklahoma. A missing soldier here could not vanish into the hills—the uniforms, the language, the very shape of his face would mark him an outsider. The fences were not wire, but foreignness itself. So he stayed close to his crew, the seven men of his gun, a small family bound to one another by duty and by chance.The news that filtered back from the front was grim. Hundreds of thousands dead in the summer battles, days when thirty or fifty thousand fell.

Artillery duels pounded the earth to mud, one side hunting the other's guns. Observation balloons and aircraft hung above the lines, marking targets, and when counter-battery fire came it was merciless. An artilleryman was both hunter and hunted, shooter and target. If a shell landed close, there was little chance of surviving whole. Hank understood it. In this war, death traveled on a screaming arc, and if it found you, it tore you apart.

He thought about his life. What he had not done, what he had not seen. The words left unsaid, the days wasted in worry or work. He wondered if he would ever stand again under the wide Oklahoma sky, bright with blue and cloud-white. He thought of fishing the Boggy, the slow river through Atoka, and told himself that if he ever got back, he would take every chance to fish again.Sleep pulled at him.

The rattle of the train became a lullaby, and he drifted. In dreams he saw his mother and father, and his brothers Walter and Benjamin, both already marked by influenza and loss. He saw the wide fields of home, the clouds drifting like sails, the still water of a pond where a line could be cast and forgotten. Home lay behind him, but in dreams it came forward, filling the gaps the war had carved open.

When Hank woke, his crew were around him—Noah steady as ever, Jesse Harjo sharp-eyed and quiet, Tinker fiddling with a buckle, Red telling a story, Miller silent and patient, Russo loud and restless. He looked at them and felt the weight of belonging. The Choctaws carried themselves with dignity, stoic and proud. Hank regretted not being closer to them before. He had seen enough of prejudice to know he would rather stand with them than with the oppressors. He was defensive of their dignity, determined not to let them be mistaken for anything less than who they were.

The train jolted and swayed on through the French countryside, past stone villages and green fields scarred by old trenches. Hank leaned against the boards, eyes closing again, and wondered how many of his seven would still be with him when the train rolled back the other way.

That night, after the train jolted to another halt and the men settled into uneasy rest, the sound of distant guns rumbled closer. Each man of the crew felt it: tomorrow would bring battle.

Hank cleared his throat. His voice carried low in the dark. 'Boys, I reckon some of us may not see the sun set tomorrow. If you ain't made peace with the Almighty, now's the time. Salvation's not something you gamble with.'

Jesse Harjo answered quietly, measured and calm. 'Corporal, our people have always walked with the Creator. We don't need saving in your way—we've got our own ways, and they've carried us this far.'

Tinker added, sharper than Jesse. 'Save the sermon, Hank. What we need tomorrow is steady hands on the gun, not preaching.'

Russo let out a restless laugh. 'Ain't nothing wrong with a prayer before a fight,' he said, half mocking, half nervous. 'But Hank—you sound like a Sunday preacher, not my corporal.'

Red jumped in, trying to lighten the mood. 'We'll get through it, you'll see. Tomorrow night we'll be laughing about how easy it was.'

Noah's steady voice followed. 'We've trained hard. We'll do our duty. That's all any of us can promise.'

Miller, quiet until now, finally spoke. His tone was flat. 'Not all of us will see it through. That's the truth.' The men fell silent, knowing he was right.

Red bragged about his brothers, already itching to hear his stories when he got back. Noah spoke softly of his wife and the farm waiting. Jesse and Tinker shared pride in their children, their faces clear in their minds even here in France

When it came to Hank, he paused. 'My ma's still living out in West Texas,' he said slowly. 'Don't have no wife, no kids. Just me.' The emptiness in his voice spoke louder than the word

The talk turned to what lay beyond the war. Red swore he'd open a bar. Russo said he'd head back to the city and never wear a uniform again. Jesse and Tinker talked of raising their children in peace, of land that would finally stay theirs. Noah dreamed only of returning to his farm.

When the turn came to Hank, he shrugged. 'Don't rightly know what comes next for me. Guess I'll just see what the Lord has planned.'

Russo broke the silence with a bitter laugh. 'You know what I still don't get? Why the hell are we here in the first place? This ain't our land, ain't our quarrel.'

Red tried to joke, but his voice wavered. 'We're here to whip the Kaiser, right? Make the world safe for democracy, or so they tell

Noah answered slow and steady. 'We're here because the government said so. Soldiers don't get to pick their wars

Miller's voice cut through. 'That's the problem. They tell us it's about freedom, but it's kings and nations arguing, and men like us who bleed. Truth is, it don't add up.

Jesse Harjo spoke with quiet weight. 'Our people fought just to live on our own land, and we still lost most of it. Now we're sent across the ocean to fight a war that ain't ours. Don't make sense.'

Hank, steady but stubborn, said, 'Maybe we're here for God's purpose. Even if we don't see it, maybe He has a reason.'

The air grew heavy. Finally, Noah asked, 'And if we don't come back? What then?

Red tried to keep it light. 'Then they'll put my name on a monument, and my brothers'll drink to me every year.'

Jesse said firmly, 'My children will remember me. That's enough.' Tinker nodded, adding, 'We live on in them.'

Miller spoke in a hushed tone. 'Some of us won't even be remembered. Just a name in a list no one reads.'

Hank clasped his hands. 'The Lord remembers, even if no one else does. That's where I place my hope.'

The men fell quiet again. The distant guns rolled on without pause. Each man lay awake, circling through questions of faith, survival, family, duty, and the reason they found themselves in a foreign land. Tomorrow would demand answers none of them were sure they had.

CHAPTER 12

THE STAGING AREA

In the forward camp, the men of Battery F were restless. They had buried their dead, replaced the fallen, and now sat in the dust with time to think. Inevitably the talk turned to why they were in France at all.

Russo, the Chicago boy, spat into the dirt. 'Back home we rent one floor of a cold flat. My old man never owned nothing. Why am I here, fightin' for this Wilson fellow? He promised we wouldn't go to war, and here I am with a rifle on my back.'

Miller, the German-Texan, nodded. 'Hill Country's rocks and dust. That's all my family's farm is. We got less than nothing. But they pulled me same as you.'

Hank shifted where he sat, feeling the others' eyes on him. 'I can vote,' he said, almost defensively. 'But that don't put food on my table neither. Don't give me land.'

That drew Jesse Harjo into the talk, his voice low, careful. 'Our families do hold land,' he said. 'But the government can take it any day. They say it's restricted, can't be sold. But I've seen the paper lifted and land gone before the ink's dry.

Noah nodded. 'So we fight here, while knowing one wrong move back home, and they'll strip us bare. We've got something to lose—but not here in France. We'd rather be at the fence line.'

Russo and Miller were stunned to learn the Choctaws couldn't even vote. 'That's not right,' Miller muttered. 'You fight, same as us. Why can't you have a say in it?' Noah only shrugged.

It was Hank who bridged the silence. 'I look white enough to cast a ballot,' he admitted. 'But I was raised with Choctaws. I know where I come from. Maybe I can walk in both worlds, speak where you can't.'

The Choctaws considered this and said nothing, but their silence carried weight. They remembered that in the past, many of their chiefs had been mixed-blood, educated to deal with whites on white terms. This was how their people had survived: not by strength of arms, but by walking between worlds.

Around that campfire the truth settled on them: they were no band of volunteers. They were a prisoner army, drafted from farms, from allotments, from immigrant quarters, and blackmailed into service by poverty, land restrictions, and laws none of them had written. They fought not because they believed in Wilson's war, but because they had no choice at all.

CHAPTER 13
THE ROAD TO THE FRONT

Orders came at dawn. Battery F was to move forward, closer to the line. Horses were hitched, limbers loaded, and the guns groaned as they were dragged onto the road. The men moved not with eagerness but with resignation—conscripts blackmailed into service, not volunteers eager for glory.

Progress was slow. The road was dry, rutted, and thick with dust. Every mile was stop-and-go, a parade of misery—infantry marching with rifles slung, ambulances rattling with the wounded, wagons piled high with shells, and refugees moving the other way with their lives strapped to carts. Children cried, goats bleated, women pulled at the reins of exhausted horses. All the while the guns thundered ahead, louder with each passing hour

The men of Battery F rode where they could—on limbers, on caissons—but more often they walked beside the gun, pushing at wheels when they struck ruts, hauling at traces when a team stalled. Sweat ran through dust until their faces were mud. Now and then they passed a burned-out wagon or the carcass of a horse, reminders of what waited further on.

Near midday came disaster. In a traffic jam, a limber slipped sideways and rolled over young Miller's foot—the German-Texan. The crunch silenced the column, then came his cry: 'I ain't quittin'! Texans don't quit!' He tried to rise, but the foot was mangled, swelling fast. He clutched his rifle like it could hold him to the fight.

The captain knelt, looked once, and shook his head. Medics were called. Miller wept with frustration more than pain as they carried him off. By sundown, a replacement arrived—a lean man with a half-French, half-Texan drawl. 'Name's Duval,' he said. 'From Castroville. My people came from Acadia to Louisiana, then out west. Huguenots, same as some of yours, I reckon. We left France to escape its wars, and here I am, sent back for another one.'

Hank heard that and felt a strange kinship. His own Darken ancestors had been Huguenots, fleeing the same persecutions centuries earlier. Now their descendants met on the road back to France, both pressed into a war neither had chosen.

By nightfall they had covered maybe fifteen miles. The last stretch was in darkness, lanterns shaded, voices hushed. At last they turned off into a stand of trees and unlimbered their gun. Tomorrow the work would begin in earnest, and none of them believed they were there by choice. They were an army of prisoners, driven forward not by faith or patriotism, but by the simple fact that they had nowhere else to go.

CHAPTER 14
BAPTISM OF FIRE AND WITHDRAWAL

The 36th Division came up to the line in the dark of October 6. It was not the smooth, orderly relief described in training manuals but a shuffling, mud-slick exchange of half-dead men for fresh ones who did not yet know they were marked. The battered 2nd Division filed back through the night, faces hollow, uniforms stiff with grime. They did not speak much, and when they did it was only to mutter warnings — "Keep low," "Don't linger on the road," "Mask up quick when the shells start

Behind them, the Texans and Oklahomans of the 36th struggled forward. Wagons bogged. Horses balked. One axle collapsed and crushed a man's foot. He was dragged off the road and left to the surgeons, the first casualty of what was supposed to be a simple movement forward

By dawn, the division was in place near St. Etienne-à-Arnes. The artillery regiments unlimbered their 75s, camouflaged them with brush, and waited for orders. Few had seen combat before. They had drilled on clean fields; now they crouched in rain-soaked hedgerows while German shells probed the ground around them. The smell of powder and wet earth mixed with the sharper tang of something acrid. Was it smoke? Gas? Men did not wait to decide. Masks went on at the first whiff, turning the world into a fogged tunnel, their own breath loud in their ears. Sightlines blurred. Orders had to be repeated twice before anyone move

October 7 opened with thunder. At dawn, the first rolling barrage leapt from the American line. The French had taught them the timings: fire, lift, fire again, move the curtain forward in careful strides. But on the ground it was chaos. Shells misfired, crews fumbled with fuses, supply wagons fell behind in the mud. The Germans answered with their own fire, heavier and better aimed. Air bursts slashed down on the batteries. A horse team went down screaming, tangled in its harness, while the gunners tried to work without looking at it.

All across the sector men labored in masks that fogged and choked them. Some pulled the straps up for a desperate breath of real air, gambling with their lungs. Gas or smoke, it did not matter; fear was the same. Confusion was everywhere. Messages from infantry runners contradicted one another. "Push ahead, we've broken through." "Hold your fire, our men are in the wire." "Counterattack coming, load shrapnel now." Officers shouted, waved, swore, tried to make sense of a battlefield where visibility was measured in yards and life in minutes

On October 8, the division attacked Blanc Mont Ridge. The artillery pounded the slopes, cutting paths through wire and breastworks. But in cutting the German line open for their own infantry, they also opened channels that enemy counterattacks could follow back toward the guns. Soon reports spread that Germans were infiltrating through the gaps. There were sudden bursts of rifle fire uncomfortably close to battery positions. Some gunners dropped shells to snatch rifles from wagon beds

In the ditches and hedgerows, men saw things they had never imagined: German storm troops appearing out of the smoke, tall shapes with bayonets and knives, slamming into stunned Americans at close quarters. Throats were cut, rifles swung like clubs. Panic surged, then discipline reasserted itself only by inches. Machine guns chattered into the gaps, rifles cracked, and artillerymen fought hand-to-hand beside the very guns they had been trained never to aband

By dusk the ridge was contested in every fold of ground. The Germans had given way in places, held in others, and everywhere the newcomers of the 36th had learned what war was. Mud clung to their boots, powder blackened their faces, masks hung around their necks like spent lifelines. They had fired until their arms shook, breathed fear through wet canvas, and seen men die in silence and in screams.

Confusion had been their first lesson, and survival their second. They had become veterans in three days.

The withdrawal came as the limbers rattled hollow. Orders came down in clipped tones — conserve, then cease, then withdraw. Men set about the work of retreat like machines, unhooking traces, tightening harness, forcing order where fear threatened to take root.

That was when they looked up and saw it: a biplane circling in the gray sky, its observer bent over his instruments. No one doubted the purpose. The little shadow in the air meant their every move was being marked, plotted, sent back to headquarters. The men felt exposed, like figures in a ledger already being balanced.

They hurried the limbers on, mud sucking at hooves and wheels, but the air itself betrayed them. Then came the sound that froze them all — the high, ragged scream of men cut off. French gunners, left behind with nothing left to fire, had been caught short. Their ammunition was gone; some of them turned and fled, others tried to stand and fight with empty hands. The Germans sensed it immediately

From the treeline came the counterattack, sudden and hard, striking the scattered French like a hammer on glass. The Americans could only watch. They saw officers step forward, shouting commands, trying to stiffen the line. They saw them fall one by one, each figure cut down in place, each effort swallowed by the tide. The noise carried across the field — sharp cracks of rifles, shouted orders that turned into cries, and then a silence that told its own story.

For Battery F, there was no choice but to keep moving. To stop was to be destroyed. The men drove the horses on, faces turned from the field where the French had gone down. The officers' sacrifice was plain: a deliberate stand to hold back the enemy long enough for others to escape. The cost of that stand weighed heavier than any load on the limber.

By the time they reached the secondary line, night had come down like a lid. The men slumped by the wheels, powder-blackened and hollow-eyed, listening to the muffled thunder of the French guns still firing somewhere behind them. They had lived through their baptism and through their first retreat, and they carried with them the memory of the men who had not.

The battle did not end on the ridge. For three weeks the 36th lived inside the thunder of guns, advancing by short marches, setting the pieces, firing until the limbers rattled hollow, then pulling forward again. The pattern was the same whether it was Blanc Mont or the low ground north of the Aisne: mud underfoot, gray sky overhead, smoke that could be gas or only smoke, and the same hammering weight of orders shouted into the din.

Losses came steadily, never in the clean blow of a single day but in the wearing drip of attrition. After Antonio was taken in the trees, two more of the crew were gone by the end of the second week — Jesse, one of the Choctaw boys from Oklahoma, and Otis, who had come down from the farms west of Atoka. Their places at the gun did not stay empty. Frenchmen detached from their own batteries, and a Belgian who spoke thick, broken English, filled the spaces. In time the gun crew became a Babel of languages, gestures, and habits, all bent to the same work of keeping the 75s firing.

It was the sameness that wore them down more than the terror. Rain in the mornings, mud at noon, smoke at dusk. Meals were cold tins, sleep was an hour stolen behind a hedge, and the only certainty was that another man might be gone when the limbers rolled again. The new faces worked without complaint, and the old faces hardened into the blankness of men who no longer measured time by days but by the count of shells fire

At the end of October the order came that no one had expected: "Relieved. Withdraw to rest area." The words moved through the batteries with disbelief at first, then a swelling release so sharp it almost hurt. They limbered the guns not to move forward but to turn away, down roads scarred by weeks of traffic, through villages reduced to walls and chimneys, past civilians who watched them go with eyes emptied by their own losses.

When the men reached billets in the rear, they fell on the small mercies as if they were treasures: hot broth, a basin of clean water, a straw mattress in a barn loft. They slept for whole days, waking only when rations were brought, and in that heavy sleep the sounds of the guns still rolled through their dreams.

The campaign was not over, and the war itself was not yet done, but Battery F had crossed a boundary that could not be uncrossed. They had entered France as raw soldiers; they came out of Champagne as veterans, diminished in number but hardened in the ways of endurance. The guns would sound again, and when they did the battery would return to its place, different men perhaps but the same machine of war.

CHAPTER 15
END OF THE WAR

Battery F did not return to the firing line again. In the final days of the war, they remained close behind the infantry, positioned as a second line of defense should the Germans attempt one last desperate thrust. No such attack came. The guns were ready, but they were never called upon to fire.

On the morning of November 11, 1918, word spread down the line that the armistice had been signed. At precisely eleven o'clock the thunder of artillery ceased. A profound silence settled across northern France, broken only by the murmur of men who had lived to see the end. For Battery F, the war was over. No more of their number would fall.

They waited in their positions until formal relief came, standing watch in the gray days that followed. Alive, intact, and grateful, they marked the end of the greatest struggle of their lives not with cheers but with quiet endurance, waiting to go home.

Yet for Hank, things were not the same. The night at the brothel had left a mark he could not erase. Lieutenant Carver had warned him to step away, and he now understood why. By remaining, he had allowed suspicion to fall on him—that his convictions had judged his men as sinners. From that night forward, he carried himself apart, a self-imposed exile among his own battery. Nothing worsened, but nothing healed. The bond between him and the others never returned to what it had been

He could see, however, that the men were relieved. They were already doing their best to forget the immediate past and to prepare themselves for going home. The Choctaw from Atoka in particular carried a quiet gladness. They had borne the burden of this war like an unwanted indenture, but now they dared to hope that their service had earned them more—that perhaps at last they might claim the full rights of citizenship, including the right to vote.

The men laughed loudest when they weren't in the barracks. A few bragged about their luck in town, others winced and muttered about "the shot" they'd been given by the medics. One fellow limped when he thought no one was looking, another joked that he'd been put on the sick list for a month with "the French fever." Hank kept his distance, listening without a word. He had no appetite for the filth of it, and no faith in the Army's chemical washes that were supposed to make a man clean again.

He was called a prude more than once, and worse behind his back. Maybe it was stubbornness, maybe pride, maybe his contempt for the others that kept him apart. But later, when the war was done and the years had piled up, it would be clear what that distance meant. Many soldiers carried their sickness home, passing it on to wives who never asked for it, to children who would suffer blindness or worse. For some, it was a slow death that haunted them long after the trenches.

Hank brought home scars of his own—scars no one could see—but he brought home no poison in his blood. His abstinence was born of anger and separation, but it became his protection. He bore the weight of loneliness so that his family, when it came, would not. In that bitter sacrifice lay the only mercy he ever gave without knowing it.

CHAPTER 16
REST AND RECREATION

When the orders finally came for leave, Hank expected relief. Instead, he found himself standing apart from the rest of the unit, watching the others scatter into the town with a hunger in their eyes. Some were determined to drown the war in liquor, others to forget it in the arms of a woman. The French villages had learned quickly that soldiers on leave were easy marks—wine flowed, beds were rented, and for a few francs anyone could believe the war was somewhere else

Hank stayed back. He did not trust the wine, nor the women, nor the idea of losing control in a place he did not understand. The other men laughed at him, called him a cold fish, or worse. They tried to drag him along, but Hank resisted. He had grown up with a rigid view of morality and a deep suspicion of strangers. That suspicion, often a burden in camp, now held him apart

As the nights went on, men returned in worse shape than they had left. Some stumbled in drunk and belligerent; others came back sick. Whispers moved quickly through the tents—so-and-so had caught something, a burning that would not go away, a sickness that spread from one man to the next. Army doctors had little sympathy and fewer cures. Quinine, injections, harsh lectures—they were all part of the routine. Still, the numbers mounted. By the end of the war, tens of thousands of American soldiers would carry venereal disease home with them, infecting wives and children, and in many cases dying years earlier than they should have.

Hank saw it all from a distance. His solitude, his stubbornness, even his bigotry insulated him. He was lonely, yes, but untouched. He could not have known it then, but his refusal to partake spared him and the family he would one day raise. While others paid a hidden price long after the guns fell silent, Hank's self-denial became a strange kind of inheritance. His children would be born free of those afflictions, his descendants spared the chain of suffering carried back across the ocean by so many.

He did not see virtue in it. He only felt the sting of isolation, the ache of being apart. Yet in that separation lay a quiet protection, one that history itself would never mark, but that lived on in flesh and blood. Hank bore the loneliness, so that those who came after him would not bear the disease.

But Hank's biggest problem was not just loneliness. It was intolerance—openly displayed in front of his men. He had never been in a position where he bore responsibility for others, and yet the army had thrust him into that role without any real training or preparation. He lacked the understanding that leadership was more than giving orders; it was about holding the respect of the men who depended on him.

The lieutenant who commanded the battery recognized it clearly. Hank's failing was not simply that he carried prejudice in his heart—many men did—but that he allowed it to show in a way that undermined the fragile bonds of trust within the unit. A soldier could think as he pleased, the officer judged, so long as his opinions did not poison the work of the battery. Hank could not manage that balance.

In an odd way, however, the flaw would serve him later. When the war was over and he returned to a life where he was responsible only for himself, his narrowness fit more comfortably. He no longer had to command men or temper his words to preserve cohesion. He lived, as he had always wanted, on his own terms—intolerant perhaps, but no longer in a position to harm anyone but himself.

CHAPTER 17
THE JEWISH CHAPLAIN'S VISIT

The rain beat steady on the roof of the barn, a gray afternoon pressing down on the village. Hank sat apart from the others, polishing a rifle with the same stubborn rhythm he used for every task. Around him the crew filled the silence with the scrape of brushes, the scratch of pens on half-finished letters, the occasional laugh cut short by fatigue. Their lieutenant, McGovern, leaned near the door, fingering a small rosary in his pocket. Jesse and Otis, the Choctaws, shared a canteen cup between them. Red hummed a tune until Doc told him to hush. They were waiting—waiting for orders, waiting for the road home.

Then the door creaked open. A chaplain stepped inside, insignia marking him Jewish. He carried a satchel and wore a calm, steady look that made him seem older than his years. "Afternoon, boys," he said lightly. "No inspections—only conversation, a blessing if you want it, and peppermints if you don't."

The men chuckled, grateful for the break. McGovern invited him in. Hank didn't look up. The chaplain set his bag down and spoke softly. "I make my rounds. Listen, pray, write letters for fellows who can't find the words. Sometimes I just hand out candy and walk on."

He looked to Hank. "What's your name, son?"

"Hank," came the flat reply.

"May the Holy One guard your going out and your coming in. That's an old blessing from the Psalms."

Hank raised his head, eyes narrowing. "You a priest?"

"A rabbi in my people's way. A chaplain in the Army's way.

Hank's words came hard and quick. "Then I don't know what a Jew's got to tell me about God. Far as I was taught, Jews killed Him.

The barn stilled. Even Red stopped shifting. The chaplain did not flinch. "That's a heavy bundle to lay on a man you just met, Ha

"It's the truth," Hank muttered. "The way we say it back home."

"Truth ought to carry light as well as weight," the chaplain said. "Jesus was a Jew. He prayed my prayers, read my scriptures. He blessed bread and wine with our blessings. Rome hammered the nails. And if you believe your preachers, it was the sins of all humanity—yours and mine included—that ran deeper than any hammer."

Doc nodded slowly. "That matches what I've heard."

The chaplain went on. "And remember, He said: 'Father, forgive them, for they know not what they do.' If you blame me, you miss His point entirely."

Hank bristled. "You don't even believe He's the Son of God."

"My prayer is simpler: the Lord is One. We are to love Him with all we are and love our neighbor as ourselves. That's the heart of the law and prophets, and Jesus Himself said those words held everything together."

Red whistled. "He's quoting both books."

"It's not two books," McGovern said quietly. "It's one root."

But Hank pressed on. "Doesn't wash. Where I'm from, we keep pure. We don't mix with folks that don't believe right."

Jesse leaned forward. "You mean folks like us, Hank? Choctaws?"

"I didn't say y'all," Hank muttered.

"You didn't have to," Otis said. "We grew up hearing it plenty—different pews, different doors. Folks calling us 'those people.'"

"I ain't hateful," Hank insisted. "I'm cautious."

"That's hate in Sunday clothes," Doc muttered.

Hank's temper rose. "Back home, Baptists say Catholics ain't Christians at all."

McGovern finally looked up. "Do they now?"

"That's what I heard."

McGovern's voice sharpened. "I carried my rosary through Belleau Wood and the Argonne. I buried men with it—Protestant and Catholic alike. If I ain't Christian enough for your hometown, then your hometown can fight the next war without me." Murmurs of assent echoed.

"I'm just saying what's said," Hank replied, defensive.

"You're a bigot, Hank," Jesse said flatly.

"I ain't no bigot."

Otis leaned in. "A bigot's a man who won't look in another and see his own face staring back."

The chaplain added, "Or worse—he prefers the story he tells about others to the real people standing in front of him. Stories don't cry. People do."

Hank's face flushed. "There's right belief and wrong belief. Right church and wrong church. Right folks and wrong folks."

"Then tell me," the chaplain asked, his voice even, "were the shells right or wrong? They didn't ask your creed before they landed."

"War's different," Hank snapped.

"No," McGovern said firmly. "War is the same matter, turned up loud."

The Choctaws pressed further. "Back home we all saw preachers thunder from the pulpit and keep a woman in town on Monday," Jesse said. "Here in France, men write letters about clean living, then spend their nights otherwise. They won't tell their wives, won't tell at the VFW either. Hypocrisy runs deep."

"Keeping yourself separate ain't the same as keeping yourself clean," Otis said. "You kept your body pure, Hank, but you kept your heart locked up tight."

Hank snapped, "What good is the prayer of a man who don't believe right?"

The chaplain answered, "What good is any prayer that doesn't make a man merciful? Micah said: 'Do justice, love mercy, walk humbly with your God.' Jesus repeated it: 'Blessed are the merciful, for they shall obtain mercy.' He never blessed men who used doctrine as a hammer."

McGovern added, "If your creed makes you cruel, it's not creed—it's armor."

Hank's voice cracked. "You're trying to talk me out of what my daddy taught me."

Jesse leaned close. "We're trying to talk you into seeing the world you just fought in. You can plant one kind of seed back home and call it a field, but you marched through a world that grows a hundred. The field ain't wrong because it's bigger than your fence."

Otis spoke gently. "Abraham left his country because God called him out. Ruth crossed borders for love and became the grandmother of a king. God isn't nervous around border crossings, Hank."

McGovern's voice was steady now. "Nor around Jews, nor Catholics, nor Choctaws. He's walked beside all of us whether you noticed or not."

The barn grew quiet. Rain softened. Hank's rag hung motionless in his hand. "Maybe I don't like being called a bigot," he muttered.

"Quit being one then," Jesse said.

"It ain't easy. Back home folks talk. They'll run you off a porch for less than this."

"Then don't preach it on your porch," Otis said. "Live it in your bones. Some things are between you and God."

Hank lashed out one more time. "What about you, Otis? You and them French girls—"

Otis didn't flinch. "I'll answer for that. That's the point. I don't get to hide it behind claiming purity. We're not asking you to like everything. Just stop disliking people you never met."

The chaplain stood. "Before I leave, may I give you the old blessing Aaron spoke? It's ours, but it belongs to any man who needs light."

Heads bowed—even Hank's, reluctantly. His voice was quiet but strong: "May the Lord bless you and keep you; may His face shine upon you and be gracious to you; may He lift up His countenance upon you and give you peace."

The word peace seemed to linger in the rafters. McGovern slipped his rosary back in his pocket. Jesse and Otis finished the canteen. Red unwrapped a peppermint with exaggerated ceremony, drawing a few small laughs. The men bent back to their tasks, quieter now.

Hank sat still. "I ain't sure I can change," he whispered.

Otis looked at him steadily. "Most folks don't. But some shift a little. That's enough to start."

"And if you don't," Jesse added, "we'll still sit by you at the VFW. We just won't let you talk foolish without a fight."

For the first time Hank allowed a thin smile. He bent again to the metal in his hands, polishing slower now, as though seeing it new in the dim light.

CHAPTER 18

THE LONG ROAD HOME

The orders came suddenly, as they always did. The regiment would be broken up for transport. Some men bound for New Orleans, others for Charleston, most for New York. The Army, ever frugal, sorted them by whatever combination of train routes and shipping schedules would save money and time. Pay would continue until they were mustered out at camps back home, but the waiting and shuffling left plenty of time for reflection.

For Hank, the reflection was bitter. He had not won friends with his talk. The men of his gun crew avoided him now, speaking in lowered voices or drifting to other circles. Even Lieutenant McGovern was cordial but distant, as though Hank carried a contagion of intolerance. Hank noticed but did not care. His thoughts were on home, where men spoke his language and believed his truths. In France he had been mocked and cornered; in Oklahoma he would be vindicated

The train east through France was packed. Boxcars rattled, straw scattered on the floor, rifles and duffels piled against the walls. Men sang, some bawdy, some holy, all loud. They joked about the trip, about the "big game won" and the prize of going home. Hank sat apart, a small New Testament open on his knee, his lips moving silently.

Jesse, the Choctaw cannoneer, sat across from him. When the noise dipped, Hank leaned forward and spoke low. "Jesse, you and me will walk the same streets again. Best thing you can do is take Christ into your heart before it's too late. He'll forgive your sins and give you a clean slate. Otherwise, you'll pay in hell.

Jesse's jaw stiffened. He was about to reply when Otis, sitting near the door, caught the words. He slid closer. "We've heard that before, Hank. Missionaries told us the same. They brought their Bibles in one hand and the surveyor's chain in the other. Preached forgiveness, then cut our land into parcels. Told us our ways were savage because we shared the earth."

"That's right," Jesse said, finding his voice. "Said we were wrong to believe the animals had spirit, wrong to think the river and the trees held life of their own. They told us only men have souls, and all else was property."

Hank shook his head sharply. "That's because it's true. Animals don't have souls. Plants don't have souls. God gave that only to man. If animals had souls, Christ would have died for them too."

Otis's eyes glinted. "Maybe He did, Hank. Maybe His blood covered more than you reckon. Our old ones said all living things carry spirit. The missionaries told us to bury that belief if we wanted to be proper Christians. We buried it in our words, but it still beats in our hearts."

Jesse added, "When I look a horse in the eye, I see spirit. When I hear an owl call at night, I know warning. When a tree falls, it's not just wood—it's a life ended. Maybe not a soul like yours, Hank, but not empty."

Hank snorted. "Superstition. Your people clung to nonsense. No wonder you never prospered. A man ought to own his own place, not share it with everyone. That's what makes a man responsible."

"That's what broke us," Jesse shot back. "We held land together. We cared for it together. Your way split us apart. Surveyed it, sold it, stole it. That's not prosperity. That's loss."

The boxcar rocked. Men nearby shifted uncomfortably at the rising voices. Hank pressed on. "Your ways were dying. Christ is the only truth."

"Then why did Christ Himself walk as a Jew?" Otis asked. "Why did He pray with our kind of people—the despised, the Samaritans? Why did He heal lepers instead of princes?"

Hank's lips tightened. He returned to his Testament, muttering. The Choctaws let him be.

The Atlantic crossing was rough. The ship rolled in gray seas, bunks stacked three high, mess lines winding for hours. Yet spirits soared. Victory, home, and survival filled the air. The decks rang with songs—"Over There" shouted by one group, "Amazing Grace" by another. Brass instruments appeared from nowhere, pieced together into makeshift bands. A group of Texans organized a dance on the aft deck, stomping in rhythm while French girls who had followed the ship out waved handkerchiefs from the pier.

Card games ran night and day. Men bet francs and cigarettes, passing bottles when they could. Others traded helmets, belt buckles, and bayonets for souvenirs. Someone fashioned dice out of a broom handle, and within hours a whole crowd was gathered around, cheering the throws. Even seasickness became a joke, with bets on who would run for the rail first. Laughter rolled louder than the sea.

Jesse and Otis joined in easily, singing Choctaw hymns that blended old chants with Methodist verses. Their voices rose in harmony, not drowned but distinct, adding to the strange chorus of victory. They laughed with others, played cards, shared stories of home. They had survived and meant to live again.

Hank sat apart. He paced the deck at dawn when others slept, muttering prayers. He read his Testament while others sang. He told himself he was pure, and that the joy of these men was false joy—bound for hell. He heard Jesse's hymn and thought it half-pagan, Otis's laugh and thought it reckless. Even McGovern, kneeling with his rosary, Hank judged as deceived. He was alone, and he wore his aloneness like a badge of honor

Still, when the Statue of Liberty rose from the mist, Hank felt a stirring he could not suppress. Bands played, flags snapped, crowds roared from the docks. Men wept openly. Jesse and Otis shouted, pounding their comrades on the back. Hank stood stiff. He whispered, "I kept pure. That's enough."

Processing was quick and impersonal. Within days, Hank, Jesse, and Otis were herded onto a southbound train, bound for Camp Travis in San Antonio. Along the way, Jesse tried once more. "If there's more than one way to hell, Hank, maybe there's more than one way to heaven too."

Otis added, "Don't fool yourself. You think you're better than us. But maybe the Lord doesn't measure that way."

Hank shook his head. "Without Christ, you're lost."

"Without humility," Jesse replied, "you are."

The train wheels hammered the words into Hank's head as the miles rolled by

San Antonio appeared in the heat of a Texas morning, Camp Travis sprawling with tents and barracks. The men filed out, laughing, thinking of home. Hank followed, solitary. He consoled himself: better to be a faithful bigot than a faithless sinner. He was saved. They were not.

But Jesse and Otis lingered a moment apart, watching him. Jesse spoke low. "He's one of ours, but he don't walk like it. He don't talk like it. I'd just as soon not claim him."

Otis nodded sadly. "His whiteness has gone to his head. He thinks he's more white than he is. Maybe he is."

They shouldered their duffels, disappointment heavy between them. Hank walked on ahead, never turning back.

CHAPTER 19

THE LAST TRAIN

The Army wasted no time in San Antonio. The war was over, the camps were swollen with returning men, and Uncle Sam was eager to clear the rolls. As soon as Jesse, Otis, and Hank set foot at Camp Travis, a clerk behind a scarred oak desk shoved papers and tickets into their hands. "Two dollars a day stops when you're on a train, boys," he said briskly. "Government will see you home, but the payroll ends here."

The tickets told their story: San Antonio to Texarkana, Texarkana to Paris, Texas, Paris to McAlester, McAlester to Atoka. Four segments, days of waiting, a route that meandered like a creek in flood. Hank scowled. "Takes longer to ride home from here than it took to get back from France." Jesse only shrugged. "We've waited longer for less

The first leg out of San Antonio was crowded beyond reason. Soldiers jammed the aisles, duffels piled to the ceiling, a baby crying in the corner. Hank sat with his Testament open, muttering about waste. Jesse leaned against the window, watching mesquite trees drift past. "Six hundred miles," he thought, "and it will take a week to walk them by train

At Texarkana, the train ground to a halt. They were told the next connection would not leave until morning. The three of them sat on the platform through the long afternoon. Jesse and Otis kept together, speaking now and then in Choctaw, their words soft and private. Hank sat apart, reading, lips moving in silent judgment. Jesse thought of his grandmother, who had been told by missionaries that her old prayers were heathen. She sang their hymns anyway, and the Lord heard her. But the memory stung.

In Paris, Texas, the layover stretched to nearly two days. The men walked into town, only to feel the weight of eyes upon them. Jesse caught the look in the shopkeeper's face—uniform or no, he was still an Indian. Otis felt it too. Hank noticed but said nothing. If anything, he seemed pleased that in their company, he was counted as white. Otis muttered later, "He thinks he's more white than he is. Maybe he is.

The train north toward McAlester rattled through fields of scrub oak and red dirt farms. In the dim light of evening, Hank leaned close to Jesse. "You'd better take Christ before it's too late. He'll forgive you yet." Jesse said nothing. Otis spoke at last: "We've heard enough of your kind. Missionaries brought the Bible in one hand and the surveyor's chain in the other. They told us to forget the spirits of the animals, the songs of the trees. They said only men had souls, and all else was property."

"That's because it's true," Hank snapped. "If animals had souls, Christ would have died for them too."

"Maybe He did," Otis said softly. "Our old ones said all living things carry spirit. The missionaries told us to bury that belief, but it beats in us still." Jesse added, "When I look a horse in the eye, I see spirit. When I hear the owl's call, I know warning. When a tree falls, I know life has ended. You can call it superstition. I call it truth." Hank turned back to his Testament, lips moving. The conversation was over.

At last, the train crawled into McAlester. The final leg lay ahead. By then, Jesse and Otis spoke little. The miles had worn them down, but hope quickened as Atoka drew near. When the train finally pulled into the small station, the platform was alive with sound. Half the Choctaw Nation seemed to be waiting—families singing, children darting between legs, old women crying for joy. Jesse and Otis were swept up into embraces, carried almost like heroes in a parade through town.

Hank stepped off unnoticed. No family waited. No cheers rose. He walked alone through the familiar streets, past houses that had not changed, past faces that did not look up. He reached the place where he had grown up, found his old fishing pole leaning by the wall, and carried it out to the buggy. At the lake, he sat in silence.

His thoughts turned not to the chaplain's words, nor to Jesse and Otis's challenges, but to his own failures: no wife, no children, no multiplied flock. He had not lived fully by the dictates of the faith as he understood them. It was not that he had thought wrong; it was that he had not been faithful enough. So he vowed that from this day forward he would devote himself to obedience: to marry, to raise children, to live as the Bible directed.

The water lapped softly against the shore. Hank set his line and stared across the lake, convinced of his righteousness, blind to the deeper truth. It was here, thirty years later, that I would find him again, still fishing, still bound by the same narrow creed.

CHAPTER 20
THE OVERNIGHT STOP IN TEXARKANA

Texarkana in May 1919 was alive with smoke, steam, and smells that told its story as clearly as any map. The train yard was a hub of rails and engines, whistles echoing through the night, locomotives hissing like beasts. The air carried the pungent tang of creosote from the tie plant, where tall southern pines had been cut, milled, and soaked to build the very rails the men rode upon. The odor was sharp but not unpleasant—an industrial perfume that clung to the town. Mixed with it was the thick, earthy smoke of clay from the great brick kilns nearby, firing red blocks that would lift houses off damp ground. And laced through it all was the briny bite of dill from the pickle factory, so strong a man could close his eyes and know he was in Texarkana. These scents mingled with the coal smoke of locomotives, a signature bouquet of industry, progress, and survival.

The town was in a boom. The Dierks timber empire fed logs by the thousands into the mills, much of it drawn from Choctaw lands wrested away by sharp deals and broken promises. Casket factories thrived, their business swelled by the influenza epidemic that had ravaged the country. Even death had become an industry here. Men like J.D. Wadley, whose fortune rose with the railroads and timber, owned wide swathes of downtown. Later his name would grace a great hospital, but in 1919 he was already among the wealthiest men in the nation. Texarkana thrived at the very crossroads of grief and industry, a place where wood, steel, and human need were turned into wealth

For Hank, Jesse Harjo, and Tinker, the layover here was their first night as civilians. The uniforms were still on their backs, but the Army no longer commanded them. Many of the Black soldiers stepped off here, greeted by families with open arms. The three men from Atoka, though, had miles yet to go. On a bench outside the terminal, under gaslight lamps and the endless churn of engines, they found the quiet space for words they had carried unspoken.

Jesse broke the silence first. 'We made it back,' he said. 'That's something to give thanks for.'

Hank nodded. 'The Lord brought us through. His hand kept us safe.'

Tinker shook his head. 'Or maybe it was just German shells missing their mark. Poor aim saved us, not any preacher's God.'

Russo, still restless, laughed. 'Hell, I'll take luck over prayer any day. Still—thank God or chance, I'm here to breathe free air again. And it sure beats mustard gas. This place smells like pickles and tar.'

Their voices dropped when Red mentioned the fellow who hurt his foot months ago. 'Never saw him again after they hauled him off,' he said. 'Hope he's all right

Miller answered, quiet as always. 'We all say we'll look him up. Truth is, we won't. But I pray he's walking again somewhere.

They let the silence hang, each remembering the ones who didn't come back, faces burned into memory

Jesse finally said, 'I'll tell you one thing. Our lieutenant was steady. Didn't waste us like so many did. I'm thankful for that.'

Noah added, 'He kept us alive. Could've been worse under another man.'

Hank bowed his head. 'God worked through him. I believe that

The talk shifted to home. Jesse and Tinker spoke proudly of their wives and children waiting. Noah described the farm he longed to see again. Each man carried visions of reunion and futures built from toil and hope.

Hank listened, a weight in his chest. 'My ma's still in West Texas,' he said slowly. 'But I've got no wife, no children. Just me.'

Tinker frowned. 'That ought to change, Hank. A man needs folks to come home to. I got a cousin—fine woman. When we get back, I'll introduce you

Hank managed a faint smile. 'I'd be grateful for that.'

Later that evening, a man passing through Texarkana recognized Hank's name. He hesitated, then told him the news: Hank's brother, Charles Bradley Darken Jr., had died back in February, traveling to Denver for the funeral of their half-brother Benjamin. Both gone, claimed by influenza's sweep.

The words struck like a shell. Hank stared, hollow. 'So I went across the ocean, faced the guns, and I come back... and my brothers are gone.

Jesse spoke gently. 'That's a hard thing, Hank. You fought the Kaiser, and they died at home.'

Hank's voice trembled. 'The flu took 'em while I lived through war. The Lord spares one man and not another. I don't understand His ways.'

Tinker's voice was blunt. 'It was pointless. Nothing gained. We bled and killed for what?'

Red muttered, 'They said to make the world safe for democracy. Feels the same as it ever did.'

Noah answered with steady resignation. 'We did our duty. That's what soldiers do. But no man can tell me it was worth the cost.'

Jesse's tone carried old sorrow. 'Our people fought to live on our own land and still lost it. Now we fight in a war that was never ours to begin with. Makes no sense.'

Russo spat. 'Funny, ain't it? Casket factories here running full tilt, men getting rich off the dead. Seems the war fed 'em just fine.'

Hank clung to the only truth he knew. 'Maybe God had His reasons, even if we never see them.'

The bench grew quiet. The irony was sharp—Hank, the only one of four brothers to go to war, was the one who lived. Two brothers lost to influenza, another gone in grief's shadow.

He bowed his head. 'Life is fragile. I see that now. I've wasted too much of mine already. I need to make something of what's left.'

The Choctaws sat with him, no mockery in their faces, only the bond of men who had survived together. Texarkana's station bustled around them—creosote, clay, dill, and coal smoke heavy in the air—but on that bench it was only three men, their memories heavy, their futures uncertain, and their gratitude for breath unspoken but deep.

CHAPTER 21
THE LAYOVER IN PARIS, TEXAS

By the time the train rolled into Paris, Texas, the men were bone-tired but restless with nearness to home. It was late spring of 1919, the nights warm and clear. The station was crowded with soldiers and travelers, and there were no rooms left to rent. The town was too small, the war too large. So Hank, Jesse, and Tinker did what they had done so many times in France: unrolled their bedrolls under the open sky. The city park, not far from the station, became their barracks for the night. Stars stretched overhead, and for once the sound of guns was gone. Only the crickets sang in the grass.

Russo shook his head, looking up the line north. 'We could hitch a buggy and beat this train to McAlester,' he joked. The men laughed, the tension breaking. Home was close enough to taste, and impatience was the sweetest burden they had carried in months.

Jesse stretched out, hands behind his head. 'This is it, boys. We're going home for real. No more France, no more mud.'

Tinker's voice was warm. 'My kids'll be taller than when I left. Can't wait to see their faces.'

Hank smiled faintly. 'Feels strange, don't it? I thought I'd never see Oklahoma again. Yet here we are.'

The laughter dimmed as Hank remembered what he had learned in Texarkana. His voice was low. 'I still can't believe my brothers are gone. I came back, and they didn't. The flu took 'em. But I thank you men for standing with me through it all.'

He looked at Jesse and Tinker. 'And don't worry. Whatever was said in France stays there. I won't speak of it. Not to anyone.

The Choctaws exchanged a glance—part relief, part unease. Hank knew their secrets, but he promised silence.

Hank's tone softened. 'I still believe salvation comes through the Lord alone. Always will. But I've seen enough now to know there are other paths men walk. And not all who walk them are wicked.'

Jesse nodded slowly. 'We each carry our faith in our own way. Maybe that's enough.'

Tinker added, 'Long as a man lives true, I reckon he's worth the Lord's notice.'

They spoke then of Atoka. Jesse laughed. 'Funny, isn't it? We lived near each other all our lives and hardly said two words. Took a war to make neighbors out of us.'

Hank answered, 'War gave me one thing I didn't expect. It gave me brothers in you two.'

The Choctaws fell quiet, but the bond between them was clear. They had shared fire, mud, loss, and now the long road home.

Tinker's voice grew playful. 'Don't forget about my cousin, Hank. I meant what I said. You need folks to come home to.'

Hank chuckled, a sound rare on his lips. 'Maybe I'll take you up on that.'

They lay back on the grass, Paris, Texas stars burning bright above them. Hank thought of the irony—two Parises in one war. One soaked in blood and death, the other a way station toward home. He whispered a prayer, not only for heaven but for earth—that he might yet find a life worth living. Beside him, Jesse and Tinker drifted toward sleep, content and eager for the dawn. Salvation, redemption, forgiveness—all of it had been spoken in their own ways. Under the night sky, they were brothers at last.

CHAPTER 22
THE MEDAL AND THE BUICK

When Hank returned to Atoka in 1919, he was not the same man who had marched off to war. The silence of France had left its mark on him, and yet he did not let his life idle. Before long he found my great-aunt May, and together they began raising a family. He seemed to take joy in being a husband and a father, and the very names he chose for his children testified to it. One was named Joy, another Happy, their middle names echoing the months in which they were born, arranged with a kind of military precision. After the long, bleak years of war, Hank built his own order out of love and famil

By the time I met Uncle Hank, it was near the end of his life. He would pass in 1960, within a year of the world itself changing—Kennedy's assassination, the Beatles' arrival, and the fading of that postwar interlude when America had stood unquestioned as leader of the free world. Atoka had grown, but not by much. Choctaw people had their vote, but little else. Only a few years later, in 1963, they would regain the right to elect their own chief and to shape their own future. Left to their own devices, the Choctaw Nation flourished. Today its programs, schools, and enterprises stand as testimony to what might have been possible in Hank's time had recognition and self-rule come sooner. His sense of belonging would surely have been stronger had he lived to see it.

I remember him as a weathered friendly man, his face marked by the years, with a broad mustache, and a crumpled cowboy hat, with a short brim pushed low over his brow. He stood by the lake beside the boat he had fashioned with his own hands, a creation unlike any other. The hull was made from the front ends of two Buick Roadmasters, their hoods joined together, the unmistakable chrome portholes still gleaming. He had painted the entire craft a deep red, inside and out, taking care to mask the chrome so it shone against the paint. The boat rested high on a stand, not only to keep it from the damp but also so he could repaint it, keep it precise, and tend to it as a man tends to something he loves. It was beautiful in its oddness, singular as its maker. One of a kind, like Hank himself.

It was there, at Lake Atoka, that he gave me his gift: a French medal, carried home across the ocean, handed to me as a token of his life and his war. I did not know then the full weight of his story, but I understood that it mattered. The medal was more than metal; it was a passage, a memory made tangible, a way of carrying Hank forward into my own life.

My great-uncle Hank passed away in 1960. Since that time, there have been massive changes in the way the Indian nations are governed. In the early 1960s, the Choctaw Nation was once again allowed to elect its own Principal Chief and to conduct its affairs in accordance with its Tribal Council. There remain restrictions—such as blood quantum requirements for both the Chief and council members—but in general, they are chosen by the people who are blood citizens of the Nation

With the exception of the old questions of land allocation and those blood quantum limits for holding office, there is now no meaningful difference between the Yowani Choctaw and the remainder of the Choctaw Nation. They share the same benefits, of which there are many.

I believe that if Hank were still alive, he would be very pleased with the way things have developed. It is true that there has been no restitution for the federal government's debt to the Yowani Choctaw—the land they were dispossessed of, and the shenanigans at the turn of the last century that swindled them out of what they were promised in return. This injustice would only have strengthened Hank's faith that a better life awaited beyond this world.

For myself, and I am certain for the rest of his relatives, there is pride in his service during the First World War. As a farm boy from Oklahoma, he found the courage and capability to stand where duty called. That was no small achievement. And more than that, he returned home, took a wife, raised a family, and lived a faithful life.

Job well and faithfully done Hank!

I should be clear: I certainly did not know Hank well. I only met him once, when I was eleven or twelve years old, and a year later he was gone. My picture of him is not drawn from long conversations or firsthand memories. It comes instead through the words of my mother and other relatives, and through the bits of history I have uncovered since. In that sense, the Hank who appears in these pages is a composite—part family story, part historical record, and part my own interpretation of what it all means.

My mother and her generation rarely spoke of being second-class citizens within the Choctaw Nation. They did not complain, nor did they dwell on it. Most of the time, they simply set it aside and lived as though it were not part of their identity at all. For them, survival mattered more than status. It was only later, in my own life, that being Choctaw became important. And when it did, proving it was no small task. Those of us who came from the reinstatement rolls were left with a thin paper trail, and establishing our rightful place required determination and persistence.

So my understanding of Hank's world is both limited and personal. I cannot know more than the fragments passed down to me, but I also do not know less than the truth I have lived: that unfairness, exclusion, and silence shaped our families. And it is through that lens that I look back at Hank, and at the faith and flaws of his generation.

There is no excusing bigotry. Hank carried it with him, and it set him apart from his comrades. But it can be explained. It came from a life where persecution was woven into every law, every ledger, every list of names written too late. It was hardened by the knowledge that others had land and security while his family had been denied. In such soil, bitterness grew easily. Yet alongside that bitterness, faith grew as well. Hank's conviction that salvation was real, that heaven promised what earth denied, was not a contradiction but a survival. To believe in something beyond this life was the one way to endure the unfairness of this one.

Hank's generation lived between everything. They were born to a frontier Oklahoma that was already fading, came of age in the Great War, raised families in the Depression, and grew old just as the modern world was taking shape. They did not receive the glory of the pioneers or the praise of the so-called Greatest Generation. But they bore the long middle years, and they bore them with stubbornness, work, and faith.

If my portrait of Hank is imperfect, it is because it must be. It is secondhand, refracted through memory and history and my own experience. But it is also faithful in spirit. Hank was a man shaped by unfairness, by exclusion, and by faith in something better. And in that, he stands not only for himself but for a whole generation—those who came between everything, and who carried both bitterness and belief to the end.

***

In the years since Hank's passing, tremendous changes have been underway for the Choctaw people, including the Yowani. I believe this is in large measure a result of the change in the Nation's governance.

The progress since 1963 can be broken down into several key areas

Rebuilding Sovereignty and Governance (The Political Renaissance)

Before progress in any other area could happen, the Choctaw Nation had to rebuild its foundational governing structure.

· Writing a New Constitution (1983): The most critical step was the ratification of a new constitution in 1983. This document re-established the Choctaw Nation as a sovereign government with three distinct branches: Executive (Chief), Legislative (Tribal Council), and Judicial (Tribal Court system). This moved the tribe beyond a simple "BIA agency" model and laid the legal groundwork for all future development.

· Expanding Citizenship and Representation: The new constitution and subsequent laws clarified citizenship criteria, growing the enrolled population from a few thousand in the 1960s to over 200,000 citizens today, making it the third-largest federally recognized tribe in the U.S. The Tribal Council was expanded to represent 12 districts, ensuring broad geographic representation across the 10.5-county reservation in southeastern Oklahoma.

· Asserting Jurisdiction: The Nation has steadily built its judicial system, including a Lighthorse Police Department, and has worked to assert its jurisdiction over its territory, often through complex negotiations with state and federal governments.

Economic Transformation and Self-Sufficiency

From profound poverty, the Choctaw Nation has built an economic powerhouse that drives the entire region's economy.

Gaming and Diversification: The launch of gaming operations following the federal Indian Gaming Regulatory Act of 1988 was a catalyst. The first bingo hall opened in 1987, and today, casinos like the Choctaw Casino & Resort in Durant are major destinations. However, the Tribe has been strategic in diversifying its business portfolio.

Choctaw Business Holdings: This corporate arm manages a vast array of enterprises beyond gaming, including:

Manufacturing: DEFT (Choctaw Defense Manufacturing)

Hospitality: Resorts, hotels, and restaurants.

Services: IT, staffing, and consulting firms.

Retail: Travel plazas and retail centers

Regional Economic Engine: The Choctaw Nation is now the largest employer in southeastern Oklahoma. Its economic activities generate billions of dollars in economic impact, providing jobs and stability for both tribal citizens and non-Native community members

Cultural Revitalization and Language Preservation

After decades of federal assimilation policies, a dedicated effort has been made to reclaim and celebrate Choctaw culture.

Choctaw Language Revitalization: This is a top priority. Initiatives include:

The Choctaw Language School: Offering online and in-person classes.

Master-Apprentice Programs: Immersing new speakers.

Language Resources: Dictionaries, phrasebooks, and digital apps.

Choctaw Language Immersion School: For the youngest learners to ensure the language continues for generations.

Cultural Centers and Museums: The Choctaw Cultural Center in Calera, opened in 2021, is a world-class facility that preserves and shares Choctaw history, art, and living culture. It stands in stark contrast to the near-invisibility of the culture just decades ago.

Promotion of Arts and Traditions: The Nation actively supports artists, singers, dancers, and stickball players, hosting annual events like the Choctaw Nation Labor Day Festival, which attracts tens of thousands of people.

Building a Social Safety Net and Infrastructure

The revenue from tribal enterprises is directly reinvested into citizen services, creating a robust social welfare system that rivals many local and state governments.

Healthcare: The tribe operates a state-of-the-art health system with a central hospital in Talihina, modern clinics throughout the reservation, and programs for diabetes care, behavioral health, and wellness.

Housing: The Choctaw Housing Authority builds and renovates homes for citizens, addressing a critical need in a largely rural area.

Education: The Nation offers extensive scholarships for higher education and vocational training. It also runs Head Start programs and partners with local public schools to support Choctaw students.

Elder and Youth Services: It provides dedicated programs, including meal delivery for elders, community centers, and youth leadership camps, ensuring support across the entire lifespan of a citizen.

National Influence and International Reach

The Choctaw Nation's influence now extends far beyond Oklahom

Political Advocacy: The tribe is a powerful voice in Washington, D.C., advocating for tribal sovereignty and the federal trust responsibility on a national stage.

Historical Legacy of Generosity: The Choctaw people are renowned for their 1847 donation to the Irish during the Potato Famine, a gesture born from their own experience of suffering on the Trail of Tears. This legacy continues through modern partnerships, such as the Nation's generous donation to Irish COVID-19 relief efforts in 2020, which garnered international media attention and deepened the special bond between the two cultures.

Global Business: Through its diversified holdings, the Choctaw Nation engages in business and defense contracting with a global reach.

Conclusion

The progress since electing Chief Belvin in 1963 is nothing short of extraordinary. The Choctaw Nation of Oklahoma has journeyed from a time when its very existence was threatened to becoming a powerful, self-determining nation that provides for its citizens, drives its regional economy, and proudly preserves its unique culture and language. It stands as a powerful testament to the resilience of the Choctaw people and the effective exercise of tribal sovereignty.

About the Author

Leaford Leven Blevins, Jr. is a passionate storyteller and cultural historian dedicated to preserving and sharing the rich heritage of the Choctaw people. With roots deeply embedded in Native American traditions, he has spent years researching and exploring the narratives that shape Indigenous identities. The Yowani Choctaw Saga is a culmination of those efforts—a vivid tapestry of lore, history, and adventure that celebrates the resilience and spirit of the Choctaw community.

Blevins believes in the transformative power of storytelling to bridge cultures and foster understanding. Throughout his writing career, he has aimed to amplify Indigenous voices and narratives, crafting tales that resonate with both history and contemporary experience. When not writing, he enjoys engaging with local communities, promoting cultural awareness, and encouraging young readers to embrace their heritage.

With the Yowani Choctaw Saga, Blevins invites readers on an unforgettable journey that highlights the beauty, strength, and unity of the Choctaw people, offering an opportunity to connect with their past while inspiring future generations.